Trick or Treat

Books by Kerry Greenwood

The Corinna Chapman Series
Earthly Delights
Heavenly Pleasures
Devil's Food
Trick or Treat

The Phryne Fisher Series
Cocaine Blues
Flying Too High
Murder on the Ballarat Train
Death at Victoria Dock
The Green Mill Murder
Blood and Circuses
Ruddy Gore
Urn Burial
Raisins and Almonds
Death Before Wicket
Away With the Fairies
Murder in Montparnasse
The Castlemaine Murders
Queen of the Flowers
Death by Water
Murder in the Dark
Murder on a Midsummer Night

Short Story Anthology
A Question of Death:
An Illustrated Phryne Fisher Anthology

Trick or Treat

A Corinna Chapman Mystery

Kerry Greenwood

Poisoned Pen Press

Poisoned Pen Press
6962 E. First Ave., Ste. 103
Scottsdale, AZ 85251
www.poisonedpenpress.com
info@poisonedpenpress.com

Printed in the United States of America

For my best friend ol' pal ol' buddy Themmy Gardner, that she should be proud of her ancestors.

With many, many thanks to the usual cast of people without whom I would write no books: David, Dennis, Jeannie, Themmy, Jen Pausacker, The Gen-X collective, Belladonna, Bron Gondwana, Eric the Fruitbat, Unique id, sesquipedeviant and catsidhe, who bear no resemblance to the Lone Gunmen for learned computer advice. Noga Nicholson for Hebrew and Samantha of Dragonfly for keeping me in writing trim. And for this book Greg Blunt, the Jewish Museum and various people who told me stories and who do not want to be named, but ought to be celebrated, which I have tried to do.

As far as I know, there is no bakery called Best Fresh, but if there is, it should be assured that this book does not refer to it. This is a work of fiction, and all things in it are fictitious. Even the City of Melbourne is an artefact of my imagination.

"There is no love sincerer than the love of food.'
—George Bernard Shaw,
The Revolutionist's Handbook

Chapter One

Four am, in my experience, contains many things. Darkness, cold, solitude, gloom, despair, madness—

I'll begin again. My name is Corinna Chapman and I am a baker, which means that in order to supply my shop, Earthly Delights, with bread to feed the suffering multitudes, I need to rise from my downy couch at four in the morning and get it all started. This has slightly soured my sweet nature, particularly this morning, because in that said downy couch reposed my dear and beautiful Daniel, a sabra of great gentleness and charm, and I could think of lots of things to be doing with him which did not involve ever leaving my bed.

But business is business, as my old mentor Papa Pagliacci used to say, and four am is four am and here I was, my apprentice beside me, bringing the bakery to life. Coffee steamed in its pot. The dough hooks clicked, the mixers mixed and the scent of spices lay heavy around Jason, who was making a mix for the Welsh bread. For an ex-junkie he had filled out beautifully. His hair was thick and curly, like Harpo Marx, though confined severely for work under his white cap. His bones were all decently covered now. His hands and arms were developing the baker's muscles, sturdy, able to knead recalcitrant rye bread for fifteen minutes without a pause which might stiffen the dough. I was so proud of him. I looked away before he caught me staring at him. Jason embarrasses easily.

It was beginning to get light outside—what our ancestors used to call piccaninny daylight. Dreary and grey, but light.

I inspected the night's massacre of vermin. Four mice and a rat. The rat was as big as a kitten. Erk. Much as I love most furry creatures, I have never been able to extend this affection to rats, though I am fond of mice and indeed used to have them as pets when I was a child. It's something about the naked tails, I believe. I disposed of the corpses in the bin and opened the street door to allow Heckle and Jekyll, my Mouse Police, out into the lane. They were going to hunt down and kill the tuna scraps which either Kiko or Ian at the Japanese restaurant were happy to give them. They belted off in a blur of black and white in search of endangered species of the Southern Ocean in order to render them more gravely endangered. There was a rather endearing scamper of hard paws on the stone floor.

Then I heard someone singing. Not the usual type heard at this hour in Calico Alley. Drunks, these days, do not sing 'Show me the way to go home', a song made to be slurred. No, they sing 'Heartbreak Hotel'. Almost invariably, in my experience. In a key of their own devising. And this wasn't 'Heartbreak Hotel' or any Elvis number. I didn't know it. But it was sweet and clear and I caught some unfamiliar words, 'Wassail, wassail, all over the town…' Then something about a 'white maple tree'. I could not see the singer. He or she was up at the other end of Flinders Lane, near the newly opened (curse its blood) hot bread shop.

The voice ceased. Odd. But nice. I went back inside to work on the bara brith, contemplating the hot bread shop.

It's not as though I have anything against the provision of new bread to the populace. The more fresh bread the better. Fewer polystyrene plastic-wrapped loaves means a better, more well nourished world. But did a hot bread shop, which was part of a chain and therefore able to keep its prices down, have to set up just along the street from me? Was there not enough of Melbourne, really quite a big city, for Best Fresh Bread to sell in that they had to come to my little corner? I felt like Eeyore talking about his sad and boggy place. *Locus tristis et palustris,* as the Professor would say.

Jason said, 'I think that's kneaded all right,' and I realised that I had knocked down the poor Welsh bread practically to its component molecules. No one could say that it wasn't worked enough. I set it aside to prove again, if the yeast had any breath left.

Jason delivered his report on Best Fresh's bread. It was succinct. 'It's crap,' he said.

'You must be able to say more than that,' I replied.

'Complete crap,' he elaborated.

Well, that's sixteen and male for you. I'd have to send a qualified appraiser to buy some for me.

The sun came up. The paper person flung the paper and missed killing anyone. I am sure that is his aim. He biked off, mumbling, 'Foiled again!' into his skimpy adolescent beard. Something huge loomed over me in the shadowy alley. A hand as big as a loaf reached for me.

But it was all right. It was Ma'ani, driver of the Soup Run bus, who oddly enough never has any trouble with rough behaviour on his shift. Even the wild boys instinctively know that it is better not to taunt someone who is over six feet in every dimension, especially across the shoulders. Those who don't have the instinct speedily acquire it. I remember seeing Ma'ani pick up a brawling fighting-mad drunk by the waist and dip him head first into a city fountain until he calmed down. Which he did, really quite fast. Ma'ani had come for the bread which I donate every day to the Soup Run, which feeds the poor and homeless. Last shift. He swung the sack easily over his massive back and grinned, teeth white in the shadows.

'All right, Corinna? Hey, Jason,' he said.

'You making a pick-up from Best Fresh?' demanded Jason suspiciously.

'That new place? Nah. They got a contract with a pig food manufacturer,' he said. 'Rather feed it to pigs than people. Sister was cross.'

'I bet she was,' I said appreciatively. Sister Mary is a diminutive nun with a will of adamant. If there is anything harder than adamant—it's just diamond, isn't it?—then she has a will of it. She would really not be impressed with Best Fresh deciding not to feed her lambs. In favour of pigs and further profit…ouch.

However, ours not to dwell on the discomfiture of others, ours to make more bread. The day was getting on and the coffee maker was getting into its stride. No coffee, no baking, is my equation. I need no funny drinks with ingredients which will be banned once Food and Health works out what they are. Just the aromatic bean, pure arabica, joy! I poured the sacred second cup which has to wait until all the mixers are mixing. Fragrant, hot and pure. Bliss.

Jason left to try to beat his record in scoffing the Trucker's Special breakfast at Cafe Delicious, where the Pandamus family clean up betting on him. I sat down to listen to the bread rising, a small sound like a crinkle in the air. So soft that I could be imagining it. A sound that comes from a very long way away in time, when they discovered leavening in Ancient Egypt and the Pharaoh's maidens sat down in a mud-brick kitchen and waited for the dough to rise, just as I was doing in my clean tiled bakery with the machines clicking. They would, however, have been drinking beer, not coffee. The other great gift of yeast.

'Blessed be,' said someone from the street door. Without turning round I knew it was Meroe, my friend and jobbing witch, as 'blessed be' is a Wicca greeting. Meroe came in. She is a thin woman with a sharply defined face and long black hair. She always wears black garments and a brightly coloured shawl or drape. Today's was a length of sky-blue silk with fluffy white clouds on it. She was carrying a basket and offered me an apple. It was a shiny scarlet apple and all too, too Brothers Grimm for this early in the morning.

'Will I go to sleep for a hundred years?' I asked, taking it.

'Probably not,' she replied. 'Anyway, it is too late for you, Corinna. You have already got your prince. Don't be greedy.'

'True, true,' I said, and bit. It was a perfect apple, crisp and juicy and just tart enough. 'And what can I offer you? Jason's date and walnut muffins, just out of the oven? Bara brith in an hour or so, poppy seed rolls? Nice loaf of rye?'

'Rye,' said Meroe. 'And one of those muffins—no, make it two. Is this a new recipe?'

'Yes, he has been working on it for a week. I reckon he's got the balance of fruit and nut just about right now. He minces the dates so that they are distributed through the whole mix. Nice?' I asked, as she broke one of the muffins and took a bite.

'Superb,' she said. 'Tell him so, will you?' She gave me some money and was about to leave when someone came stumbling down Calico Alley, wailing.

The Mouse Police belted inside as though wolves were after them and cowered in their bed of sacks. The wailer got closer. It was an eerie noise. Not like someone crying or screaming, but keening in a tired little voice that sounded like it had been going on forever.

Meroe stepped out into the alley. Witches never run away from anything, even when it might be wiser to do so. I had to go with her, though I didn't want to and the noise was, as the girls say, creeping me out. The wailer was a young man. He was wringing his hands and wailing, and now he was closer I could hear words. 'Gone, gone,' he said. 'Gone, gone, gone. My hands. My hands! Gone, gone, gone...'

Meroe stepped in front of him and took both of his hands in her own.

'Your hands are here,' she said in a clear tone, calculated to pierce through a drug-affected fog. 'Here. Look at them.'

'Gone, gone,' mourned the young man. He seemed unaware of Meroe's existence. He kept bumping against her in a vague way, as though she was a wall in his path. She turned him gently so that he was facing an actual wall and he continued to try to walk through it.

'Call an ambulance, Corinna,' she instructed me and I went inside to do so.

I have the number on my speed dial. The drug-fucked are not unknown in Calico Alley, though usually they just lie down and go blue, or spend their energy fighting the air. The irritating wail continued, setting my teeth on edge. It was getting to the Mouse Police, too, and I would have said they were as tough a pair of streetfighting moggies as one could wish not to meet down a dark alley. But they didn't like this, and they had huddled together, buried in their flour sacks, and clearly weren't coming out until the noise went away. I wished I could do the same.

In ten minutes the ambulance was in Flinders Lane and two competent ambos were jumping down. The young man wailed at them, too, and they also attempted to demonstrate to him that he had hands while he insisted that he didn't.

'Not the usual run of junkie,' commented one ambo. Her name was Julie, and I had met her before. Her mate was Tom.

'No,' I said, actually looking at the wailer. He was dressed in a good grey suit, shirt and tie fresh on today, shiny black shoes, designer haircut. 'Not at all. I wonder what he's taken?'

'He can't tell us,' said Tom. 'Might be ice. Might not be anything at all. Might be a fruitcake. Plenty of them around. Load him up, Jules, and we'd better get on. Nice to see you again, Corinna,' he said. He collected their reward of two muffins, and the ambulance left. The wailing died away, to my considerable relief.

'That was strange,' I said to Meroe.

'Very,' she agreed.

'And unsettling,' I went on.

'Yes,' she said. We looked at one another for a moment. Real insanity is the most frightening thing in the world.

Well, except for large homicidal maniacs with machetes. They are bad, too. But that faint, relentless voice from that dried-up throat, mourning the loss of his hands—I shook myself.

The Mouse Police burrowed up out of their sacks and began a relieved and slightly embarrassed wash. Yes, we are tough, they implied, but no cat could be expected to put up with that frightful noise, I mean, could they? Not with ears like ours. And I had to agree with them. I poured myself another cup of coffee. Jason came back. Meroe took her leave, and baked bread began to happen.

Once we had the orders sorted out and the wire racks of the shop all filled, it was time to meet my shop assistant of the day. It was either Goss or Kylie who was jumping up and down with impatience in the street, both hands under armpits, getting some warmth out of her shrug. The girls change hair colour and even eye colour so often that I am not at all sure what they actually look like. Since they have taken to covering their navel rings, I have no chance, and just ask who it is every day. This girl had pink hair and bright blue eyes and said she was Kylie. And I had no reason to believe that she was fibbing. I unlocked the shop door and the scent of baking flooded out into the cold street. Kylie took a deep, appreciative sniff.

'Scrumptious!' she said. 'What's the muffin today, Jase?'

'Jason,' said Jason sternly. Names were important to him. 'It's date and walnut. Want one?'

'Half a one,' temporised Kylie, who was on a perpetual diet. 'Corinna can have the other half. It doesn't matter to her.'

This was true. I weigh about a hundred kilograms, am as healthy as a horse, and have no truck or any other kind of vehicle with diets. People who intend to offer me their latest weight loss miracle diet, pill, rare oriental herb or tea can find another sucker. Daniel thinks I'm beautiful. So there.

Jason tore a muffin in two, gave half to me and half to Kylie, and went back into the bakery to meet the carrier who would take my bread to all corners of the city. I don't really need a shop to make a living—my bread sells very well to restaurants and cafes—but I like to see the smiles on the faces as the poor starved peons of the city buy a little mouthful of pleasure to sweeten their long, long days.

My own view is that everyone works too hard and too long and they ought to get out more. There isn't time in their improverished lives to do anything creative, or even to just sit and stare, one of my favourite occupations. And how the wired-in young—never without their music, never out of touch because of mobile phones, constantly sharing everything, even pictures— are going to cope if they ever encounter solitude and silence is another thing. They might easily go mad…which brought me to the handless wailer again. What could send someone off into that sort of delusion? It didn't sound like a drug. Perhaps he just cracked. Working in the city at present was enough to make anyone break down…

Meanwhile, Horatio, my tabby and white gentleman, had descended to the shop, where he took up his position next to the cash register. I removed the float from the mop bucket—no adolescent male burglar was going to look in a mop bucket—and Kylie pulled the blinds on a new day. Earthly Delights was open for business.

Which was slow. Despite the admirable muffins, created by Jason the Muffin Master, despite the scent of fresh baking and caraway seeds and fruit, the hordes failed to arrive. I went out into the lane to see if my suspicions were correct, and saw that they were. Best Fresh was doing very good business.

But the faithful eventually did arrive at Earthly Delights in sufficient numbers so that the day was not a total loss. Some people valued organic ingredients, fine spices and perfect skill over a fifty cent price difference.

'They'll get sick of it,' said Kylie. 'They're just going there because it's new. Don't stress on it, Corinna,' she said, and I decided not to stress on it. There was nothing I could do about it anyway, short of firebombing the place. Which I was trying not to consider.

We all live in an eccentric building called Insula, which is Latin for an apartment house, and it is a Roman apartment house. Every flat has a theme and a name—I, for instance, live in Hebe, the handmaid of the gods—and we have an impluvium full of goldfish in the lobby and a roof garden with a temple of Ceres, complete with a statue of the goddess. How it escaped the vandalism of the sixties I do not know, but it is perfect, sparkling, very comfortable and home to as rich a collection of interesting people as I could ever imagine. They were all, I could tell, going to come in and buy bread today, to make me feel better about Best Fresh. Even, perhaps, Mrs. Pemberthy, who is always accompanied by her rotten little doggie, Traddles. Horatio ignores Traddles as beneath the notice of a nobly born cat.

And here they came, my fellow tenants. Mrs. Dawson, back from her bracing early morning walk, was the first. She bought a loaf of rye bread and a muffin, tendering, as usual, the correct money. She caressed Horatio briefly. He allowed this with royal condescension.

'I should not be concerned about them,' she told me. Elegant as ever, she had marked the tentative beginning of spring by changing her bitter chocolate leisure suit for dark trousers and a priceless cashmere jumper in soft apricot. I loaded her bread into a broad, willow-leaf peasant basket. 'Quality will prevail,' she told me, and went out. I hoped she was right.

Jason had dispatched all of the bread orders and was beginning to clean the bakery. There was a time when I had done this myself, and it was nice to hear someone else clanking about with buckets of hot water. He was singing gently to himself. Jason had never heard gospel or work songs before he came to me. Now he likes them. Instead of trying to sing hip hop, which is hard without an accompaniment, he was singing spirituals.

'Deep river,' sang Jason, 'my home is over Jordan! Deep river...oh, shit.' There was a louder clank as he dropped the mop. I stifled a laugh.

My next customer was tall. She had long legs clad in fishnets, six-inch spike heels, cascading black ringlets and studded bands around wrists and throat. Her mouth was painted blood red.

'Mistress Dread!' said Kylie, pleased. 'What can I get you?'

'Wholemeal bread. And rolls. Got a supplier for lunch,' she replied in her deep voice. Mistress Dread (in private she prefers to be called Pat) runs a shop which sells leather wear for the discerning customer. She also runs a very well patronised dungeon where the very best S&M people gather to suffer and be suffered. When she said she was having a supplier for lunch, the mind boggled.

We supplied her with wholemeal bread. Kylie was thinking the same as me.

'You don't think she meant…'

'I don't know what she meant,' I said firmly. 'He'll be lucky if he isn't cooked and eaten. What a woman, Kylie!'

'Yair,' she sighed. 'Strong. Here's the Professor,' she added.

My very dear Professor Dionysus Monk came in, beaming goodwill. He is the nicest man I have ever met, as well as the most learned. He came in with a parcel which he put on the counter next to Horatio, who sniffed and settled down with all four paws upon it. I hoped it wasn't chocolate.

'I promised to lend this book to Daniel,' he said. 'Rolls, please, and a muffin or two. Nox delights in your cheese scones, by the way, so perhaps I ought to have some of those too.'

By the time they had all come through I was almost sniffling. Therese Webb came down from her flat Arachne in a flurry of home weaving, for date muffins. Jon and Kepler had descended to ground level from their flat, Neptune, and bought bread. Jon was about to fly away to another one of those godforsaken, pox-ridden, starving places where he went to bring kindness, water treatment plants, high protein biscuits and trade to the lost, stolen, enslaved and oppressed. I admire him immensely. Kepler is his shadow, a willowy, beautiful Chinese man who was expressly created, it seemed, to be Jon's soul mate. They are very sweet together.

Then, as the day's trade did begin to pick up, more fellow tenants came to show the flag. Andy and Cherie Holliday, father and daughter long parted and now back together, bought two loaves and news that the queue outside Best Fresh had dissipated. Perhaps it was just an early morning novelty thing.

The ham and cheese rolls vanished fast. Jason went off to engulf all the leftovers at Cafe Delicious. I ate a ham roll. Horatio graciously accepted some of the ham. Well, most of it, really. Mrs. Pemberthy (and her rotten little doggie Traddles) did come in, to tell me that Best Fresh's loaves were ninety cents cheaper. But she bought muffins.

The day wore on. By three, when I was usually sold out, there were ten loaves left. The Soup Run was going to do well tonight.

But then Del Pandamus rolled into the shop, filling it nearly from side to side. He is quite big but he is also Greek, with an expansive personality. I am always glad to see him. I love his Eleftherios Venizelos moustache.

'Corinna!' he boomed. 'We need bread! Seven loaves!'

'Del,' I said, 'you never run out of bread. You're just doing this to make me feel better.'

'Me?' he cried, flinging his arms wide. His moustache bristled. 'Me, lie to you? I would never do such a thing. Yai Yai, she sent me. You want to argue with Yai Yai?'

'Not a chance,' I said hastily, parcelling up his bread. The secret of success in Greek society is always to remember that Yai Yai is never wrong.

So, all in all, it was with a not too heavy heart that I closed the shop, returned Kylie's iPod and mobile phone to her and sent her off to do the banking, then farewelled the labouring Jason and ascended to my own apartment. There I washed, dressed in a long blue robe and, taking my cat under one arm and my esky under the other, ascended further to the temple of Ceres. It was glass sided and always warm.

I sat down on a marble bench under the shadow of the goddess, whose generous arms held a whole swathe of corn, and poured myself a drink. When a certain tall, dark and gorgeous man appeared, walking like a cat, my pleasure was complete.

Daniel and gin and tonic. Wonderful.

Chapter Two

Daniel accepted a glass and sipped slowly. Horatio removed himself from my knee and shifted to Daniel, putting one paw imploringly on his chest. Daniel caressed his whiskers. He purred. So far, the encounter was going well. Horatio is sometimes quite fast with a clawed snub if his ears are stroked when he wants his tummy tickled.

With the world as it is, with climate change and water shortages and wars over oil and ideology, ruin and death and distrust and lies, moments of perfect peace are rare and to be relished. We sat and savoured. The purring of the cat, the taste of the gin and tonic, the nearness of the beloved person, the warmth of the temple, the play of light on the marble arm and hand of the goddess. The sight of all those poor people in their offices, working for The Man. The snuggle of tired feet into sheepskin boots. We had a lot to be thankful for. The moment extended in serene silence.

Then Daniel sighed, Horatio shifted to the marble bench nearest the heating vent and began an elaborate wash, and I sat up.

'Well,' I said.

'Well indeed,' he replied. 'How have things been?'

'Trade is down because of that thrice-damned hot bread shop,' I said. 'Oh, and we had a madman in the lane this morning.'

I told him about the handless wailer.

He shook his head. 'I don't recognise that one,' he said. 'Must have been a real madman. Poor creature. Not something you really needed at that hour, however.'

'He was harmless.' I shrugged. I wasn't going to tell him about my moment of real fear because…well, I wasn't going to tell him. For some reason. 'Meroe was with me. The ambulance came and took him away.'

'But he gave you a fright,' he diagnosed. I am never going to get used to being so relentlessly understood. 'Madness is scary,' he added, hugging me.

'You are right,' I said, leaning my head against his shoulder. 'It is.'

'And it's on the increase,' he told me. 'There must be something new out there in the clubs and pubs. The Soup Run picked up three nutters last night. Two were just out of it but one fought like a…well, madman. Dragons, he said. Eating his heart.'

'One of the ambos mentioned it, too. Nasty.'

'Very. I recall that we had a surge of insanity when ice arrived. Must be something like that.'

'What's ice?'

'A new kind of ecstasy,' he explained. My turn to sigh.

'There seems to be nothing that an all-hating demon could do to humans which they aren't already doing for themselves. Must be disheartening for the demon,' I said.

'CS Lewis,' he said, incomprehensibly. Then he put me aside gently and stood up, placing his empty glass down on the bench. 'Got to go. I picked up an old friend from the airport last night and need to get home to see how George is doing with the jet lag.'

'Can I come too? Perhaps we could have an early dinner,' I suggested. I had never seen Daniel's apartment.

'Why not?' he said airily. 'Come on then, Horatio, time for a nice afternoon nap.'

He lifted the cat, I lifted the esky, and we descended.

I didn't bother with good clothes, as Daniel seemed to be in a hurry and I have unaccountably lost one of my good shoes.

Horatio loves to leap upon open shoes, landing with both front paws inside, and then cat and shoe slide across the floor until stopped by Newton's Third Law, usually collision with a wall. Therefore it was boots or…boots. I drew on jeans and a pullover patterned with red and green parrots and grabbed my backpack.

Ten minutes and an encounter with Carolus, Therese Webb's regal King Charles spaniel, who was waiting for Therese in the atrium, later, and we were on our way. Daniel, it appeared, lived in Elizabeth Street. Down the market end, which is filled with dingy backpackers' hostels, garages and dubious enterprises, and is redeemed by the Victoria Market and the Stork Hotel.

'It's not a very nice flat,' he told me. 'I really only needed a place to dump my things, set up all my electronic gear and to sleep occasionally, and it's cheap and central. I don't know what I am going to do when some developer takes over the buildings and makes it into upmarket apartments at three times the rent.'

'Always a problem,' I agreed. I wasn't ready to have anyone live with me and Horatio. It made sense for someone with a nocturnal profession to have his own place, especially since my hours were so unsocial and my rage, if roused from my rightful slumber, volcanic. I even threw a pillow at Horatio once when he woke me by tipping my bedside glass of water into my face. I missed but he didn't speak to me for the whole day.

Elizabeth Street during the afternoon was a fascinating melange of languages and faces. The YMCA housed the respectable traveller, the student, and those paid for by their doting parents, and the hostels housed the rest. There were little shops selling tacky souvenirs like stuffed koalas, kangaroo paw bottle openers and snakeskin belts (erk) and more selling liquor and junk food. Daniel stopped before a dingy entryway and led me up three steps.

The Buildings was not so much dingy as grimy, and not so much grimy as dirty, with that ground-in, institutional dirt of a building which no one either cares about or is responsible for. It had not been repainted since its original coat of old stone in about 1930, and still had a sign stencilled on the inner wall which requested the patrons to refrain from spitting. It could have been a charming place if it was cleaned and decorated and loved, but I could tell it wasn't going to be.

'Stairs,' said Daniel apologetically. 'I don't trust that lift.'

'Stairs? Fine,' I said, inspecting the iron-doored 1930s lift. 'I like stairs.'

'You won't like these,' he promised and he was, of course, right. Filthy and smelling strongly of urine and phenol, not a nice combination. But they were well built and safer than that lift. I wondered how my cleanly Daniel liked his surroundings. I asked.

'It impresses the clients,' he said with a wry grin.

'Yes, indeed,' I said, as we came out onto the landing and saw the familiar etched glass door with the name on it. Familiar from hundreds of black and white movies, usually starring Humphrey Bogart. 'I see what you mean. Let me guess—can you see a neon sign saying Eat At Joe's from your window?'

'No, it's a neon sign saying Garage, and there is no bottle of Old Grandad bourbon in the desk drawer. It's a bottle of ouzo. Otherwise...'

He unlocked the door and it was, indeed, the perfect mean streets private eye's office: the scarred desk, the unmatched visitors' chairs, the uncurtained window with the blinking sign. Cleaner than one would have expected from the rest of this dump. The floor had been swept inside the millennium and the window glass was actually polished. The room smelt of Mr. Sheen, coffee, generic Melbourne City and the crisps and Twisties always present where nerds congregate. The computer and electronics were not period, but the blonde entering by the other door certainly was.

She was tall and slim and willowy, with long, long legs. She was patting at her long golden hair with a blue towel. She was wearing the royal blue silk dressing gown I had given Daniel for his birthday. On her it looked devastatingly sexy. This could have been enhanced by the high heels. She turned and revealed a cleavage which would have made Sam Spade fall off his chair. She could have come straight off any Carter Brown cover. I looked at her. Then I looked at Daniel.

'Hello, George,' he said easily. 'This is my friend Corinna.'

'Nice to meet you,' said the blonde, extending a languid hand. I took it. Warm and scented. Her nails were perfect, like little drops of blood.

'George?' I asked. My voice squeaked.

'Georgiana,' she explained in a flawless Sloane accent. 'Sign that Daddy wanted a boy. Only thing Daddy gave me, actually. Georgiana Hope, in fact. Danny's an old friend of mine.'

'Oh,' I said. I could not for the life of me think of anything else to add. Danny? Old friend?

'I told you about George,' Daniel reminded me. 'She ran a catering company in England.'

'Oh, yes.'

'She taught me to make radish roses,' he said, smiling, aware that something in this meeting was not going well. 'Feel like an early dinner, George?'

'Couldn't eat a thing,' declared the blonde.

'You'll be hungry later,' warned Daniel. 'And there's not a lot to eat here.'

'So I see. Tinned beans, dried noodles, bottled pasta sauce. I can see I shall have to do some shopping.'

'Er…don't do it on my account. Anyway, if you aren't coming, I've got to go out. Corinna has to go to bed early.'

'Very well, dear boy,' she said, and enveloped him in a hug, kissing him on the neck. 'Come back to me soon.'

Daniel did not answer and I didn't know what to say. George was moving in on my lover, and she might have had a prior claim. I had to find out and did not know how to phrase the questions.

'Stork Hotel,' decided Daniel. 'We need real food.'

'All right,' I concurred. We went out. On the staircase, I could still smell her perfume. I identified it. It was called Poison. How very suitable.

'So, how long is George staying?' I asked, as artlessly as I could.

'Until she finds an apartment. She's sold the London business and moved to Australia, got a business visa.'

Another reason to loathe the Minister for Immigration. Not that I needed one, as it happens. I tried to think of how to frame my next set of questions as we went down the mud-coloured staircase and finally achieved the street.

'Nice little flat, if it was decorated,' I said. 'How many rooms do you have?'

'A kitchen and a bathroom, the office, a lounge room and a bedroom. I've got a fire escape just like those New York tenements. And the rent is very cheap.'

So Georgie wasn't necessarily sleeping in Daniel's bed. With Daniel. Oddly enough, I wasn't jealous, not that curdled green bilious feeling. But I did feel hurt, as though something precious had been lost, as though I was bleeding.

'I suppose I should have at least washed and painted the walls,' said Daniel self consciously. 'But I almost never have visitors. Clients come because someone I know has sent them, and they don't care about the office, just the results. Actually I was going to suggest that she ask if there was space in Insula.'

I paused to stare at him, the sort of stare that women have been giving men since eyesight was invented and the first man brought an uncleaned stegosaur and seventeen mates home for an impromptu dinner when his wife was nursing a baby and a cold and trying to finish a song for the women's corroboree. A look that said, surely you can't be serious? Oh, you are. Goddess have mercy.

'There's nothing available,' I said flatly. 'Is she starting a business here?'

'Yes, she's looking out for an established place to invest in.'

'She might like Docklands,' I said hopefully. 'Lots of flats there, nice view of the river, plenty of restaurants, too.'

We were brought up short by the door of the Stork, which was, exceptionally, closed for redecoration.

'Damn,' I said.

'Corinna, what's wrong?' asked Daniel, taking both my hands in his and swinging me round to face him. 'You're not yourself today.'

'I don't think I like your old friend,' I said. Honesty in everything, Corinna.

'You're jealous?' asked Daniel, with an edge of laughter in his voice. The amusement stifled any further revelation I might have made.

'Don't be ridiculous. Now, where are we going to eat? Or shall we buy some supplies and go back to Insula and have a picnic?'

'Let's wander back towards Insula and see what happens,' he said. 'If there's an enticing cafe, we can eat there, otherwise the New York is on our way.'

That had my vote. Someone had finally noticed that lots of people were now living in the city and most of them had enough money to buy, as it might be, kalamata olives if they wanted olives, and Jindi camembert, saucisson sec if they wanted sausages, and organic tomatoes rather than those plastic supermarket ones. Thus the New York Deli was born. It stayed open almost all night and it sold all the best of the *delikat essen* one's heart could desire. And when Daniel and I came in, the intervening cafes being uninviting, there was a display of German sausages which decided our dinner. Bratwurst. Weisswurst, my favourite.

'Corinna, you look terrible! What's the matter, this big hunk not treating you good?'

'Just tired, Uncle Solly,' I smiled. Uncle Solly looked like every Yiddish uncle anyone had ever described; rounded, dark-eyed, fluent, with fluffy white hair and a big white apron. He knew every customer by name after they had been into his shop more than once and most of the surrounding populace called him Uncle Solly. He had a throng of apparently willing nephews, nieces and cousins who kept the shop going during the day and Uncle Solly did the night shift. Someone had tried to hold him up once, and Uncle Solly had overwhelmed the thief with hospitality, so by the time the cops arrived the robber had handed over his knife and was drinking *caffee mit schlag*, nose deep in whipped cream. Then the attending police officers had some coffee too, and some ginger cake, and it ended with no charges being laid after all. It was a mistake, everyone makes mistakes...

I really loved Uncle Solly. When it was his turn for the Soup Run sandwiches, the homeless ate really well on his donated ingredients. As we were going to, I could tell.

'Sausages!' he exclaimed, looping them into a greaseproof-wrapped bundle. 'A good meal, if you also have maybe just a mouthful of my potato salad, look, mmm! Creamy! I won't insult such a lady, such a baker, by asking if you got rye bread. But busy woman you are, maybe you like my already made green salad with this little sachet of the special Uncle Solly thousand island dressing like you never tasted.'

'All of that,' I said greedily. I hadn't brought a bag so he put everything carefully into one of his white canvas bags.

'And some coffee cake,' said Daniel. 'It's just like my mother's.'

'Coffee cake as well, *bubelah*, you're living large. And who was that blonde I saw you with yesterday? Blondes I don't think you should be squiring round the street, people talk. What's your Corinna, who is a good woman, going to think of you, eh?'

Daniel stared at Uncle Solly. Solly stared back. There was one of those masculine silences. I have no patience with them.

'It's all right, Uncle Solly, I know about her, I just met her. She's an old friend.'

'Friends he's got,' muttered Solly, ringing up the total and giving me change. 'Bring the bag back next time you come,' he told me. 'And you, *bubelah*...'

He said something in a language I did not understand and conducted us out of the shop.

'What did he say to you?' I asked.

'Nothing,' said Daniel. 'Just a proverb, a Yiddish proverb.'

'Right,' I said.

We got back to Insula and my apartment. Horatio woke from one of those little day-long naps which cats take and politely intimated that it was dinner time. Which it was. He accepted a ration of kitty dins while we grilled sausages. I found the French mustard and the rye bread. Daniel opened a bottle of Rhine style wine to accompany our German food.

Uncle Solly was right. His potato salad was creamy with just the right amount of fresh dill, his green salad with the thousand island dressing was delicious, and his sausages did make a good meal. Our constraint vanished when Horatio, whom Daniel had been ignoring while he asked politely, grabbed a piece of bratwurst which Daniel was using to emphasise a point about the war in the Middle East and took it under the table where he could be alone with it.

We laughed as though George had never appeared in our lives and ate more sausage and drank more wine. Then we went to bed, to make love slowly and sleep sweetly, until the alarm shattered the peace and it was four in the morning again.

I woke more abruptly than usual and listened, once I had thumped the alarm into silence. If I had been a cat, I would have said that my whiskers were tingling. Something in the world was subtly wrong, and I did not like it. But I heard nothing and a search of the apartment revealed nothing amiss, if one did not count a starving tabby who was about to expire of inanition unless that milk which I had taken out of the fridge was for him, in which case he could hang on for a few minutes longer. I left him with a bowlful and tried the door and the balcony French windows but everything was locked up tight, just as I had left it the night before. Daniel was sleeping as though stunned, and he had Israeli-army trained reflexes. I was just nervous, that's all. As any woman would be whose livelihood was threatened by one rival and whose relationship was threatened by another, and who had probably eaten too much weisswurst the night before.

Shaking my head, I made coffee, drank it, toasted the leftover rye bread and ate it with slightly failed microwaved blood orange marmalade. Then I dressed in my tracksuit and carried the next cup of coffee down into the bakery.

My apprentice, Jason, now lives in one of the upstairs flats, so he always gets to work late. The principle is the same everywhere: children who live across the road from the school are always late at first, as are housemaids who live in the hotel or conductors who sleep on the train. It's a passing thing until you work out that even if you are on the spot, you need at least ten minutes to find your glasses or keys or have a quick last minute pee, and still descend the stairs on time. I was letting this go for a few weeks. Jason wasn't used to having a permanent home. After that, he was going to refine his last second arrivals to last minute arrivals or I would start docking his pay. I could easily do this by cutting off his credit at Cafe Delicious, run by the Pandamus family of happy Hellenes and his primary source of nutriments.

I dead-heated Jason. I heard the outer door clang open as my foot touched the bottom step. Jason flung himself inside and dragged on his baker's overalls, ramming the cap down on his curls, flipping switches so that the machines rumbled into life and trying to look like he had been in the bakery for an hour, whiling away the time by reading cookery books and waiting for his boss to rise from her couch. It wasn't a bad imitation and I let him get away with it.

'Good morning, Jason. Better open that new sack of rye flour, we've got a big order for rye bread. Also, you promised chocolate orgasm muffins today, have we got enough chocolate?'

'Yep,' said Jason, all snap and polish. 'Checked it yesterday. And the new packet of caraway seeds.'

'Number of vermin removed?' I asked, as he gathered up the dead mice from their designated place and bunged them in the bin. The Mouse Police were enthusiastic hunters, bless them. They were sitting at attention before a small scene of rodent massacre, tails twitching in anticipation of breakfast.

'Five mice, no rats, and a bloody big spider,' reported Jason. The lid of the bin clanged. I heard the rattle of dry cat food hitting the Mouse Police ration tins. 'Cat food supplied, sir!' He saluted, looking unbearably cute in white overalls and cap and shining morning face.

We were being naval this morning, it appeared. 'Carry on, Midshipman,' I said wearily, flipping open the order book. Jason took the Evil scissors and went to attack the flour sack.

It's just a whimsy. Everyone has heard the cry 'Where are the *good* scissors?' echoing through the house or school or workplace. Daniel, in a theological discussion we had drifted into one night, opined that if there were Good scissors there must be Evil scissors, this being a Manichean universe, and I had to agree. The Good scissors were used for cutting cloth and nothing else. The Evil scissors were used for opening sacks and snipping bacon rind and cutting out recipes from *Good Weekend*.

Orders were bearing up. I sell most of my bread to cafes and restaurants. I don't really need a shop. But I liked having one and I resented being outbid by a hot bread shop. Some of them are doubtless excellent, but my reports of Best Fresh had not been encouraging.

Machines on, rye bread on, I heard Jason ripping away at the top of the rye flour sack for the big order. I was just wondering how I could have used so much cream when he said, 'Captain?'

'Yes, Midshipman?'

'There's something crappy about this flour.'

I really must teach Jason some more descriptive words when we have a spare moment, I thought. I rose with a groan to inspect it. He was right. I buy rye flour in smallish paper sacks, as even in the heaviest bread it is an addition, not the main ingredient. Jason was right. The opened sack smelt mouldy and slightly acid, not the right scent at all. Rye ought to smell sour. I damped a small amount of it and the smell was marked, enough to make the Mouse Police sneeze, and the flour was greyish and slightly greasy, not the fine dry meal it should have been.

'Quite right, well spotted, that man. Damn. Where are we going to get another sack of rye flour at this hour of the morning?'

'We could go and ask Best Fresh,' he suggested, ducking out of cuffing range.

'Over my dead body.'

'Well, we can't use this stuff, Cap,' he told me. He was right. 'And we've only got enough rye to cover the standing orders,' he said, 'not the new one.' Right again. And I would hate to disappoint a new big order, which might then go over to a lesser baker. As it might be, just down the lane.

'Where did that sack come from, sailor?' I asked. Now that I looked at it, it wasn't the usual supplier. Their lettering was red, this was black.

'Just says "rye mixture",' read Jason.

I am going to need glasses soon and I am resisting firmly. It's not that I am getting short sighted, it's just that the rest of the world wants its print too small. 'Wait a tick. Aha,' said Jason triumphantly.

'Do you know what the penalties are for saying "aha!" to a superior officer?' I demanded.

'No shit, Corinna, look,' he urged, dropping the naval affectations. He hoisted the sack onto the bench. 'It's not for us, anyway. It's for Best Fresh. The van must have mixed them up.'

'So they've got my sack of unrefined special organic rye flour,' I said. 'Expensive unrefined organic rye flour. And we've got...'

'Their crap,' said Jason with admirable nicety. 'I'll just seal it up again and go over and get our flour.'

'Tell them there's something not right with it,' I said.

'After I get our rye flour back,' he replied. So young and so cynical.

He sticky-taped the sack, lifted it into his arms, and I opened the alley door. The Mouse Police rushed out and Jason followed, walking easily away in the darkness with his load. I went back into the bakery and put the coffee machine on. Today was not going to be a good day, I could tell.

But it improved when Jason came back with our flour, which had not even been opened.

'They were going to send it back,' he told me, engulfing three ham rolls and a couple of leftover muffins with his can of Coke. Coke! At that hour! The boy has the digestion of an ostrich. 'They don't use neat flour. All their stuff comes in mixtures. Just upend it into the mixer and add water, yeast included. There was only this one guy Eddie there to mind the machines. Don't reckon he knows a thing about bread.' There was a pause as he chewed briefly and cut himself a doorstop of bread and cheese. 'He scammed me ten for bringing the sack, said he'd be in deep shit if the boss came in at nine and found the rye mix not started.'

'And you told him the flour was iffy?'

Jason widened his eyes in an affectation of innocence which verged on the extreme. 'Yeah, Boss, I told him. Twice. I said, "Don't use that stuff, it's shitty", and he said, "Thanks", and gave me the money and I came back.'

'Well, we can't do any more than that. We told him and he's in charge. If the boss doesn't come in until nine…' I said with a certain complacency, noting that it was now getting on for five thirty and we had better get cracking on the rye or we wouldn't make the new order. 'Nothing more that we can do. Is our rye all right?'

Jason had anticipated me and produced a teaspoonful of the new flour. I sniffed and tasted. Perfect. Sour and silky.

'Then prime the mixers, Jason, we're making bread,' I announced.

'Aye, aye, sir,' he grinned around his last mouthful. 'Captain?'

'Yes, Midshipman?'

'Do I get to keep the ten?'

'You carried the flour,' I said, getting out of my chair. 'You keep the fee.'

'Aye, sir!' he said, and we sprang into action.

Chapter Three

Morning came. It was one of those Melbourne spring mornings which make everyone long to be somewhere else: in the country, by the sea, sitting on a suitable mountain. Sunrise was as pink and soft as Jason's raspberry icing, with delicate blues behind and above and streaks of pure gold which John Martin could have used for *The Plains of Heaven*. I stood in my lane gazing at the sky as the Mouse Police bounced back inside for a little snooze, smelling of tuna scraps and uninterested in aesthetics.

Calico Alley was empty. I could see all the way to the steps which lead up into the arcade. Yet someone was singing, quite near, a song about wassailing. The voice was a clear, honey-sweet tenor: 'God bless the master of this house and the mistress also/ And all the little children that round the table go…'

I listened until it faded away. Someone walking along Schmutter Alley or Flinders Lane, perhaps, caught in one of those odd inner city soundscapes which make St. Paul's whispering gallery so famous. Nice. Very nice. And my day was further improved by the scent of cooking rye bread and the appearance of my most glamorous neighbour, Mrs. Dawson. She was wearing a rough silk leisure suit which was a sonnet in burnt umber and carrying her terracotta coloured jacket and the umbrella without which spring in Melbourne is a very soggy thing.

'Spring,' she observed with a smile.

'For the moment,' I agreed.

'I met our witch and a few friends in the Flagstaff Gardens,' she told me. 'Dancing in a ring.'

'Must be a solstice or a festival or something,' I replied. 'Er… clothed?'

'Completely,' she said.

This was a relief. Meroe was a solitary amongst witches, not belonging to any coven. If she was dancing with others it meant some occult celebration was in the offing and most Wicca ceremonies are carried out skyclad, which struck me as unwise in the Flagstaff Gardens at dawn, or indeed at any time.

'Rye bread,' said Mrs. Dawson with as much greed as a refined lady should exhibit at dawn in an alley.

'I can only spare one loaf,' I said. 'I've got a special order. And it nearly didn't happen at all.'

While I was fetching and wrapping a loaf of the first batch of bread I told her about Jason's return of the odd flour.

'The thing which is now worrying me,' I confessed, 'is that I should have made sure the idiot in charge didn't use that rye mix. It was definitely off.'

'Not your responsibility,' said Mrs. Dawson, deftly relieving me of guilt. 'Jason told the man that the flour wasn't good. And if their rye bread fails, my dear, that is not your fault either. Price for confession and absolution…?'

'One loaf of rye bread,' I agreed promptly, handing it over. 'Eat it in good health, as Uncle Solly says.'

'I do like that man,' Mrs. Dawson observed. 'The reason I wanted your rye is that I bought some of his gravlax yesterday. Divine with sour cream and capers. Well, I have done my exercise and my detective story has to go back to the library today. I intend to make myself a few open sandwiches at about ten and eat them in the roof garden.'

'With Russian tea?'

'Of course,' she said. 'Do come and share it with me if you can get away,' she added, and walked on.

When Mrs. Dawson drank Russian tea, she drank it from an elaborate silver samovar which Trudi wheeled up to the garden for her. It had tea glasses in silver holders and dispensed a delicate straw coloured beverage, drunk with lemon, which would entirely complement Uncle Solly's gravlax and my bread. It would be a very civilised morning tea. I would see how business went today.

Soup Run Donnie came sidling along just as she left. He had probably been watching for her departure from around a corner. Before the adamantine Sister Mary had reformed him, he had been a lookout man for many a burglary, and he just didn't feel comfortable standing brazenly visible, even in Calico Alley at this hour. I hauled out the sack of bread, heavier than usual, and he lifted it onto the trolley which everyone but Ma'ani used to transport food offerings from the charitable.

'Been a good night,' he said. 'Lots of customers.'

'Any madmen?'

'One,' he said, smiling nervously. 'But they took him away. Bye,' he added, and was gone.

Sunrise had gone, too, and I ducked back into the bakery to see how the chocolate muffins were coming along. I had an order for a tray of princess cakes for a child's birthday. Bless the little darling, she insisted on my cakes, resisting the temptations of the very good patisseries in her area, who would have happily made her a cake in any shape whatsoever including—to judge from their window display—trains, planes, armoured personnel carriers, subatomic particles, geese with brooms and Barbie dolls. But it was princess patty cakes for Karina, and I had to concentrate while making them. They have to rise nicely and evenly or the whipped cream filling tips the pink icing top off. I started my seldom used cake mixer, which makes a loud clatter, so the love of my life had to shout to be heard over it.

'Can I help?' asked Daniel.

'By all means, separate those eggs for me,' I shouted back. Daniel came in, gorgeous in a pair of jeans and a white t-shirt emblazoned with a slogan in an unknown script. He began on the eggs. I watched him long enough to be confident that he wasn't going to spill yolk into my egg white, in which event it would never whip. He could break the eggs with one hand, I noticed, green with envy. So was Jason.

'Cool! Can I learn to do that?' he asked.

'Just practice,' said Daniel modestly. 'I squashed a lot of eggshell learning to do it. But I can show you how.'

'Don't practise on this mixture,' I instructed. 'Wait until we make challah again and it doesn't matter if some yolk gets spilled. Isn't it time for your breakfast?' Jason's appetite is usually as good as an alarm clock. In which event either the clock was fast or Jason was ten minutes slow.

'Just waiting until I get the choccie muffins out of the oven,' he answered, watching Daniel as he gripped an egg in his hand, squeezed, and spilled the white out of the half-shell, dropping the unbroken yolk into the second basin. Poetry in motion.

Jason dragged himself away from the spectacle to slide his muffins out of their tins and lay them in reverent rows to cool, then shucked his cap and overalls and went off to renew the inner boy. Which took a fair bit of renewing. Due to a frightful childhood and a period of drug abuse, Jason had interrupted his adolescent growth spurt. Now that he was clean and employed and amused and had a nice bed to sleep in every night, he was growing at an alarming rate. His overalls were already snug and by next week would be too tight.

I compounded the princess cakes carefully, giving Daniel the job of beating the egg whites into peaks. When they were safely in the oven and we could hear again, I greeted him with a kiss.

'Good morning,' I said. 'What does your t-shirt say?'

'*Shalom*,' he replied.

'Oh, so that's Hebrew writing. Or was that just a greeting?'

'That, too,' he said, kissing me on the cheek. 'Sheer luxury,' he added. 'To kiss you whenever I like. And you like, of course. *Shalom, süsselah!* There's a mixed language for a fine morning.'

'What does that mean?' I snuggled against the pacific t-shirt.

'Peace be unto the sweetie,' he grinned.

'And also with you,' I answered. 'What do you have to do today? We can drink Russian tea with Mrs. Dawson at ten.'

'Begone, tempter. It's a hardworking world.' He kissed me again to comfort me for the hard work of it all. 'I might be able to drop back at about three, if the lady would honour me with the company of her so-distinguished cat and self?'

'Three it is,' I agreed, and he washed egg off his hands and sauntered away.

The bakery always seemed emptier without him. But soon it was augmented with a Jason, as replete as he ever is, which was not as replete as all that. He was carrying a large basket and laughing to himself.

'What's that? A midmorning snack? And what's funny?' I asked.

'From Mama Pandamus. For someone called Old Spiro. And they were having this Greek argument about this Old Spiro, Yai Yai yelling from the kitchen that he was a prostitute—well, that's what she said—and Del yelling back that such things were a long time ago and far away and he was an old man on his own and Grandma coming right back at him that if Old Spiro was alone it served him right. I just grabbed the basket and went before they started throwing things. I might have missed a bit of the argument,' said Jason, lifting a corner of the white cloth which covered the basket. 'Mmm! Baklava.'

'No, you don't.' I removed the basket from my young omnivore's questing nose. 'It's for Old Spiro.'

'Yeah, I s'pose,' Jason unwillingly admitted.

'Leaving us with only one puzzle.'

'What?' asked Jason, clanging the main oven door open to remove the last of the rye and put in the pane di casa rolls.

'Who's Old Spiro?'

We looked at each other blankly.

'Fucked if I know,' he said.

'Me neither.'

I put the basket up on top of the clothes dryer, out of the way of any greedy cats or apprentices. 'We'll ask about it later,' I decided. 'Don't swear in the bakery, it's bad luck. I told you that.'

'Ouch,' said Jason, burning the back of his hand on the oven door. 'Okay, okay. I believe.'

Time to open the shop. I unlocked the outer door to reveal an awful lot of someone who said she was Goss. Today's hair was blonde and eyes blue, which I believe were the original colours. She was wearing about half a t-shirt in bright pink and approximately ten centimetres of pink skirt below a broad leather belt suitable for a brickie, bikie, or one of Mistress Dread's clients. I will never understand fashion. I refrained from comment.

'Nice day!' said Goss, greeting Horatio with a polite caress of the regal whiskers. We opened the till, put in the change, put up the shutters and started the day peacefully. Customers came. Goss reported that there was a queue at Best Fresh, who were advertising two muffins for two dollars. But the discerning came to buy Jason's chocolate orgasms, which were five dollars each and worth every delectable crumb. And really, did I want the custom of people who bought their muffins for size not taste?

Of course I did. There is no room for hypocrisy in baking, which is a magical process. It is surrounded with superstitions, every one of which I obey, even to the extent of telling Jason about the unluckiness of blaspheming or swearing, which must be centuries old. As Meroe told me once, 'I don't know if the spoken charms add to the effectiveness of this dill water I am making for that child with colic, but dare I risk leaving them out?' And, covering my ears against infant roars of agony, I had had to agree. Never point a naked blade towards rising dough. Never leave a flame burning in the bakery—not difficult with mine, because apart from the old style bread ovens, the machines were all electric. Never burn snails in the oven—again, not a common request, but I would refuse it if someone asked for some charred shells. Never allow bees in the kitchen. Not a lot of them in the city. Never allow a cat to leap over rising dough. I had forbidden the Mouse Police such antics and they couldn't, anyway, the warm air riser was set in the wall.

I mused thus as I counted out the loaves for the courier, the zappy Megan, who would be running transport in Australia by the time she was forty. The rye bread had come out glossy and fragrant and I regretted not making a few more for the shop. And, of course, for me. Megan went off on her motorbike rickshaw with a cheerful toot and I found Professor Monk in the bakery, talking to Goss about luck. I know a cue when I hear one.

'What about the baker's beliefs?' I asked, enumerating some of them. His eyebrows lifted and he smiled his beautiful scholar's smile.

'Snails? How interesting. Virgil in one of the Eclogues says that one should not burn shells near a beehive. Leaving aside the reasons why anyone should want to burn shells, that's a very old belief. Ah, here comes our expert on the occult. Good morning, Meroe.'

'Blessed be,' replied Meroe. 'To Corinna, Dion, Goss and of course Horatio. Do you think you could make this recipe, Corinna?'

She gave me a handwritten piece of what looked like parchment. Meroe was in a hurry. I wondered if dancing in the gardens at dawn had delayed something important. I studied the paper, holding it at arm's length. It was English, at least: 'Tak yr pure wheaten manchet dough and strew thereon saffron and raisins of the sun, cloves cinnamyn sugar if they be hadde, a handful, pounded wel. Knead soft and make yr cakes as many as ther be singers.'

'It looks like it's white bread dough mixed with some fruit and spices and sugar and made into buns,' I said. 'Does that sound right? There's no instructions about how long to cook it or anything like that.'

'When this was written down, cooks knew their own business and would not have appreciated amateurs learning too much of their craft,' said Meroe, unsmiling. 'Can you make me some?'

'Yes, but I'll need to experiment a bit. How many do you want, and when?'

'Thirty-seven, and not until the end of the month. Perhaps you could try the recipe out for a few days until it's right? I'm happy to pay extra for your trouble.'

'No trouble, I'll give it to Jason. He loves experimenting. And that's about his standard of spelling, too.'

'Wonderful,' said Meroe, and relaxed, unloosing her hold on today's wrap, which was a silk-screened length of Monet water-lilies. Clearly these buns were important ones, though I could not imagine how buns could be important. She happily joined in Professor Dion's discussion on superstitions, informing me that it was thought very unlucky to let a cat leap over a corpse, in case the cat was a necromancing, shape-changing witch who had something nasty in mind for the deceased's soul.

'But over bread dough?'

'It might not rise,' said Goss. 'I remember when I got sent to stay on a dairy farm. One of those colonial ones where they do things like the old days, so dirty and horrible and no toilets, I never want to live in those times, it was my mum's idea, rotten bitch, she was just getting me out of the house so she could screw her new boyfriend, that's when I got Dad to give me my own flat, where was I? Oh yes, well, the lady showed us how to churn butter and there was this little rhyme you had to say while you were turning the handle…' Her forehead wrinkled. 'Now I can't remember it.'

'Come, butter, come,' said Professor Dion unexpectedly. 'Come, butter, come! Peter stands at the gate, waiting for a but-tered cake, come, butter, come!'

'That's it,' said Goss.

'Where did that come from?' asked Meroe.

'From a very long way away. From Wales, in my childhood,' said the Professor. 'Well, must go, dear ladies. I have an appoint-ment in the city and I must be back by ten.' He put on his tweed hat and left.

I knew why he had to be back before ten. Mrs. Dawson was not going to be consuming her Russian tea alone, which made me feel better about not going.

The morning continued. Trade was down, but not out. All my regulars came. Sarah Jane and her charming husband Michael-the-Musician wandered in about ten, craving chocolate muffins and a cup of my filter coffee, because the Pandamuses' *cafe hellenico* kept everyone but the hardened addict awake for twenty-four hours. I, personally, loved it, but even I only drank Greek coffee before noon.

While I was discussing her honeymoon (with elephants) with SJ, who seemed happier than I had ever seen her, little Anna came in from that same cafe, carrying a plate covered in cling wrap and a cup of that same caffeine-rich brew from her grandmother. We watched, charmed, as the child moved with the religious certainty of the young, the very tip of her little pink tongue poking out of the corner of her mouth, until she reached the counter and laid down her burdens safely. She drew a deep breath of sheer relief and said, 'Yai Yai sends the coffee to Corinna and these to Mrs. Pappas.'

'She does?' I asked, bewildered. Anna nodded emphatically, which made her brown fringe fall over her eyes. She shook it back impatiently.

'To Mrs. Pappas and tell her to call Yai Yai,' said Anna, repeating her lesson. Then she grinned. She had a delightful grin. She noticed Goss' pink costume and held out the rosy skirts of her own. 'I've got more dress than you,' she told my assistant. She had, at that. Goss giggled and pulled down her inadequate hem.

We gave Anna a princess cake for her very own and she went out, cupping it between her hands as though it was a flower. I drank the coffee. Wow.

'Who is Mrs. Pappas?' asked SJ.

'There you have me,' I answered. 'This sort of thing is probably going to go on happening,' I added. 'It's been a very strange day.'

They left with an invitation for me and Daniel to go to a concert and Goss said, 'I would like to have a little girl like that. Isn't she just so cute?'

I agreed and we went on selling bread. The rye sold well, the pasta douro fled out the door, the ham and cheese rolls were popular and the cakes vanished. I wondered if I should concentrate more on cakes. Jason was a natural cake-baker. He had invented a fruit icing made of mashed berries and icing sugar which exploded in the mouth. There was no cake-maker anywhere near us in this part of the city and I was cheered by our next encounter. A young man dressed in an Italian suit demanded, 'Can you make good muffins?'

'We make the best you have ever tried,' I said immodestly.

'Have a taste of that,' he snarled, flinging a paper bag from Best Fresh at me. I fielded it. Inside was a very large chocolate muffin with one bite taken out of it. I tore off a piece and tasted.

Oh, dear. Sawdust with cocoa flavouring. I couldn't choke down more than one mouthful. I passed it to Goss, who nibbled and grimaced. Only her extensive training in ladylike behaviour constrained her from spitting it out.

'Euw,' she commented and dropped the bag in the bin. 'Tell you what,' she said, taking the incandescent young man by the double pleated French cuff and handmade silver cufflink, 'you have one of our muffins for free. Here you are. It can come out of my wages. And I'll give you a cup of coffee, too.'

I nodded and poured the coffee. Clearly this was one of those highly strung characters, stock exchange or merchant banker, if I was any judge, who only allowed himself a few treats. But they had to be premium. One haircut, but it had to be from Le Paris. One serve of soup, but it had to be Porelli's. One car, but it had to be a Porsche. One steak, but it had to be Vlado's. One tie, but it had to be Gucci. One definitive Vienna schnitzel, but it had to be Le Gourmet's. And one muffin—and the poor boy had chosen Best Fresh.

Already much comforted by Goss' attentions, he sipped some coffee and then bit into a Jason chocolate orgasm muffin. This is not only a chocolate muffin but has chocolate ganache inside, which fills the mouth with the essence of pure chocolate. I cannot imagine eating more than one, but they are superb. If he gets into the pastry-makers' guild, they will be Jason's masterpiece. They would earn him a hat in any sensible food guide.

Goss and I, and Jason, who had come in from the bakery, watched him in suspense. First there was the raising of the eyebrows, denoting astonishment. Then there was the gradual realisation that this was, indeed, a chocolate orgasm. There was the blissful consumption of the rest of the muffin. Finally he swallowed the last crumb and sipped some more coffee.

'Yes,' he said crisply. 'You do make the best. I'll send someone in every day for a dozen. Any flavour. Thank you,' he said to Goss, handing her a twenty dollar note. 'No, keep the change. Benson,' he added as he went out. Evidently we should have known the name. 'Stock exchange. A dozen. Every day.'

Goss fished in her own purse and found a ten. 'Half for the muffin man,' she said, handing it over to my apprentice. He laughed and stuffed the note into his pocket.

'I'm cleaning up today,' he said. 'Thanks, Goss. That was nice of you,' he added, and went back into the bakery in case I noticed that he had learned some manners.

Goss patted me. 'See?' she encouraged. 'I told you. The nice people won't want to eat that Best Fresh stuff. That was a really awful muffin.'

'It was,' I agreed. 'I wonder how their rye bread turned out?'

Goss was interested in the story of the rye flour mix-up. She agreed with Mrs. Dawson. I felt freshly vindicated.

Soon the lunch trade flooded in, seeking bread for their soup or something to take home to their starving families. We sold all the cakes and I yelled to Jason that he might think about some small cakes with his raspberry icing tomorrow. Which sent him out to buy some frozen raspberries before he got on with the cleaning and mopping.

Then another visitor arrived, a very tired Greek lady with a lot of shopping bags. She had been to several sales. I knew old Greek ladies and sales. My ribs still occasionally ached from their forcible use of their elbows in securing the towel or sheet on which they had set their Hellenic heart. They always got it, too, to the tune of small yelps of pain from the shoppers around them.

I came out from behind the counter to direct her to the loving arms, familiar food and comfortable chairs at Cafe Delicious when she passed me a bag and said, 'For Mr. Pandopoulos,' and then staggered out in the direction of the cafe.

'It's getting weirder, like you said,' commented Goss, putting the bag behind the counter. I took over so that she could collect herself some lunch as well, and when she came back she did not bring any more gifts from Greeks but just the usual village salad, my favourite food in the universe, and I went into the bakery to find a real fork to eat it with. Nothing is better than black olives, feta cheese, tomatoes, radishes and cucumbers in a lemon, oregano and olive oil dressing. You can just feel it doing you good. I crunched and slurped myself into an equable frame of mind.

By about two thirty business had dried up, and I sent Goss off to the bank with the takings. It's my shop, so I can shut it when I like. I gathered the various offerings to strange Greeks and carried them upstairs, leaving Jason with the cleaning and Meroe's recipe. Jason plugged himself into his iPod and went off into another world, and I carried Horatio up the stairs to my own apartment, as he intimated that he was too fatigued to climb.

I had missed Mrs. Dawson's Russian tea, but I made some of my own. I drank it on the balcony, where Trudi has planted some Corinna-proof plants which Horatio does not relish. He ate a few blades of the soft green grass which Trudi grows for all the Insula cats in their very own flat terracotta bowls, then lounged over to a sunbeam and lay down in it. Actually, was captured by it. I am sure that he meant to perch on the arm of my chair, which he likes to shred, but he never got there. The sunbeam ambushed him and he collapsed and fell asleep instantly.

I was dozing over my detective story, re-reading the Jade Forrester about Harry and whatever his name was—begins with S—and their unlikely love affair, when I was woken by a kiss. It was Daniel. He seemed tired and made himself a drink. Stronger than usual, too. It seemed only civil to join him. Then he noticed the basket from Mama Pandamus and the bag and the cling wrapped plate and said, 'Is that all for Old Spiro?'

Chapter Four

There was a silence. Then I chuckled and poured myself some more gin.

'All right,' I said. 'I should have known it had something to do with you, mystery man. Tell me, before I rupture a gusset. Who the hell is Old Spiro?'

'He's an old man who lives alone and I promised to go and see him this afternoon,' said Daniel, an answer which wasn't as full of information as I could have wished.

'I see. So Mrs. Pandamus sends him a basket of goodies and Yai Yai says that he is a prostitute.'

'I think she meant another word,' said Daniel gravely.

'In all probability,' I agreed. 'Then Anna P comes in with a plate of goodies for Mrs. Pappas,' I went on.

'Who is the lady who takes care of Old Spiro,' Daniel informed me, and poured himself another drink. It was unusual for him to gulp, but he was gulping.

'And the shirts and underwear delivered by the third Greek bearing gifts was for Old Spiro Pandopoulos,' I guessed. He nodded. 'And I do know, by the way, that *timeo Danaos et dona ferentes* actually means "I fear the Greeks and especially those bearing gifts" because Professor Dion told me, but the conventional translation fits this situation better,' I added.

Daniel leaned back and closed his eyes and it seemed a pity to disturb him so I let him sleep for almost an hour and read more of my Harry story before I got up, made coffee, and brought him some. He woke, rubbed a hand over his face, and accepted a cup.

'So where are we going?' I asked.

'You don't have to come,' he replied. 'I didn't ask you to.'

'But unless there is a reason why I should stay away, I am,' I told him. 'You don't look like you are anticipating a pleasant encounter so at least I can take you to dinner and make you feel better.'

'Oh, Corinna,' he said, taking my hand.

And he didn't say anything more but in half an hour Daniel, me and all the parcels were in Timbo's car, on our way to Fitzroy.

Daniel had helped Timbo, an ex-getaway driver, to regain his licence when they let him out of jail, and he acts as Daniel's wheel man. In size he is a smallish Sumo and in tempera-ment a rather soppy labrador dog. I like him very much. He accepted the bag of leftover little gem cakes with which Jason was experimenting. He gave me a big smile and on Timbo a big smile is like one of those huge ones on a drive-in screen. That concluded the conversation and we went off to Fitzroy in a mood of gentle efficiency.

Timbo found the house and stopped.

'About an hour,' said Daniel. 'If you go down Brunswick Street, the best ice cream is at Charmaine's and the best hot chocolate is at Mario's.'

'Okay,' said Timbo and the car slid away.

Daniel squared his shoulders and took up my parcels.

The house was small and old, one of those brick houses evi-dently designed by someone who hated tenants. The windows have looming stone brows which keep out the light and the steps up to the door are uneven and high. There was a light on in the hall and we rang the doorbell.

After a long interval the door opened a crack and a suspicious voice spoke in Greek. Daniel replied. The door creaked open.

That was strange, because what the voice had said was, 'Go away.'

I don't recall whether I have mentioned my only friend at that frightful girls' school to which Grandma Chapman consigned me, once I had learned basic table manners and how to plait my own hair. Her name was Soula and she was Greek and desperately bullied and terribly unhappy, which made an instant bond between us. She had taken me home to her family at weekends sometimes and I had joined in the joyful Greek scrimmage known as 'the kids'. It had been so nice. They had just accepted me and I had learned many things, like how to milk an uncooperative goat (it needs five children, one to milk and the other four holding a leg apiece) and that spinach can taste really good in spanakopita, rather than being the strange blackish stuff which curdled on our school plates and was universally loathed. Soula had gone off and married an Irish artist, of all things, and now raised paintings and children in a palatial villa just outside Florence. Her textiles are greatly valued and she is making a name for herself as a landscape gardener, and if you can do that in Italy, you are good. The thing I had never even thought of telling Daniel was that I spoke a little Greek, and understood a lot more. '*Fighe!*' the old man had said, and that meant, 'Go away!'

And yet he was letting us in. Odd. I followed Daniel inside and we were met by a gnarled old man, presumably Old Spiro. He was small and twisted and looked like he had probably been a mere slip of a lad when he greeted the Turks as they entered Salonika in 1754. He was completely bald and wore a great uncle's hand-me-down blue suit, greasy and threadbare. He inspected Daniel narrowly, and then gave me an unpleasant once-over. His eyes went immediately to the basket and he reached out rude hands for it. This was a social solecism. He probably didn't care about manners, having outlived them. I hung on to the basket so he had to lead us into his parlour.

It was stuffy and unused but clean. I put my basket down on a table draped in sugar-stiffened antimacassars and asked, 'Mrs. Pappas?'

In answer Old Spiro bashed on the adjoining wall with a shoe. A female voice shrieked something in response. Old Spiro did not speak or invite us to sit. Presently a middle-aged Greek woman came in through the back door, halted when she saw us, then hurried forward.

'Mrs. Pappas?' I asked again. She nodded, breathless. I handed over the plate.

'Mrs. Pandamus sent these to you, and asked you to call her.'

'That was kind,' replied Mrs. Pappas in English. 'Come, come into the kitchen, leave the men to their talk. I make you lemonade, such a hot day.'

'And coffee for them?' I asked.

'He's not to have coffee, the doctor said,' she replied. 'He's very old. My grandmother married his brother. His younger brother.'

'I was also given these.' I caught her up at the kitchen door. The kitchen was clean and shabby and looked comfortable. She inspected the shopping bag.

'Good, his old ones are in rags. Kyria Elena always get them cheap enough so he'll pay. He's a mean old devil,' sighed Mrs. Pappas, opening the fridge and getting out ice and home-made lemonade syrup. 'But the Devil looks after his own. There, sit here while I make up a tray and find the *glykos*. Would you like some?'

I have never turned down *glykos*, a confection made of candied citrus peel. This one was made of orange peel and was delightfully chewy. The lemonade was also excellent. By custom, having offered me refreshment which I had accepted, Mrs. Pappas could now ask me what I was doing at Old Spiro's house. She struggled to form the question. I saved her the trouble.

'My friend Daniel wants to talk to him,' I said. 'I haven't the faintest idea what it's about.'

'I hope it's not trouble,' she said. 'I'll take in the tray and if we sit here we can hear what it's all about. I can't give him coffee but maybe some ouzo. The doctor hasn't got around to telling him he can't have ouzo.'

She collected glasses and the bottle and the little dishes of *glykos* and went into the parlour, was not thanked by Old Spiro but got an '*eftharisto*' from Daniel, and came out, not shutting the door. We could hear quite well.

Mrs. Pappas might have been forty, but while the men were talking she aged twenty years in front of my eyes. I couldn't understand all of the words, but she could, and even I caught the dreadful tone of the story from Daniel's soft questions. Sometimes she whispered a translation.

They were talking about the German occupation of Thessaloniki, Salonika, where most of the Jews in Greece had lived since 1492 when that Columbus-loving King Ferdinand and Queen Isabella expelled them from Spain. A little later they had been driven from Portugal. With their sophistication and languages and capital and trading skills they had made Salonika the Mother of Israel and a very prosperous and beautiful place.

'Then the Germans came,' whispered Mrs. Pappas. 'They wanted the Jews. We gave them the Jews. Who needs Jews? *Christofonos*.'

I knew that word. Christ-killer. Until very recently all the Christians blamed the Jews for killing Christ, carefully forgetting that Christ was also a Jew. And that they were getting their information from only one side. The Polish Pope, who knew Jews personally, apologised. Soula had told me that most of the really anti-Semitic stuff had been left out of the Orthodox liturgy. Everyone was a bit embarrassed by the Holocaust. The hateful old voice was going on. Old Spiro was gloating and I wondered that Daniel could bear to be in the same room, or house, or country with him.

'All of them. Mothers and fathers and little children. I saw them go. It was Commandant Mertens. He was very good at getting rid of them.'

Mrs. Pappas fumbled for a handkerchief to wipe her eyes. Her translation dried up for a moment but I heard the words for 'child' and 'mother'. And *nekros*, the word for 'dead'. Daniel was talking, his accent soft and educated, his Greek too fast for me to even pick out words. Mrs. Pappas abruptly shoved back her chair, got up, opened a vegetable bin, and brought out a bottle of whisky. She opened it with a twist of her strong wrists and spilled a lot into her lemonade. I followed suit.

Then I picked out more words. The word *Ebraois*, Jews, and the word *chrysafi*, meaning 'gold', also the names of jewels; *amethystos, thiamandes, rombeeni, zahfeeri*. Amethyst, diamond, ruby, sapphire. Mrs. Pappas took a gulp and began translating again. 'They were all gone at last. It took weeks. But they all went away to slaughter. I knew they were going to die because I was a friend of Max Mertens. I translated for him. He didn't speak Greek. Oh, you old demon,' she interpolated. 'You old devil! How could you? Mothers and children! I curse you,' said Mrs. Pappas in a cold white undertone. 'I curse you with the leprosy of Namaan, the sorrows of Job, the pangs of death, the noose of Judas, the whale of Jonah, the shivering of the dying, the horrors of Hell...'

Someone had told me that Greek was a wonderful language to curse in, and it was. Over her incantation I could catch a few more words. One, I am sure, was *ploio*, ship. Then *psarema*, fishing. Then I took a last gulp of my drink because it seemed that Daniel had heard enough. The parlour door opened.

'Time to go?' I asked.

'More than time,' he answered, one hand steadying himself on the wall.

'People will know,' promised Mrs. Pappas. 'They will know what he has done. They will curse him too. Take this,' she said, giving me the open bottle of whisky. 'Tomorrow I bring the priest. He must confess. Monster! Offspring of a goat and a sea-serpent! Cruel heart! We never knew,' she added, pushing us out of the door, tears streaming down her face.

We left. It was quiet in the street. Timbo had not come back. I looked at my watch. We had only been inside for half an hour.

I sat down in the gutter, which was one of those high stone Fitzroy gutters, and drew Daniel down to sit beside me. He slumped.

'Drink,' I instructed, handing him the bottle. He obeyed. I could have given him straight hemlock and he would have swallowed it down. The air was warm and the atmosphere pleasant, a sharp contrast to the evil clogging the air inside. 'I probably forgot to tell you that I know a little Greek,' I told him. '*Ligo*, just a little. And Mrs. Pappas was translating until she started cursing him. If all of those fates fall on Old Spiro he won't survive the night.'

'He does not deserve to survive the night,' said Daniel quietly. He leaned his head on my shoulder and closed his eyes and we sat there in the Fitzroy dusk, not speaking, sipping the whisky, until Timbo came back full of ice cream (the Charmaine flavour of the day was hazelnut) and he asked us where we wanted to go.

'Out or home?' I put it to Daniel.

He did not reply at once. Then he sat up with a great effort and said, 'I don't think I will be very good company tonight.'

'Back to my place, Timbo, and spur the horses,' I instructed, and the car sped into the night. Timbo loved someone to tell him to drive fast. We were back at Insula in a very short time. I paid Timbo and let him go.

Daniel allowed me to lead him up the stairs and lower him onto my couch, where Horatio courteously made room for him. Then I warmed some chicken and barley soup and watched him drink it. I hesitated over a DVD, turned on the television and found that an old Star Trek movie was playing, the one about the whales. Perfect. It even had a happy ending.

I ate my own supper in the kitchen, watching Daniel slowly slipping into relaxation. By the time Captain Kirk was telling the girl that he *came* from Iowa, he only *worked* in Outer Space, Daniel was asleep. I covered him with the mohair rug and took myself to a punitive shower, in which I scrubbed as much of the memory of Old Spiro off my skin as Mr. Pears could cope with.

My shell-shocked lover did not wake enough for me to move him so I lowered the lights and went to bed. I had to get up at four.

I surfaced as Daniel slipped into bed behind me, curled himself around me, and fell asleep again. With Horatio warming my stomach and Daniel warming my back, I closed my eyes. Very pleasant, if a little claustrophobic.

Four o'clock and the alarm brought Daniel awake and screaming. I grabbed at him as he leapt out of bed and he swung around glaring, and for a moment I thought he was going to strike me. Then Horatio hit him with a full-strength, outraged, all-claws-extended swat across the naked thigh and he flinched and woke up.

'Oh God, Corinna,' he cried, 'I didn't hurt you?'

'No, Horatio hurt you,' I said. 'I feel just the same when that bloody alarm rings.'

I stomped into the kitchen and put on the coffee, wondering where I had hidden the painkillers. I had a hangover, my first in many years. Do not drink cheap whisky in Fitzroy gutters after emotional shocks, someone should have told me. My head throbbed and my mouth tasted like incontinent parrots had roosted there overnight. I poured out a large glass of water and drank it, then another. I went and brushed my teeth. I slurped some more water. Daniel found his underwear and came into the kitchen just as the coffee was ready.

'I'm sorry,' he mumbled. 'I was dreaming.'

'Coffee,' I said. I drank a cup standing and then put on the kettle again. This was going to be a caffeine-laden morning. Daniel sipped, wincing at the electric light.

'You need to go back to sleep,' I said, kissing him. He smelt like nail polish, the stench of fear. That must have been a very bad dream. 'But have a shower first, and a little breakfast.'

'I stink,' he agreed, and stumbled off to the bathroom. I went in to get my painkillers and found him standing in the stream of scalding water, letting it pour over his head. I noticed again the massive scar where Palestinian shrapnel had gutted but just failed to kill him. Oh, my precious Daniel. Hundreds of thousands such as he were trucked off to the death camps and murdered, lost forever. I could imagine what he had been dreaming. A thin trickle of blood from Horatio's claws ran down his perfect thigh. I dragged myself away.

More coffee, more water, a couple of pills and I was able to contemplate toast. Horatio was unwilling to contemplate kitty dins and was still affronted, growling softly. His tail was still bristling. I offered him what Professor Dion calls 'a solatium' in the form of cream and watched his fur subside as he licked delicately, making it last. My hackles were going down, too. That was not a nice way to rise from the downy couch.

More coffee, sourdough toast with cherry jam. I found I could contemplate a day's baking after all. To complete the cure, I dug my last and only packet of Gitanes out from under my jumpers, took one and went onto the balcony with it. I hardly smoke at all now. But sometimes one needs a cigarette.

It was a dark morning. The streets were silent. Every city, even all-night ones like Athens, has an hour when the last of the night people have staggered home and the earliest of the day people are just getting up. Four am is Melbourne's changeover hour. I lit the Gitane and sat puffing luxuriously. It was still too early for mosquitoes. In any case Gitane smoke will keep off anything but sandflies and Amway salesmen.

I had just begun to wonder why Daniel had gone to see that loathsome old man when I ran out of Gitane. Slightly dizzy, I rose and went back inside.

My kitchen looked cosy. A rough-dried young man was feeding cream to a cat. The air smelt of toast and coffee. Horror was being abolished by hot water and soap and ordinariness, which is just as it should be. Daniel smiled and passed over a plate of fresh toast and the gruyère cream cheese I like.

'I took a couple of your pills,' he said softly. 'I can't tell you how sorry I am.'

'Stop being sorry,' I snapped. 'You were asleep. I'm sorry that my ill-mannered cat sliced you across the thigh. I'm going to put on my working clothes. How are you feeling?' I asked, kissing him on the neck. Now he smelt of my cleansing soap, wet hair and coffee. A great improvement.

'Better,' he said. 'It was that old man. I never met anyone like him.'

'Me neither, and I hope that means there aren't many of him around. I suggest that you grab a few more hours' sleep. I'm sure Horatio will be glad to accompany you.'

'I hope he's forgiven me, too,' said Daniel. Horatio, hearing his name, gave my lover an assessing look, licked at his whiskers in case there was any trace of cream left, then tucked his paws under him as he paid close attention to his kitty dins.

'I'd say the chances are pretty good,' I said. I kissed Daniel again, and went down the stairs to the shop.

There was no chance of catching Jason being late today, because I was late myself. I walked brazenly into the bakery a full half-hour beyond my usual time and found that all was in motion. Mixers mixed. The air conditioning hummed. Jason's clothes were in the dryer and Jason himself was taking a tray of small buns out of the oldest oven.

'They smell very good, spicy and fruity,' I said.

'It's that old recipe you gave me to try. Since I had some time to play with it yesterday, I worked out some proportions,' he told me. 'How are you, Boss?'

'Shipshape and Bristol fashion,' I said, saluting.

'Aye, aye, sir,' replied Mr. Midshipman Jason. 'Buns at five o'clock, sir!'

I tore one apart. The bread dough had accepted the spices and sugar, though it seemed a little dry. I bit. Really nice. Just what a hungover woman needed. Perfect texture, hot, filling, sweet.

'Good,' I said. 'Maybe a bit more moisture for the next batch. These are a teensy bit dry. But the balance of fruit and spices is excellent. Can I have another?'

'Nice to see you eat them, Captain,' said Jason. 'I've got all the bread on. I thought I might try some of those little cakes, but...'

I knew his tricks and his manners. 'You need to practise breaking eggs with one hand. Right. Break each one over a clean saucer. That way you can collect up the failed ones and we shall make challah later.'

'Where's Daniel?'

'Asleep, I hope. We had a rather action packed night. No, not that sort of action. Haven't you got something you should be doing, Midshipman?'

'Aye, aye, sir.' He saluted and then took a dozen eggs over to the sink, where spills would not be so tenacious as on the floor. I had a feeling that breaking eggs with one hand wasn't as easy as it looked.

I was right, by the way that Jason was risking injury by cursing in the bakery ten minutes later. Still, eggs weren't expensive. And I had things to think about, the primary one being, why had Daniel gone to see that evil old man? What was his reason? Who was his client? And why had he agreed to do it when he must have known how it would make him feel? It was probably one of those 'a man's gotta do what a man's gotta do' things which rendered the casualty rate so high in *Gunsmoke*.

I got on with my challah. There would be plenty of egg for the egg-mixture. After about twenty minutes of cracking noises and solid swearing, Jason called me over.

'Look, Cap! Mission accomplished!'

Just as Daniel had done, he broke the egg and separated it, all with one hand.

'Brilliant,' I said.

'Only thing is,' said my midshipman slowly, 'what do I do with the other hand?'

I was about to say something I might have regretted when there was a stir outside in the alley. Someone was screaming.

'Wash your hands—I mean, hand—and find the mobile, Jason,' I ordered.

'You're not going to open that door!' he exclaimed. 'Some dude's being killed out there!'

'Not in my alley, not on my watch,' I said firmly, sliding the door open a crack. I grabbed the baker's friend, a long, heavy slide used to take loaves out of the oven, just in case of argument.

It was still dark in Calico Alley. The one feeble light only made the darkness visible. But the screaming was coming towards me. I gripped the slide, ready to fell any attacker with arms made strong by years of kneading and hauling sacks. I could hear Jason scrabbling through my bag for the phone. A handful of coins rang on the stone floor.

Then I saw her, a woman out of her mind with pain or rage, tearing her hair, shrieking that her feet were burning, burning! But there was no flame. I could not smell smoke. She was entirely alone.

Windows began to open in the building above me, lights coming on as apartment dwellers were shocked out of sleep. I hoped that Daniel would not hear.

'Ambos on their way,' Jason called. 'What's happening?'

'Fucked if I know,' I replied honestly. Oh, dear. I was courting bad luck in my bakery by using language like that. But the bad luck seemed to have already arrived.

She was young. She had been out to a disco or a club. She was wearing what Kylie or Goss would have worn, a minimum of clothing, with spangles, bubble skirt, tights and high platform shoes. Her dark hair was torn and dishevelled, and she limped and stumbled and shrieked until I had to fight down the impulse to belt her with the slide and put her out of my misery. At least to silence that dreadful noise.

But I went out and threw my arms around her because she was young and human and female, and instead of fighting me she collapsed into my grasp and sobbed and fumbled for her feet and mumbled about burning, burning. It was unpleasant to be near her. As Daniel had smelt of fear, she smelt strange; a musky, mushroomy smell. I've got a good nose and I'd never smelt that odour before. She was sweating like she had a breaking fever and the scent was in her skin, and now on mine.

Mrs. Dawson called down to me, her voice as clear as if she had been standing next to me.

'Corinna? Do you need assistance?'

'No, it's all right,' I replied. 'Ambulance is on its way. Thanks,' I added.

The girl writhed and whimpered. In all it was with great relief that I handed her over to the ambulance officers, who loaded her into their vehicle.

'What is it about this end of town lately?' asked Jules. 'You been poisoning the customers, Corinna?'

'I doubt that she ate any of my bread,' I told her.

'Eleven cases in a week,' said Jules. 'There's something new on the street which is converting citizens into fruitcakes. Well, off we go. You got a muffin for a poor hardworking chick?' she asked Jason.

'And her poor hardworking non-chick partner,' put in Tommo.

'Two left,' said Jason, and gave them the last of the chocolate ones. 'Making jam ones today, drop in later.'

'No offence, but I hope not,' replied Jules, and the ambulance light bobbed away down the alley. When they got out into the lane, they put on the siren and it shattered the night. I heard more windows slam and voices complain. Mrs. Pemberthy would be calling a tenants' meeting, I just knew, to demand that ambulances be banned from the alley.

'Phew,' said Jason.

'Phew,' I agreed.

'You can have the shower first,' he offered. 'As a superior officer.'

He was right. I needed a wash. I smelt like a mushroom farm. I showered in the bakery bathroom, put on clean trackies and stuffed the others into the washing machine.

'Me, too?' asked Jason, as I dried my hair. 'I feel all crappy, seeing something like that.'

'Full steam ahead, Mr. Midshipman,' I ordered.

I wondered if I was going to regret giving him Hornblower to read. Jason had not really had a childhood and he was only passingly literate. I would have started with something simpler but he had lit upon Hornblower and was puzzling his way through it with manful determination. And who was I to discourage him? Enough people had already tried to discourage Jason without me putting my oar (sorry) in. He was getting a massive kick out of all this naval stuff and was showing a fine natural talent as a mimic.

'Aye, aye, Captain,' responded Jason.

The day came, calm and bright. Only homely noises could be heard; the twittering of Melbourne sparrows, the world's most indestructible bird. The Mouse Police padding out for their morning fish. The paper boy hitting the door dead centre with his plastic wrapped missile. Kiko of the Japanese restaurant putting on Radio Nippon as she always did at six sharp. Nice, normal. Humdrum. Humdrum is soothing. The bread cooked, smelling superb. There was a sharp scent of fruit as Jason compounded his raspberry icing.

Ordinary. I *like* ordinary.

Chapter Five

Too good to last. The baking proceeded with efficiency and dispatch, the loaves went into the oven flabby and came out shiny, the muffins smelt heavenly. The little cakes rose evenly and when Jason went out for breakfast I ate one with my next cup of coffee. The compounded fruit icing was sharp and almost sour, setting off the sweetness of the cake beautifully. The icing doesn't last well, but then it usually doesn't hang around for too long.

Time to open the shop. I had my hand on the shutters when someone spoke, far too close and directly behind me, and I jumped a mile. If I had been Horatio I would have sprung up into the curtains.

'Miss Chapman? Are you Corinna Chapman?'

'Part of her,' I said, putting a hand to my breast to check that my heart was still inside. It was. I could tell from the way it was thumping. Two blue-clad ladies looked at me evenly.

'Senior Constable Bray, Constable Vickery. Can we come in?'

'Surely,' I said, unlocking the shutters and letting them slide up with a click. I unlocked the bakery door and allowed the officers to enter.

The speaker, SC Sharon Bray according to her nametag, was a small, stocky woman who looked as though she had survived an eventful childhood with three older brothers and was consequently not going to be frightened of anything, ever again. She was good-looking, with humorous brown eyes and cropped, curly brown hair. Constable Helen Vickery was thinner, paler and solemn. They both sniffed appreciatively as they became aware of the divine scent. Jason peeked out of the bakery and slid back into it like an eel into mud. Despite his present state of virtue, Jason did not like cops.

'Well, what can I do for you on this cold morning?' I asked. 'Cup of coffee and a muffin?'

'We're asking about the girl in the alley,' said Sharon Bray. 'And coffee and a muffin would be very nice. It's been quite a night. And it's still not over.'

Kylie came in, dressed in a long strange garment apparently made of purple fishing net with feathers knitted into it. She widened her eyes at the sight of blue uniforms in the shop and hastened to supply coffee and two of the new jam-filled muffins. There was a pause as proper reverence was given to the pâtissière's art, then the senior constable put down her cup and produced her notebook.

'Tell me about it,' she said, and I told her everything I had observed, including the odd scent of the girl's skin. Sharon Bray made notes. Constable Vickery poked around the shop, picking things up and putting them down again in a manner calculated to drive the guilty into confession. And the innocently nervous into conniptions.

'The ambos said this was the eleventh,' I told my interrogator. 'Is there something new on the street?'

'Yep,' she replied soberly. 'Something very nasty. Trouble is, none of them have been able to tell us what they took. I've seen stuff that sends them mad, but with this stuff they stay mad. Tox screens are coming back with "unknown compound" in them.'

'That's bad,' I said inadequately.

'Have you seen anyone hanging around, perhaps dealing?' she asked. 'You're here very early, aren't you? Patrol says you start at four.'

'So I do,' I said. 'But I haven't seen anyone in the alley except the people who are usually in the alley—you know, the night people, security guards, cops, the paper boy, no strangers but the ones who collapse on my doorstep. I wonder…'

'You wonder?' she asked sharply.

'I wonder why here?' I reasoned it out. 'I mean, this alley only leads into the arcade and the arcade is closed from about eleven until eight am. But there is a little linking back alley where the rubbish men come to collect. That leads around a dogleg into Schmutter Alley and out into Flinders Lane again. I wonder if the dealer is there?'

'You can't see into the link from here?'

'No. Come into the bakery,' I said, determined to show everything I had to the police in case they got ideas. They followed me. Jason dropped to his knees and pretended to be taking bread out of an oven.

'This is my apprentice, Jason. Say hello to the nice ladies, Jason.'

He scrambled up and mumbled, 'H'lo.'

Sharon Bray eyed him narrowly but didn't say anything. I led them to the alley door. The Mouse Police woke up and blinked and Constable Vickery cooed at them and stroked their heads. They purred. I preceded Ms. Bray out into Calico Alley.

'See, the link's right at the back, where the arcade stairs are. I can't see into it from this angle. But the victims have come down the alley towards me, and there's no other way they could have got into it.'

'We'll certainly take a look,' said the senior constable, snapping her notebook shut. 'Thanks, Miss Chapman. Come on, Constable. Say bye-bye to the puddy-tats.'

Constable Vickery blushed and followed and I watched the strong blue-clad figures move away toward Kiko's. I hoped they found that dealer. He would know that he had been in a fight.

Excitement over, I went back into the bakery to soothe Jason's shattered nerves and get on with the day's work. There were people to feed, and it was up to us to feed them.

'Cops!' he was muttering. 'In our kitchen!'

He sounded like a scruffy male version of Lady Macbeth: *Ah, woe, alas! What, in our house?*

'You've changed sides,' I reminded him. 'The police officers are now required to protect you, Jason dear, from people like the—'

'Person I used to be,' he finished.

'Well, yes,' I agreed lamely.

Kylie interrupted and saved my face. 'Those jam cakes are fantastic,' she told Jason. 'Can I have another one?'

'S'pose,' he grunted, mollified.

'Don't forget the dozen muffins for the stock exchange.' I told Kylie about the elegant young man. 'Benson. Of course. I should have known the name, indeed. He's a wunderkind. Supposed to have the stock exchange equivalent of perfect pitch. Makes millions in a day.'

I went back into the shop. Horatio had taken his place by the cash register and the first customers were already caressing the royal whiskers. Something about my statement worried me, but there was a rush of business and I forgot about it.

The morning continued in the usual way. The police did not return. I went out into the alley to empty the bin into the big skip—yes, all right, I was curious—and found that, as I had said, the little alley only linked Calico and Schmutter alleys and didn't go anywhere else. Why anyone would want to hang about in this small, badly paved and malodorous place was beyond me. But addicts will be addicts and drugs will be drugs and I took my bin back with no further information. Except that I noticed, written on the wall in small, beautifully formed letters, the word 'wassail'. Probably not important.

We sold more bread and Megan the courier came for the restaurant orders.

'Cops all over,' she remarked as we loaded the trays into her motorcycle rickshaw. 'Had my licence checked four times.'

'All in order, I trust?'

'Of course, Corinna, this is my living. What are they doing? They wouldn't tell me anything.'

'Looking for a dealer whose drugs have sent eleven people off their rockers,' I told her. 'Should you be going to a club any time soon, I'd buy my pills somewhere else.'

Megan gave me a censorious look. 'I don't take drugs,' she said. 'I get high in perfectly legal ways. On chocolate, mostly. Especially Heavenly Pleasures Cafe Noir. That stuff could fuel rockets. Bye,' she added, and sped off, driving more circumspectly than usual in view of the police presence. Which meant that she rounded the corner on both sets of wheels.

I was mildly worried about how Daniel was managing and took a moment off from the baking consultation over the spiced buns Meroe had requested to climb the stairs. But he was fast asleep and would, with any luck, remain so until I had time to ask him some questions.

We sold bread. It was a quiet day. I opened the mail. Nothing but the usual bills, an invitation to a book launch, a few people interested in my fiscal future offering me shares in various doomed enterprises and my copy of the accountancy newsletter which my professional body occasionally sends for the edification of us numbers people.

Article by that same Benson. Strange little bump in gold exploration. Bendigo. Someone had told me that there was a lot more gold in the ground in that area than had ever come out of it, but it was in deep veins in quartz and not worth winning. In fact, hadn't someone discovered a really rich vein of ore and would have made a fortune except that the Bendigo people selfishly objected to him burrowing under their houses? Someone now thought that they could float a company on what they had found. The newsletter was noncommittal. Might be, might not. Wait and see what the Navarino Gold Company's assay turned up. Sound advice. Navarino? I had heard the word before. Some sort of orange, perhaps?

I heard Daniel coming down the stairs and put the newsletter away. He looked better. The dark marks under his eyes had lightened. He was wearing his Shalom t-shirt and jeans.

'Hello!' I kissed him. 'Lunch?'

'Got to go,' he replied. 'Have to report to the client.'

'About Old Spiro?'

'Yes,' he said uneasily.

'Well, what about dinner?'

'Not tonight,' he said, shifting his gaze. 'I have to—'

'There you are, Danny,' said a Sloane voice triumphantly. 'You're late.'

Standing in the doorway of my bakery was a vision in dark grey: bubble skirt, tights, tall shoes, cropped blazer, string tie enclosing creamy throat. Her long hair was folded into a perfect French pleat. She looked taller than I remembered and Kylie, beside her, seemed diminished and shabby. This did not make me like Georgiana Hope any better.

She reached out an immaculate hand and took Daniel by the arm. 'You promised to show me Melbourne,' she reminded him. The scent of Poison enveloped me, overruling the earthy smell of baking bread.

'Oh,' said Daniel. 'Yes, I suppose so. Bye, Corinna.'

And he followed her out of the shop without a backward glance. Jason swore. Kylie, however, had clasped her hands to her nonexistent bosom in rapture.

'Did you see her clothes?' she breathed.

'They were boring,' said Jason. 'Like a school uniform.'

'What do you know about it?' snarled Kylie.

'I know you look better than that bitch,' said Jason stoutly. 'Behave better, too.'

Kylie gave Jason the sort of look one gets when announcing a large lottery win to the lucky contestant.

'I never knew you looked at what I was wearing!' she exclaimed.

'Can't help it, can I?' asked Jason sensibly. 'You're right in front of me. You look like the girls in magazines. She looked like a schoolgirl. An *old* schoolgirl.'

I could have kissed him, but he doesn't like emotional scenes. Kylie, who was immensely flattered, patted Jason on the cheek. There was a moment of silence.

'Muffins,' I said. 'For the stock exchange wunderkind. You choose the muffins, Jason, will you? You pack them, Kylie, use the dark brown tissue paper and make them look pretty. Mr. Benson's PA is waiting.'

They got busy, and so did I. But I wasn't happy. It was, after all, Thursday. I have never really got the hang of Thursdays, as Arthur Dent said. Daniel hadn't seemed enthusiastic about going along with that 'old schoolgirl'—I would love Jason forever for that description—so I dismissed the incident from my mind as far as such things can be dismissed, and left Kylie and Jason with the shop. Kylie was still examining Jason as though she had never seen him before. Jason was thinking about Meroe's spiced cakes and ignoring her. That can be very attractive. Not, however, to me.

Nothing I could do about one rival, so it was time for me to have a look at the other. I went upstairs and donned polite daytime clothes, my jeans, a t-shirt and a fleecy jacket, and went forth, basket and purse in hand, to sample the wares of Best Fresh Bread. And I had found my other good shoe wedged under the dressing table, so that was a plus for the day.

On the way out through the lobby, I paused to watch Trudi and her kitten, the death-defying Lucifer, feeding the fish. That is, Trudi was feeding the fish with sweeps of her gardener's gnarled hand, and Lucifer was fighting his harness, attempting to get free and convert the koi into entrees. He was perfectly capable of leaping in and taking the fight to the fish, so the harness was a wise precaution. The coloured fins rose up, eying the cat warily. They knew those clawed ginger paws. He had almost got them on several action-packed occasions.

'Corinna!' Trudi greeted me. She is stocky, sixty-five and Dutch, our gardener and maintenance worker, the only person whom the freight lift obeys. She is always dressed in blue. Blue cotton shirt and trousers for summer and blue woollen jumper and jeans for winter. And, of course, a boldly contrasting cat, who rides on her shoulder most of the time as though he has just eaten her parrot. 'The scarlet tulips, they are out! Such beauty!'

'I'll go and see them this afternoon,' I promised. She had extorted extra gardening fees from us for those tulips, and promised they would be superb. I don't think they would have dared be otherwise. If Trudi tells something to grow, it grows.

'Bad cat,' she said to Lucifer, who had rolled into a tangled ball with one paw waving insouciantly out of the mass of tethers. 'I tell you already, no fish, I give you fish in your dinner! Not these ones!'

I left her to unravel the kitten and went on my way, refreshed. There was something fundamental about Lucifer which was very charming. He was a cat with no nuances. If it moved, he either chased it or chewed it or ate it or slept on it.

Best Fresh was located just beyond Heavenly Pleasures in Flinders Lane. It had been an old tailor's shop and someone had gutted it and built a new shopfront in place of the old workshop. It was pinker than one could have wished but certainly clean and shiny, with several small iron tables and chairs and a long counter, behind which one could see into the bakery. I looked at their prices and sighed. I could not match them even operating at a serious loss. Two muffins for two dollars! Mine cost eighty-five cents to make and I sold them at five dollars each. They were, of course, superior muffins, made by the Muffin Mage, but for one of mine you could get three of Best Fresh. I leaned the basket on the counter and a bored blonde girl in a pink uniform, nametag Janelle, said, 'Can I help you?' through a mouthful of chewing gum.

I bought a loaf of white pane di casa, a selection of rolls and three different muffins. This did not come to much. I surveyed the action in the bakery, which seemed to consist of one working mixer and one spotty youth putting trays of rolls into a new electric oven. I could not see anyone who looked like the boss. They had a list of their products and I took one and fought off a lacklustre attempt by the girl to enlist me in a loyalty program. Hypocrisy can only go so far.

I was in the street when someone said, 'You're buying Best Fresh?'

I turned swiftly and it was Meroe. I put a finger to my lips. 'Shh, I'm undercover.'

'Come to Pandamus for a cup of chakra-tarnishing caffeine?' she suggested.

This was so unusual that I agreed and we fell into step.

'Anything bothering you?' I asked as delicately as possible.

'No more than you, my dear, with Georgiana and Best Fresh on your plate. I've got witches.'

'Yes,' I said. I wasn't going to ask how she knew about Georgie and Best Fresh. Meroe always knows. She and the Delphic Oracle would have had a lot in common if they'd sat down for a cup of ouzo and a chat about prophecy. 'That's because you're a witch.'

'I'm a solitary,' she told me. 'I don't belong to a coven. And the reason I don't belong to a coven is…'

'You don't like other witches?'

She drew in a quick breath, was about to deny it, then laughed. 'Well, yes. And they are all here in Melbourne for the Hallowe'en festival. We call it Samhain. The feast of the dead. It's Melbourne's turn to hold it this year.'

'And you are organising it?'

She halted suddenly and I ran into her.

'Goddess, no! I'm just on the edge. I don't like large groups of people. I only had to find someone to make the soaling cakes for my group, and I found you and Jason so that's all right. We shall certainly have the best cakes of the festival. No, it's some of the people. They are having a working every night.'

'Why is that a problem?'

She waved her beautiful hands. 'There's…too much magic around,' she tried to explain. 'Magic isn't like oxygen, you can have too much of it. It's interfering with my perceptions. And…I don't trust some of these New Age practitioners.'

'Too vague?' I asked, as we came in through the doorway of Cafe Delicious and found ourselves a pair of seats. Del insists on broad-bottomed cane chairs for his broad-bottomed clientele, for which we thank him.

'Too ambitious,' said Meroe darkly. 'These ones are convinced that they have found treasure.'

'Yeah, right,' I said scornfully. 'The mahogany ship, is it?'

'Funny you should say that,' said Meroe. 'Hello, Del, can we have *cafe hellenico metriou*, please, and maybe…what's the special today?'

'Yai Yai had to go to see Mrs. Pappas,' said Del darkly. 'Katya's cooking. We got goulash and we got veggie soup with pebbles. What you want?'

'Pebbles,' said Meroe.

'Goulash,' I said. I wasn't going to pass up Katya's goulash, which was wonderful. It had to include, she'd told me, a stolen ingredient in order to be authentic. She stole her rosemary from the gardens on the way to work. A neat solution. Then I realised that Yai Yai's Mrs. Pappas was the woman who looked after Old Spiro. 'Wait, Del, is Mrs. Pappas all right?'

'She's a good woman,' Del told me.

'I know,' I said, surprised. 'Why, what's wrong with her?'

'That old man, that old Spiro, he's dead.' Del distributed plates and cutlery to our table like a man dealing cards. 'Kyria Pappas, she upset. She look after him a long time.'

'Dead?' I repeated.

'And good riddance, him,' growled Del. 'But bad death like bad life.'

'Why, how did he die?'

'Choke,' said Del, making a far-too-realistic noise to illustrate. 'Yai Yai, she says he ate her baklava that she put a curse on. You say it in Australian, that curse.'

'Hope it chokes you?' I quoted. Del nodded. He bellowed to the daughter behind the counter to send us some lunch and went to make coffee. He is happy to allow his son to make that wishy-washy inferior espresso coffee with the Gaggia. But he makes the Greek coffee himself, as is proper for the host.

Meroe and I looked at each other.

'You, clearly, have things to tell,' she informed me.

'And you too.'

'After lunch,' she said.

Without asking, Del gave us a small heavy glass of red wine each. Meroe accepted a big white bowl of vegetable soup with the tiny fluffy noodles, *knödlen*, which Del calls pebbles. I ate my goulash, rich, fragrant and heavy, in small mouthfuls while I considered what Del had said. Choked to death. If Old Spiro's story was important, then Daniel had heard the very last account of it. I tore off a piece of my own pane di casa and mopped up garlicky paprika-flavoured sauce. Treasure-hunting witches and treasonous old men. What a world.

Still, it had goulash in it.

Chapter Six

I returned to Meroe's shop with the proprietor. The Sibyl's Cave is very small and crammed with whatever the working witch might need for any spell except those nasty voodoo ones involving dolls, which Meroe does not stock. Her view is that anyone who wants to cast that sort of spell can make their own *poupée* and overload their own karma without her assistance. It's not that she doesn't know how to curse, or objects to cursing if the reason is a virtuous one. She just doesn't like using dolls. I mentioned Mrs. Pappas' curses as I was telling her about the death of Old Spiro.

'Oh, they're good,' she said admiringly, stroking her night-black cat Belladonna, who was occupying the arm of her big chair and looking inscrutable, a thing which black cats can do without even trying. 'Fine, strong, ancient curses, those.'

'Yes, and they seem to have worked,' I commented. 'If he choked before the priest got there to absolve him, he has gone to hell.'

'Seems an appropriate destination,' murmured my witch. 'He'll like the company. Must be stuffed with Nazis by now. They'll be having Bund meetings and trying to oust Satan by putsch. Which won't work,' she added.

'Which is why it is hell,' I agreed.

Bella purred and angled her chin for a scratch. I brushed aside the hanging shells of a charm to attract maritime luck and said, 'Well, that's it. What do you make of it?'

'Georgiana or the Old Spiro story?'

'Both. Either. I feel…hurt.'

'That's men for you,' sighed Meroe. 'I sometimes believe that is what they were designed for. I question the wisdom of the Goddess, but perhaps she was distracted that day. He doesn't sound infatuated with this Georgie.'

'But she definitely has designs on him,' I objected. 'She would love to steal him from me.'

'Corinna, Corinna, one can't steal a person,' she chided me. 'Not unless they want to be stolen. People can be seduced only if they are seducible. If that is a word. You had no reason to doubt Daniel's love before Georgie turned up. You have no reason now. This other matter has clearly upset him. I'd leave it for a few days and see how he recovers. He must have got a severe shock.'

'He did,' I concurred.

'Well, then. People under stress behave badly, it's an axiom of witchcraft.'

'I suppose so,' I said, conscious of sounding like Jason. 'All right, then, what about your glut of witches?'

Meroe rubbed her hands over her face. Belladonna gave her a cool, pitying look and butted the witch's wrist with her nose.

'Yes, Bella, it is silly of me,' she confessed to the cat. 'But I don't like these rituals. It's not that they follow the left hand path deliberately, you understand, but they are…'

'Greyish?' I suggested.

'Grey,' she agreed. 'Tending to darkness. Perhaps it is just their pursuit of worldly wealth that bothers me. Corinna, do me a favour? Come with me tonight. They are having a working on Williamstown beach. I'd really value an uninvolved opinion.'

'Does this mean I have to take off all my clothes in public?' I demanded with deep suspicion.

'No. Only the practitioners will be skyclad. You just have to wear blue and stay silent.'

'I can do that,' I said. A night's sleep was something I cherished, but I could sacrifice it for my friend Meroe, who really was worried. And in any case, Daniel was not going to be in my bed. Which might make it far too empty for sleep.

'Thank you,' she said. 'Be blessed! I'll meet you in the atrium at eleven thirty. Wear blue or black, no jewellery or metal, seashells if you have any.'

I patted Belladonna, kissed Meroe on the cheek and fought my way out of the Sibyl's Cave, ducking under the hanging chimes and amulets in a jangle of sweet sounds. The Tibetan soul-changing bells over the door always got me, as they did anyone over one metre high, and their strange sound, which seemed to contain its own echo, accompanied me into the lane.

Back to Earthly Delights, where Jason and Kylie were holding the fort. The day had proceeded well. Most of the sweet things were gone. Jason was beginning the cleaning. Kylie was loading the remaining loaves into the racks and counting up the unsold.

'Not bad,' she told me. 'Like, Corinna, we nearly sold out of all the muffins and the little cakes. Only eight loaves left.'

'Good,' I encouraged. 'You can take the banking on the way out. Jason? I'm going out with Meroe tonight so I need a nap. Can you factor in more muffins and cakes for tomorrow?'

'Aye, aye, sir!' he said. 'Need to buy more ingredients. Sir!'

'Take a fifty out of my purse,' I told him, paying Kylie from the till.

'Then can I get him some new overalls?' asked Kylie. 'And some other clothes?'

'Yes, provided that you don't overspend,' I told her. 'Jason has to buy his own casual clothes and he doesn't earn much.'

'Because you don't pay me much, sir!' came the voice from the bakery, accompanied by a clanging of buckets.

'Quite right, Midshipman Jason!' I called back. 'Any time you want to renegotiate, say the word.'

'No problem here,' he replied hastily. Cheeky boy. Kylie giggled.

'Just a shirt, I thought, like, a good shirt, and maybe one of those…I don't know, though, maybe Goss'll come too.'

She demonstrated indecision by standing on one foot.

'Just return Jason in good condition in time to do the baking,' I said and left them.

I had meant what I said about a nap, but when I laid myself down, I couldn't sleep. Do not drink *cafe hellenico* if you want to close an eye any time soon, I knew that. After half an hour I got up and took Horatio with me to the roof garden. We sat contemplating tulips and drinking a gin and bitter lemon. I felt that it matched my mood better than the usual tonic.

The tulips were superb. They were scarlet and yellow, strong and upright. Some were splashed with red and white. Some were smooth, some ragged. Splendid. However, one can only spend a certain amount of time staring at tulips and I had spent it. The rest of the garden was blooming with spring flowers, the last of the freesias, the blossom on the linden tree, the profusion of those little mauve stars. The ground was watered by the ingenious recycling system which the original builder had installed, along with his waste-heat-dump temple of Ceres and his air-moisturising impluvium. Those old Romans knew about houses. Apparently they knew about steam, too, but they didn't need it, what with a thousand slaves ready to leap to it on command. Wondering what the world would have been like if the steam train had been invented two thousand years ago, I drifted off into a pleasant daydream.

Horatio woke me an hour later. It was time for his nap. I went down to my apartment and found a letter on the floor. It had evidently been pushed under the door. I opened it, not without trepidation. The last anonymous missive I had received had threatened to kill me. But this was written in pacific blue ink and just said '*Sweet Corinna, how I love you*'. And that was a nice thought, too. I folded the half sheet of plain white paper and put it on my desk. I had a secret admirer. How very encouraging.

There being no prospect of sleep while the Greek coffee was working in my veins, I decided to give the apartment a good clean. After I had got out the bucket and the mop and the cleaning fluids, I decided against it, put them away again and sat down on my couch with my Jade Forrester and three Heavenly Pleasures chocolates. There are days when you need ferocious action, and there are days when you need a new detective story and a chocolate. Today the chocolates won.

I did manage to get five hours' sleep before the alarm went off and I rose to find some blue clothes, farewell Horatio and join Meroe in the atrium. She surveyed me carefully. I had left off my watch and was dressed simply in a dark blue tracksuit and backpack. She wore her usual black with a marvellous blue wrap, almost indigo shot through with paler tendrils like seaweed. She was carrying a large bag stuffed with I know not what which clanked slightly when she moved.

'Good,' she said. 'A blessing on our journey and our returning.' She flung a pinch of salt over our heads. Then she led the way to the lane where a bright green car was waiting. Meroe loaded us into it, told the driver, 'Yes,' and we drew out into the street.

'Williamstown beach,' said Meroe, and shut down. She does this. She just withdraws. As it is no use talking to her when she isn't there, I stared out of the window as Footscray Road flew past. I saw piles of shipping containers like Lego blocks, proclaiming strange ports—Murmansk, Rio de Janeiro, Haifa—and tall cranes straddling the trackway like daddy-long-legs.

I hadn't been to Williamstown since I was taken to the Williamstown festival perhaps five years earlier. Even then I hadn't explored, as I had been escorted by my annoyed then-husband James, who was there to judge a cooking competition and was in the throes of extreme indigestion and a near-terminal fit of the grumps. This limits one's appreciation of landscape. But I remembered the greenswards down to the sea, the boathouses, the cannon on the foreshore in case of invasion from Russia, the yachts from many nations all lined up along the marinas, and the ice cream, which was first rate. Whatever James had said.

It appeared there was more to Williamstown than the Esplanade and the pier. We swept around the Time Ball tower and went uphill to a point no different from any other that I could see, but Meroe told the driver, 'Here,' and she stopped the car. We got out. The driver was a tall, lanky young woman in a blue sarong and swimsuit.

'This is Neraia, our lifesaver,' Meroe introduced me.

'You must be freezing,' I commented, shaking her hand.

She shrugged. 'You get used to it,' she told me. 'Poseidon is my father, Galatea my mother. I like sea water.'

There didn't seem to be any ready reply to this.

Where were we? It looked prosperous. Big houses lined one side of the road. The other was a verge with trees and rough grass, leading down to a rocky coast. I had no idea that such wild landscape existed so close to the city. The wind had dropped. It was dead quiet. On the calm salty air, I could hear chanting, and smell incense.

'This way,' said Meroe, and led us across the turf to the shore.

The sea foamed and splashed on sharp broken boulders. This was the blacksoil plain, of course, the rocks would all be volcanic. Black basalt by the look of it, and if anyone intended to ask me to tippy-toe out onto that slippery knife-edged barrier, they had another think coming. But Meroe gestured to me to sit at the edge of the sea and I sat, able to see all that was going on and probably invisible to the eye in my dark blue garments. Neraia shed her sarong and waded into the sea.

There were twelve naked people in the water, pale as moonlight. I shivered in sympathy, but they seemed to feel no discomfort. They had formed a ring, hand in hand, and were chanting in an unknown tongue. 'Evoe! Evoe!' they called. 'Poseidon Evoe!'

It was cold and oddly boring as well as uncomfortable and interesting. I shifted my weight as different bits of my spine impacted the gravel I was sitting on. In fact, since nothing whatsoever seemed to be happening, I scooted uphill until I was sitting under a thrawn tree, where the ground was hard but not actively pointy. Three people on the shore were tending a small, hot fire, on which they were burning an incense that smelt seaweedy and musky. It was not a nice smell but it was compelling.

The chant was heating up. Meroe was standing with her wrap drawn close over her head and her arms folded, concentrating hard, like a fisherman's wife watching for a returning boat.

The wind picked up. The waves creamed and then folded. There was a slap and splash of water. Out at sea the lights of the big ships moved slowly on their voyages out or home. And the sea existed, uninterested in these brief, fragile humans who could not survive underwater for more than a couple of minutes. Who were these importunate idiots, I wondered, to dare to call upon the lord of the sea? They could all be obliterated with one casual slap of a sea-monster's paw.

I didn't like my train of thought. I also didn't know where it had come from. I stood up. If Poseidon resented being summoned, I wanted to be out of the backwash when he annihilated the coven.

The chanting was rising to a shout. The figure in the centre, crowned with shells, suddenly vanished and the whole ring was dragged underwater with him. Neraia slid forward like a seal. But they came up again, after a breath-catching interval, shedding water, gasping and laughing. Meroe stood like a highly disapproving pillar of salt as the coven waded ashore and grabbed at wraps and towels and exclaimed at the cold.

The man with the crown of shells was imposing. Solid, big, wide shoulders, a broad face with a black beard. I was nose to loin with him as he climbed the back. Nice loins, if a little chilled and shrunken. He laughed hugely and opened his hand to show us what Poseidon had sent him.

'Success!' he boomed. 'What do you say now, Meroe?'

'What I have always said, Barnabas,' she replied tartly.

'Where luna shines, there is silver,' he said.

In the palm of his large hand was a jewelled plate, fully the size of a cigarette packet. It was studded with precious stones. Cabochon, not faceted. Hard to tell colour in the moonlight but they might have been emeralds. It looked very old. A fragment of chain hung from each top corner. I wondered what it had been. Not the usual run of pendant, that was for sure. Meroe looked at it without touching.

'And how do you explain this?' she asked. I had never heard her voice so harsh. She was croaking like a crow with tonsillitis.

Barnabas laughed again. He would make a wonderful Father Christmas, I thought, a big jolly man in a red robe.

'Jealous, little witch?' he teased, and swung the object up out of Meroe's reach.

Just then a lot of things happened at once. Meroe stepped back and tripped, falling into me so that we tumbled together under my tree. Five, or perhaps more, men in, I swear, black clothes and black balaclavas attacked the coven in a running assault, moving very fast along the edge of the sea, leaping from rock to rock, and landing on Barnabas so hard that all the breath went out of him in an 'oof!' Then they were gone. So was the pendant. I heard a car start and roar off into the night. Meroe and I untangled ourselves and drew away from Barnabas, who was getting his breath back. His accusing finger shot out.

'You!' he shouted at Meroe. 'You did this!'

'Don't be ridiculous,' she answered with the sort of chill which starts ice ages. 'I don't know who your attackers were but I suggest you dismiss this working properly and go home to scry for your treasure. As I shall do,' she said, withdrawing up the hill. He seemed about to follow, in which case he was going to get a kick on the shins, at least from me, but he thought better of it and turned back to soothe his offended coven.

'You take the car,' said Neraia to Meroe. 'I'd better talk to the nymphs. They don't like violence.'

She chose a place further away from the escalating argument on the shore. I saw her dive in, straight as an arrow. Meroe took the keys and we got into the car and moved off just as we heard sirens.

'Well, I can tell you one thing,' I said. 'That was the most unmagical magical thing I have ever seen.'

'Yes,' she said, turning the car into Melbourne Road. 'Odd, isn't it? There's such a lot of latent magic around that it's curling my hair, but none of it was in that working. Barnabas usually does better than that. Of course a lot of his success is pure personality. People like big, jovial, confident witches.'

'Yes, but, Meroe, what about the men in black? I saw them. Didn't you?'

'Oh yes,' she said airily, as we turned off Melbourne Road for the city. 'I saw them.'

'Who were they?'

'I don't know, as I told Barnabas. Some emanations from the underworld, perhaps.'

I didn't think so. Few emanations from the underworld say 'bugger!' when they slide on slippery rocks.

'They were humans,' I stated.

Meroe shrugged. 'Someone must have been talking,' she said. 'Nothing more likely with these loose-tongued, undisciplined witches. Mention the word *treasure* in a cellar at midnight and someone will hear it. They were organised, I'll say that for them. That was a textbook assault, along, in and out with the jewels and no one injured. Except Barnabas' pride, which could do with a puncture.'

'I have seen that sort of jewelled plate before somewhere,' I told her.

'Oh, so have I,' she said. 'It's an ephod. Read Exodus,' she said, and disappeared into one of her silences for the rest of the way home.

It was too late to read Exodus, but I put the Bible out on the table so I could check up on it after I finished baking. At least it was Friday, and I did not have to get up on Saturday, because I close Earthly Delights for the weekend. There aren't a lot of people about in the city and I need the rest. Best Fresh, I had no doubt, would be operating. With only one worker and a shop assistant, it wouldn't cost the chain a lot to keep the shop open. But there it was.

I was coming down from all that maritime excitement. A few hours' sleep would have been nice, and I was only going to get two. I fell into bed and grabbed them while I could.

Four am and I rose and did the zombie routine which gets Horatio fed, me washed and dressed and partially caffeine-enriched and down to the bakery without the intervention of any higher intelligence. Such as it is. Jason was already there, Goddess bless him, the mixers were all on and the orders book laid out on the counter.

'Captain on deck!' he said, springing to his feet and saluting.

'Carry on, Mr. Midshipman,' I said.

'Permission to make an observation, sir?'

'Go ahead,' I said warily.

'You look like crap, sir!'

'It matches how I feel, Midshipman. I was up until all hours with a magical problem of Meroe's.'

I poured myself another cup of coffee. The first ones had gone down without touching the sides. Jason gave me a considering look from under his white cap.

'All the bread is on, muffins are ready to be mixed, we've just the fairy cakes and the carrot cake. You could grab a couple more hours' sleep,' he suggested.

'Nice thought, but I can manage. Thank you, Midshipman.'

'You said there was a magical problem, Captain?' he asked hesitantly.

'Yes?'

'There's a horrible thing stuck to the door of Insula,' he told me. 'I saw it when I went out to empty the bin. Maybe it's a curse or something?'

'Show me,' I said, and he led me round to our elaborate front door.

Horrible was right. A lump of red tissue, smelling strongly of blood, was fixed to our beautiful Roman ironwork. I didn't want to, but I examined it more closely with the aid of my torch. It was, I judged, a sheep's heart, wound around with barbed wire.

It had thorns or nails stuck in it. Altogether as nasty an object as I had seen since I last saw the Attorney-General smiling.

'I'm going to put on gloves and get this off,' I told Jason. 'Someone might see it and have a heart attack—sorry. Then we can take it to Meroe when she wakes up.'

'You're going to touch it?' He recoiled.

'Only as much as I have to,' I said, hurrying him back to the bakery. 'Go get me a cardboard box and the red-handled pliers.'

I left Jason to compound muffins in the nice safe lighted bakery and went back to the door with my pliers. Someone had gone to considerable trouble to make sure that this…thing, this fetish, was going to be hard to remove. It was pitch black, and I could feel a cold breath down the back of my neck. The dark lane developed odd clunking and cracking noises, like footsteps. I wished that someone was with me, even the Mouse Police. I had to hold the torch in my mouth to see what I was doing because I needed to use both hands, and I wondered what the police patrol would make of me if they saw me.

Eventually I untwisted all the wires and dropped the heart, with a sickening thud, into one of my nice cardboard boxes, and I took it away. What to do with it? The person who had attached it to our door meant us ill, that was clear. The whole object was soaked in malice. I didn't want to take it inside.

I left the box by the back door in Calico Alley, peeled off the thin plastic gloves and dumped them in the bin, and washed my hands very thoroughly with rose-geranium scented soap and water.

'You got it?' asked Jason nervously.

'I got it. It's outside. Not to worry, Jason. If this is a magical duel, we've got Meroe on our side.'

'Oh, right,' he agreed, a smile beginning to dawn on his face. 'We do, don't we?'

'Yes,' I affirmed.

'Boy, is that dude going to be sorry,' he said.

'He is,' I agreed.

Chapter Seven

The Mouse Police had investigated the box, sneezed, and left it alone, which led me to believe that it wasn't just a lump of meat, upon which they would have dived with cries of joy. On the occasions I have brought them the trimmings from a steak, for instance, there has been a scrimmage which would have disgraced a parliamentary banquet or Roman orgy. I rescued it from the hands of Ma'ani when he came to collect the bread. It is no part of my charitable duty to curse the homeless. When he saw what was in the box his face drained of colour, leaving it grey.

'Bad magic,' he stammered, backing away.

'Yes, and when Meroe sees it, the curse will be winging its way back to the sender with additional postage,' I told him. He smiled.

'That Meroe!' he said admiringly. 'She's a strong-minded woman all right. Good morning, Corinna,' he added. He hefted the sack of bread and went away down the alley, keeping to the side away from the object.

Jason said hopefully, 'Can I go and call Meroe? It's seven am, she ought to be up to feed the cat by now.'

'No, she gets to sleep as long as she likes,' I said firmly. 'You're safe in here, Midshipman. Show some command of yourself, man!' I snapped, and his spine, I swear, stiffened. After he has read his way through Hornblower I am getting him onto the works of Patrick O'Brian. I always wanted to be the captain of a sailing ship.

'Aye, aye, sir!' said Jason, showing backbone, pluck and grit.

Bread happened. Because it was the end of the week, I sat down to do the accounts, and found that things were bad. Not dire, but not good. If Best Fresh continued to take my custom away for a few months more, I would be barely breaking even. I could, of course, close the shop and tout for some more bread orders from the restaurants. That would mean I'd have to sack Kylie and Goss though, and until their film and TV careers took off, I was their sole source of revenue, apart from their parents. I really didn't want to disappoint them. Damn.

I was still staring at these uninspiring calculations when Meroe came in and I gladly left the books and escorted her into the alley, where sunlight now fell on the cardboard box. She knelt to open it with the tips of her fingers and then shut it again, very fast.

'Where was it?' she asked tersely.

'On the front door,' I said. 'Jason saw it first, and I went and got it before anyone else could see it. It's a curse, isn't it?'

'Oh yes, a very old one,' she answered, still on her knees. 'I'll take it. You didn't touch it with your naked hands, Corinna?'

'No, I had gloves on. Why? Is it poisoned? The Mouse Police sneezed at it.'

'As well they might,' said Meroe abstractedly.

'Does this have anything to do with your treasure hunters?' I asked.

'Hard to think not,' she said. 'But we shall find out soon enough. Bella and I will be busy tonight. Well done, Corinna, it would not have been at all fortunate to leave that object where it was. And brave of you to go near it,' she added, getting to her feet and picking up the damp cardboard box.

'Not at all,' I said, and watched her walk away, very glad to banish my doorstep of that horrible burden.

'Good riddance,' said Jason, echoing my thought.

I wondered what Meroe was going to do with the heart and what she would subsequently do to the person who sent it, then decided that I didn't really want to know, and it was time to open the shop and let my poor starving midshipman run to the galley for his breakfast.

Today I had Goss in a blue miniskirt and matching sort of tied up at the front bodicey thing. In eyelet lace. When I think that Grandma Chapman's grandma used to make reams of that eyelet lace to trim the unmentionables of the virtuous, I could giggle. Fashion doth make fools of us all. Except, of course, me. In the event that shabby blue tracksuits become fashionable, I may have to resign from the human race. And I should be careful with that sort of comment, because look what happened with Ugg boots…

Goss bounced into the shop, clanged the racks apart, slammed the cash float into the register and announced at the top of her voice, 'I've got a part! Me and Kylie both! It's, like, excellent!'

'Wonderful,' I said, much soothed in conscience. 'When do you start?'

'Monday,' she said. 'But Cherie said she could do the shop for you, Corinna. Some of the time. But isn't it great?' she demanded, launching herself at me and hanging around my neck. 'I'm first shop girl and Kylie's second shop girl in a new soap called *Visitors*! We've got three lines!'

'Wonderful,' I said, hugging her thin little body. 'Each or between you?'

'Each,' she replied, giggling.

'Great.'

She skipped into the bakery to tell Jason.

Daniel came at about eleven, just when the shelves were beginning to look empty. He seemed pale and distracted.

'Come to dinner tomorrow night?' he asked. 'George is cooking. She's hauled in a whole load of stuff.'

I was about to snap that I was in need of sleep rather than George's company, that in fact I would rather dine with the prime minister or any other pond dweller than George, when I saw how drained he looked and relented. Whatever George wanted with Daniel, it wasn't making him a happy camper.

'All right, tomorrow is fine,' I said. 'I'll be in bed early tonight. I was up late last night.'

'Trouble?' he asked, taking my hand.

'Trouble,' I agreed. 'Magical trouble. Meroe is dealing with it,' I added.

He smiled faintly. There were dark marks under his eyes and his hand had a gash across the back. 'That ought to make it really sorry that it bothered you,' he said. 'Come up to my place about seven?'

'Seven it is,' I agreed, and Daniel went away. Damn. I hadn't asked him why we had gone to see Old Spiro, which I had meant to do as soon as he surfaced.

'What's wrong with the dude?' asked Jason. 'I used to look like that when—'

'No,' I said firmly. 'I don't think so.'

'No,' Jason concurred, shaking his head. 'But he's not good, is he?'

'No,' I had to agree with my apprentice. 'No, he isn't.'

And there being nothing else I could do, I sold bread until three, when I closed the shop, loaded the sack for the Soup Run, paid my helpers and bade them have a happy weekend, and carried myself and my cat up to my own apartment, where we needed some lunch and a quiet afternoon reading our detective story.

And that is precisely what we got. I settled down on the sofa with Horatio initially on my lap, and then snuggled in next to my hip, where he likes to be. He does not trust me not to leap up if the phone rings, and this way he is not displaced if I move. I made myself a cup of herbal tea which Meroe had prescribed for stress. It tasted like old, curried grass but seemed to counteract the effects of the coffee I had been drinking. I read, enthralled, of the impossible romance about which Jade Forrester writes so convincingly, and when her Harry got together with his lover, it was both triumphant and utterly likely. In another universe,

of course, but that was where I had been for the last four hours.
And very nice too. I did not much admire the universe I was
coming back to inhabit.

And I was dining alone. I put a block of my own sauce into
the microwave to thaw and put on the pot for orecchiette pasta.
I was not in the mood to struggle with anything, much less fet-
tucine, by which I have been defeated before.

The bell rang. It was Meroe. She held up a basket.

'I've got half of dinner,' she told me.

'And I've got the other half,' I said. 'Puttanesca, if that suits
you.'

'It does,' she said.

I added another block of frozen sauce to the microwave and
threw the pasta into the boiling water. Meroe laid out plates,
put her salad leaves into my wooden salad bowl and poured the
dressing over it. I know that this dressing is only composed of
lemon juice, virgin olive oil, salt, pepper and oregano, because
I have watched Meroe make it, but it tastes better than any
combination of those ingredients I have managed to produce. I
left her to crush garlic for the garlic bread and stirred my pots.
I heard a thud and turned to see Meroe enjoying this culinary
task. She was crushing garlic with the flat of a knife and her fist,
and that garlic knew it had been in a fight.

'That's one allium bulb which will never threaten us again,'
I said.

'I'm full of negative emotions,' she confessed.

'Because of Barnabas?' I asked.

'Because of Barnabas, and this whole flood of witches into
my space. In the old days in Rumania the number of witches
in any coven was one and if a witch strayed into another witch's
territory she would be warned off.'

'Or turned into a frog.'

'That, too,' she agreed, slathering garlic and butter into slits
cut in a baguette. 'But here there are a hundred witches, all
proclaiming that they are witches, and it…'

'Makes you nervous?'

'Yes,' she admitted.

'And you think they might have something to do with the outbreak of madness in the city.'

'That's very astute of you,' she observed, wrapping the bread in foil and stowing it in the oven. 'You must have been watching my reactions.'

'I watch everyone's reactions,' I told her.

She dragged back her long black hair and knotted it behind her neck.

'True. Yes, I did wonder. It's only been happening since they came to town. All this magic must have some sort of psychic effect.'

'Yes, but…hang on, the pasta's done.'

The next few minutes were spent in decanting and lavishing the thin, spicy tomato sauce onto the pasta, adding freshly ground pepper and Parmesan cheese and the laying out of the garlic bread and the salad. I know that garlic bread is a fashion which has come and gone, but I don't give, as Jason would say, a flying. I like garlic bread. So does Meroe. And garlic is good for you. It keeps away colds, although that may work by repelling all other humans who might breathe germs on you.

I poured myself a small glass of chateau collapseau, but Meroe only wanted water. The pasta was perfectly cooked, just beyond al dente. If I want something to bounce back when bitten, I'll eat erasers.

'Why do they call it puttanesca?' Meroe asked, taking a big mouthful and relishing the taste.

'In the manner of whores? Because the working girls came home to their apartment and made a sauce out of whatever was in the cupboard—olives, anchovies, tomato *passata* doubtless sent from their home village by their doting mothers. Some people put chili in it but I don't like chili. I cook up a big pot of it now and again and then freeze it in one person serves for when I don't feel like cooking.'

'I'm glad you do. I didn't feel like cooking either.'

I helped myself to a large spoonful of the fairy salad. Marvellous. We kept eating until most of the food was gone and I was nibbling the end of the garlic bread. Meroe was sipping her austere glass of tap water.

'I never got around to looking up Exodus,' I said idly. 'There's quite a lot of Exodus. Can you give me a reference?'

'Twenty-six, I think,' she said. 'Or twenty-eight.'

I got the Bible and leafed through it, holding it at arm's length and squinting.

'Twenty-six is about the building of the temple. Goats' hair curtains, that would have kept out the heat and dust. And linen in purple, scarlet and blue.'

'The most expensive dyes,' said Meroe. 'Blue would have been woad or indigo, both of which had to come from very far away. Purple from conch shells, traded with the Roman empire. And scarlet was probably madder.'

'Rough on the madder plant,' I observed.

'But a very beautiful colour,' said Meroe. 'The makers of the temple wanted the best for their god.'

'So they did. "A veil of blue and purple and scarlet and fine twined linen of cunning work: with cherubims shall it be made". Sounds like we'd need to ask Therese Webb how to embroider cherubim.'

'She'd know,' said Meroe comfortably. 'And she could probably find us twined linen. And her work is always cunning.'

'That's true.' I scanned further. 'Aha, here we are. "Thou shalt make a breastplate of judgment with cunning work... foursquare shall it be...and thou shalt set in it settings of stones, even four rows of stones: the first row shall be a sardius, a topaz, and a carbuncle: this shall be the first row. And the second row shall be an emerald, a sapphire, and a diamond. And the third row a ligure, an agate, and an amethyst. And the fourth row a beryl, and an onyx, and a jasper: and they shall be set in gold in their inclosings...and the stones shall be with the names of the children of Israel twelve...and thou shalt make upon the breastplate chains...and rings on the two ends..." Meroe! That sounds very like that flat jewelled plate that Barnabas had in his hands last night.'

'Had briefly in his hands,' she corrected me. 'Yes, it was an ephod. Part of a high priest's regalia.'

'And have you any idea what it was doing in the sea off Williamstown, Victoria, Australia?'

'Not a lot,' she said.

'What?' I was confused.

'I mean, I don't for a moment believe that it was there in the first place.'

'You suspect Barnabas of the old "the quickness of the hand deceives the eye"?'

'I do,' she said. 'Much as I am loath to accuse a fellow witch of chicanery, I feel that in this case…'

'Indeed. Anyone that big and jovial almost has to be up to something.'

'I shall investigate further tonight. Bella is already preparing.'

'Bella? Your cat? How is she preparing?' I asked, then wished I hadn't.

'She is entering her deepest trance state,' said Meroe, getting up and picking up her empty basket.

'You mean she's asleep?' I asked. My witch gave me her most inscrutable smile, compared to which the Mona Lisa's is a broad grin.

'You could call it that,' she said. She kissed me on the cheek and left.

I washed the dishes and put them away. I wiped the table. I finished my book and made myself a nice cup of Ovaltine, awarded Horatio a saucer of milk, and put myself to bed early. It seemed the sensible thing. Whatever Meroe was doing, I wanted to be safely asleep before she did it.

And I slept all night without stirring and didn't wake up until eight am, scandalously late. And only then because someone was tapping on my door.

I stumbled out to open it. There was a delivery person, with a box to be signed for. I signed. When I brought it inside, it contained a note—'Corinna, sweet Slug-a-bed, how I adore you!'—and four fresh, hot croissants *au naturel* from the only French bakery left in Melbourne which can make them. Someone loved me...

I went to make coffee and find the cherry jam with a lighter heart than a woman who faced an empty day and a difficult evening engagement should expect. Breakfast was very pleasant. The croissants were so good that I ate two, saving the rest for lunch. Then I did a little housework; greeted, paid, and farewelled my grocery deliveryman, and put away the shopping. The Mouse Police, freed for the day from rodent operative duties, joined Horatio on my balcony for a little day-long snooze with breaks for grooming.

Sweet Slug-a-bed? Wasn't that one of those cavalier poets? I went to my bookcase to scan my prized collection of second-hand poets. The books were second-hand, not the poets, who were as fresh as the day they were born. Cheeky boys, all of them...

I found the reference. Robert Herrick. 'Corinna's going a-Maying':

Get up, get up for shame, the Blooming Morne
Upon her wings presents the god unshorne
See how Aurora throwes her faire
Fresh quilted colours through the aire:
Get up, sweet Slug-a-bed, and see
The Dew-bespangling Herbe and Tree.

That sounded like good advice. I put on some clothes and went forth to the Flagstaff Gardens, found a tree with deep shade, and sat down to read my book and watch the people going past. It being Saturday, there were a lot of children and dogs, but I could put up with some rough company for the pleasure of the sun, the open air, and the red and gold of the Flagstaff cannas, which almost hurt the eye and left orange after-images on the retina.

I walked back into the city and decided to buy my lunch at Uncle Solly's New York Deli. Solly was not there, but several of his charming nephews were. They bore a family resemblance: tall, slim, darkish, and very friendly.

'Corinna!' one hailed me. 'You looking for lunch? How about some of Solly's salt beef, fresh sliced, on a bagel, and maybe a little pickle or three?'

'Sounds good,' I agreed. 'Are you John?'

'You're confusing me with my cousin,' he said. 'I'm Yossi. How's Daniel?'

'Largely absent,' I said frankly. He looked concerned, which was nice of him.

'You don't have to worry about that Daniel,' he told me, handing over the bagel and adding a free extra pickle. 'He's all right. Just busy, is all. I bet.'

'I hope you're right,' I replied.

I took the bag, and went out. Back, this time, to Insula, where the roof garden had several lunchers. The rose bower was bursting into blossom with Cecile Brunner thornless pink flowers. I sat down with my paper bag near Therese Webb, who laid aside her tapestry to welcome me and pour me a cup of chai. She makes it with milk and sugar in the Indian manner and it's superb, rich and fruity and spicy.

'So how's Daniel?' she asked.

I was getting tired of the question. 'I don't know,' I said, as crossly as one can while drinking the questioner's chai.

'He didn't look well when I last saw him,' she explained.

'I'm dining with him tonight,' I answered, to deflect further enquiry. 'How's the tapestry business?'

'Doing well,' she said.

I felt a cool nose touch my hand. Carolus, the regal King Charles spaniel, was requesting a little of my salt beef. I detached a small piece. He ate it with condescension and returned to his cushion. He is not a greedy dog.

'Carolus, really,' said Therese. 'A dog with your lineage, for shame.'

'One small bit of salt beef in homage,' I said, stroking the silky ears. Carolus is exempt from my usual strictures on dogs. He is more like a feline than a canine, anyway. He is a perfect pet for a craft worker, being all colours of autumn and furred in the very best plush.

'Corinna, have you felt…well, odd, lately? In Insula?' asked Therese.

'Yes,' I said. 'As though there's someone watching. But all my bolts have been bolted and all my locks have been locked. I think it's the high magical ambiance that's making us uneasy. Meroe's got a hundred witchy relatives visiting.'

'I suppose that could be it,' she said doubtfully. 'Carolus always barks if there's someone at the door, and he hasn't barked, so…'

'There's no one there,' I said bracingly.

'And I keep hearing this little song,' she confessed.

'Wassail, wassail?'

'Yes, how did you know?'

'I've heard it too. Out in the alley, early in the morning. But when I look for the singers they aren't there. And I don't think it's supernatural. It's one of those acoustic effects you get in cities. I have no doubt that the singer is a human.'

'You've heard it too, that's a relief,' said Therese, picking up her tapestry. It was red waratahs on a green field, very eye-catching. 'I thought I was going mad.'

'If you are, I'm coming with you.'

'Always delighted to have your company, my dear,' she said comfortably. 'I was thinking of this for Cherie Holliday's room, what do you think?'

'She's still in love with pink,' I said. 'And going into interior design on her own account. It would suit the Prof's Roman couch, though.'

'And Nox would look very decorative asleep in the middle,' said Therese.

A tiny black kitten, Nox ruled the Professor with an iron paw, not even bothering to conceal it in a velvet glove. She had begun life in the roof garden where her mother Calico had dined on rats, then spent a distressing week in the air conditioning ducts, subsisting on condensation and mice. Once rescued, she had clearly formed the resolution that the rest of her life was to be lived in luxury and was enforcing this with an uncompromising view on cheap cat food and substandard accommodation. Which meant she ate only gourmet treats and slept under Professor Monk's chin, not in the padded cat bed which Meroe had lent him.

He, of course, loved it. He had bought her a little red harness into which she allowed him to strap her for her daily constitutional in the garden. She had already given Mrs. Pemberthy's rotten little doggie Traddles such a look when he came barking up to her that he had retreated behind his mistress' lisle-clad ankles and whined, while she shrieked at Professor Monk to call off his nasty cat. Nox was a familiar, like Belladonna, and such animals are formidable.

I wandered down to my apartment for a shower and to dress in nice clothes for Daniel's dinner. What to wear? I could not compete with long legs and curls. Finally I found loose black trousers, a white kurta, and a filmy cobweb drape which Therese had made of fine feathery thread in silver and purple. It had a tendency to shed but it looked beautiful. And after all, it wasn't going to be shedding in my house, but that grotty flat of Daniel's, which could do with some colour in the decor.

I found a bottle of cab sav, a wine suitable for any food, and one of white and loaded them into my backpack. I fed Horatio and the Mouse Police, watched the news, which was no worse than usual, watched the other news, which was even worse than usual and full of North Korea and snipers and climate change, and then I could delay no longer. I dragged my unwilling feet out into the lane and set off for Elizabeth Street and Georgiana Hope's dinner party. I didn't want to, but I went.

Chapter Eight

Perhaps it might not be as bad as I feared. In fact, unless she stripped naked and ravished Daniel in front of my eyes, it couldn't be as bad as I feared. I climbed the stairs of the Buildings slowly, carrying my backpack with my two bottles of wine, moving like someone invited to the deathbed of a dear friend.

The office had been cleaned, but it still looked agreeably rumpled, as though Sam Spade had just clapped on his fedora and gone out with the mysterious woman diffusing a Parisian scent. The mysterious woman, however, emerged from the other room wearing, I swear, higher heels than last time, the tightest of blouses in lime satin, a simply schoolgirl grey bubble skirt and the first pair of seamed stockings I had seen since I caught Audrey Hepburn on the Late Late Late You Are Severely Insomniac Movie Show.

'Danny! Corry's here!' she called over her shoulder, not greeting me at once. 'And you said she wouldn't come!'

'Not so lucky,' I murmured, handing over my bag.

She peeked inside. 'Oh, Australian wine,' she said.

'This is Australia,' I replied firmly. 'This is your vin du pays, if you are staying.'

'Of course,' she said. 'Do come through. I'm just putting some finishing touches to the food. Danny can entertain you.'

'Hello, Danny,' I said, not without a touch of malice. 'Why not entertain Corry by opening this bottle?'

'Why not?' he answered.

He had dressed up for the occasion, I saw, in the charcoal-grey shantung suit which Kepler had coaxed a Chinese tailor into making for him. The distressed artisan had complained the whole time that he did not have any patterns for giants, just ordinary sized men, but Kepler had persisted and Daniel was worth dressing. The Mandarin collar outlined his smooth throat and I had to fight down the urge to fling myself into his arms and kiss him so thoroughly that it might take weeks to reach his toes. I could tell that he was thinking the same thing. I began to blush. I touched his cheek.

'I miss you,' I whispered, which was not at all what I had been going to say. I forgot what I had been going to say, something sharp and modern and sassy, I have no doubt. Possibly even feisty.

His smile, which had warmed, warmed further and he reached out a hand to me just as Madame ankled back into the room and called us to the table.

Said table was laid with a new white cambric cloth. A new set of David Jones' pure white dishes, ditto Flatware new cutlery, Bistro One new glasses, and salt cellar and pepper grinder just out of the box from House. If Daniel was paying for all of this, she had set him back a couple of thousand dollars, which I didn't know that he had. I had never, in fact, asked about his finances. It didn't seem to be any of my business and it still didn't, so I sat down, opened my crisp white (new, double damask) napkin and said, 'Smells good!'

'I quite like your market,' she replied, 'but there's nowhere to match the Food Hall at Harrods, or even Sainsbury's, here,' she commented. I refrained from a shriek of outrage on behalf of Myer, David Jones and multiple remarkable food shops within easy staggering distance, because she was putting down a serving dish (new, white) full of prawns which looked like they'd had the same sort of day as I had: enough to make you curl up and lose your head. I took one. There was a dipping sauce which had a suspiciously familiar green tinge.

'Wasabi?' I asked. I looked at Daniel. He knows I can't stand the stuff. He shrugged.

'I'm sure you'll like this,' said Georgiana. 'There's only a little touch of wasabi in it. Do try,' she coaxed.

I tried. It was the same old wasabi, which exploded in my mouth and abolished my tastebuds. I muffled my scream of pain and swallowed, mopped my streaming eyes, then ate the rest of the prawn naked. It had an odd, grassy taste.

'I've been having such fun with all these new spices—bush foods, they call them,' she informed me brightly. 'That one is lemon myrtle. Perhaps you might like the lillipilli or bush pepper ones better.'

I tried all three. They tasted foul. Bush spices are a condiment, not a food group. To be used sparingly. By the taste, I might have been chewing a branch. I wondered what to say but didn't need to comment, because Georgie was enthusing about the dear old dead days in London with Daniel, and Daniel was replying. He tried to drag me into the conversation, but every time I said something, Georgie would block me out again.

The second course was contained in a perfectly round white (new) cup: three broad beans, a measure of greenish stock and a dollop of something white which I took to be yogurt. I swallowed the soup. The white substance was not yogurt or sour cream but horseradish, which scalded my mouth afresh. I wasn't going to count this dinner as one of the great culinary delights of my life, I could tell.

I drank another glass of my good Otways sauvignon blanc and plotted dark poisonings. Georgie first, of course, but after that, how about the proprietor of Best Fresh? I still hadn't met him, her or them, and I really ought to go and say hello. All bakers together, after all. They couldn't be less amusing than Georgie's conversation about London galleries. Which I knew, as it happened, a lot better than she did.

The next course was salmon, which had clearly died hard before being undercooked, smothered in a sauce made of pesto and kiwi fruit and wrapped inside a banana leaf. Kiwi fruit and fish? Well, it might be delicious…

It wasn't. I noticed that this was clearly the slimmer's version of dinner. I had already put a ritual curse on the inventor of cuisine minceur, so I didn't need to do it again. Each tiny offering—three snow peas, three fanned leaves of radicchio, a transparent slice of fish—was laid with grave solemnity in the middle of a great big plate, as though that made them any bulkier. Or was this some comment on my weight? Surely even Georgiana Hope wasn't that crass. No potatoes, avocado, nothing starchy: no bread of any kind.

Then came a salad. In a sparrow's nest of leaves were three thin slices of rare steak. The dressing was a Thai concoction so hot that I had another glass of wine while trying to put out the fire. Meanwhile the conversation went on and I had had enough of it. 'No, it's in the Courtauld,' I said, rudely interrupting her discourse on Italian naive painting. 'It's the large marriage chest, in the third room. You'll recall that it has an icon of Christ Pancrator over the door? That room.'

I had eaten my three slices of steak so I poured another glass and went on, determined to grab some conversation with my only love. 'My favourite is the Wallace collection. So interesting and individual. There's been a tendency lately to put away most of the art works and display the remains very carefully—rather like this salad. Not a lot of substance, but very pretty to look at and one can appreciate every nuance of the flavour. But I much prefer the old-fashioned sort of museum, where all the things that the person collected are all crammed together and you don't have to walk ten miles to see the Botticellis. I like Mr. Wallace and his arms and armour and paintings and Mrs. Wallace's fire screens in Berlin wool-work.'

'Absolutely,' agreed Daniel. 'Like the Bourdelle Museum in Paris, where the painter's studio is upstairs and the sculptor's downstairs, and you can imagine the washing hanging out the window.'

Georgiana collected the plates and brought in dessert. It was a soupçon of coconut ice cream with nasturtium petals around it and a thin slice of mango. It was nice, if you like coconut ice cream. I ate it in one mouthful and Daniel and I continued to enthuse about crowded collections, and I began to feel better.

Over a demitasse (new) of very weak coffee from a home barista (his own) and a tiny curled sliver of chocolate-coated orange peel, Georgie settled the two of us down on the couch and began to interrogate me about Earthly Delights. Daniel was bidden to do the washing-up and I wondered that she had not yet made him buy a dishwasher.

Georgie shed her high heels and draped herself over the sofa, long legs and short skirt. She was very beautiful. I sat next to her like a lump. Of what, I had not decided. Granite, perhaps? Or maybe just jelly. Envious jelly.

'So, you are making a profit now?' she asked cosily, twiddling a red-painted toenail and admiring the effect.

'Yes, after a couple of years of very hard work,' I told her.

'You see, I am looking for a business—' she said.

'And you don't want mine,' I completed her sentence.

'Oh, but I am beginning to think that I do,' she cooed.

'No, you don't,' I told her. 'I don't want a partner.'

'But you're working yourself to death, Danny says.' She seemed concerned. 'If you have a partner you can hire more help.'

'I don't need more help now that Jason is getting to be so skilled,' I said. 'Besides, if I have someone else making the bread, it isn't Earthly Delights bread, it's their bread, and that's not what the customers pay for.'

'Silly,' she chided me. 'Jason's bread isn't your bread, by that argument.'

'Yes it is, because I am there watching him make it,' I said, never actually having thought of this before but firming in my view that any partner would be better than Georgie and I didn't want one anyway. 'Would you be proposing to get up at four and make bread with me?'

'No.' Her nose wrinkled, ever so slightly. A woman who needed her beauty sleep, evidently. 'I am thinking of being a silent partner. You'll never know that I'm there. And when there is more capital, you can franchise.'

'And destroy everything that people value in a niche market?' I said. 'People want to know who made the bread, they want to see—so to speak—my thumbprints in the dough. They want to talk to me about the weather and about yeast and about Jason's latest muffin. Otherwise there's no difference between Earthly Delights and Best Fresh, and they're cheaper. My customers are not only paying for my quality flour and original sourdough and interesting recipes, they're paying for me. Furthermore,' I added, warming to my topic, 'if I had a partner I'd need to put every important decision before her. What, for instance, would you say if I told you I was proposing to employ a recovering heroin addict, first as a cleaner and later as a baker?'

'I'd say, not a chance, you can't let someone like that into your kitchen,' she replied honestly. For which, for a moment, I liked her.

'Precisely. Jason might have worked out and he might not have worked out, but he was my risk and my decision. No, thank you, but you need to find another business. Plenty of them around! Have a look down at Docklands, there're restaurants galore down there, and it would be a lovely place to live, too. You can see all the way across the bay.'

I got up, before I lost my temper. She put a manicured hand on my arm.

'Is that your final word?' she asked, blue eyes imploring.

'Certainly,' I said. I shook the hand. 'Thank you for dinner. Sorry that I have to leave, but I have to get up early. Goodnight,' I added, and went to the door, collecting my bag and calling farewell to Daniel on the way.

I didn't draw breath until I was out in the street, at which point I sighed as if I had escaped from some terrible danger. Then I became aware of the fire below my girdle and realised that I would have to find something to eat and some antacids or I might actually burst into flame.

It wasn't late, but somehow none of the cafes attracted me. Which meant that I washed up on the beach of Uncle Solly's New York Deli, as many famished mariners have done before me, and he recognised my expression instantly.

'Heartburn, dollink?' he asked, gesturing at one of his nephews. Yossi, I think. The young man began to mix something in a small glass. 'You drink down a glass of Uncle Solly's Infallible Heartburn Cure and you feel better in a sprinkling.'

'Twinkling, Uncle Solly,' said Yossi patiently. 'I've told you before.'

His uncle shrugged. 'Sprinkling, twinkling! Then maybe we get you some real food, Corinna. You been eating that pagan stuff again?'

'Not by my choice,' I said, gulping down the chalky white mixture and then a sparkling red mixture. The result of which was to immediately damp the fire in my stomach and then to make me burp. Uncle Solly beamed all over his face and two of his chins wobbled with delight.

'There! Good, *nu*? The cranberries give it body. Now, what you want? You eating alone?'

'Yes,' I said sadly.

'No,' said Yossi. The shop doorbell tinkled and Daniel came in.

'I thought I might catch you here,' he said, panting. 'You walk fast!'

'She was poisoned with pagan spices,' reproved Uncle Solly. 'You do that to a woman, she walks fast. And away from you,' he added, pointedly.

'I know, it's all my fault,' said Daniel impatiently. 'I'm so sorry, Corinna.'

'You wait a moment before you forgive him,' advised Uncle Solly. 'Let Yossi make you a malted. You want a milkshake, Daniel?'

'Yes,' said Daniel, sinking down into one of the fancy wicker chairs which Uncle Solly says are good for the customer's behind, which must be considered as well as his stomach and his soul. 'Yes, please. And can Yossi make me a heartburn cure as well?'

'For you,' said Uncle Solly with a broad gesture, 'the world.'

He went to the back of the shop to yell at another nephew. Yossi compounded drinks without comment. The city rushed by outside. I sat with Daniel and did not speak.

In due course I sipped my malted, which I had not tasted since I was at school. It was lovely. The embers of the spice-induced fires went out. Daniel was holding my hand in the one not occupied with a glass of chocolate milk and ice cream. I was suddenly, blindingly, happy. I did not trust my voice.

Finally Daniel ventured, 'If you can actually forgive me, I can sort of explain.'

'You don't need to,' I assured him.

'Yes, but I want to,' he said. 'I have told Georgie that I am not coming back to sleep in the flat while she is there, so she should make some other arrangements as soon as she can. I didn't realise that she wanted to buy into your business or I would have told her that she hadn't a chance. But she didn't ask me. I could have told her that she didn't have a chance with me either, being spoken for, but nor did she ask me about that. She didn't mean to insult you. She just doesn't understand people at all. Never has. I think it's part of being a Sloane. And I have let her hurt your feelings and scald you with wasabi and I am so sorry.'

'Apology accepted,' I said.

'Nice phrasing,' approved Uncle Solly, popping up from behind the tall fridge. 'Spoken for—I haven't heard that in years. Not since my Aunt Miriam told my father that she was spoken for and he said, spoken for what? You mean you talk too much? It took days to sort it out. *Nu*, lovebirds, to important matters. What you want for dinner?'

We settled for pimiento cheese sandwiches and salads and wedges of orange and poppyseed cake and ate them watching the city walk past. I began to feel tired as well as very happy.

'Good night, Uncle Solly,' I said gratefully. 'I never had an uncle, can I adopt you?'

'Gladly, an honour,' he said. 'Now, niece, you better let this lout walk you home. After,' he added markedly, 'he takes off his adornments.'

I looked at Daniel. Daniel looked down. We all began to laugh. He was wearing a frilly, blue-checked gingham apron.

When we got back to Insula the building was quiet, and we lingered in the atrium, watching Horatio watching the fish. He wanders out through his cat door occasionally and sits on the edge of the impluvium, favouring the goldfish with a stare which stops just short of being hungry. Unlike, for instance, Lucifer, who dives in to try and catch them on the fin, or the Professor's delicate little black kitten Nox, who has a deep atavistic appetite for anything piscine. She has been known to dive from a height onto a seafood pizza and wrestle the prawns off even before the box was fully opened. The Professor does not like to risk her near the pool, in case she falls in. My personal view was that Nox was as tough a feline as one was likely to meet in these post-sabre-toothed times and that, if she fell in, she would come up with her sweet little fangs full of fish.

Horatio, of course, has no need to hunt. Unlike the Mouse Police, his job description is limited to amicable coexistence with the other tenants, pleasant companionship, not clawing the curtains unduly and, when necessary, beating up Mrs. Pemberthy's rotten little doggie Traddles. He stood up and greeted us politely and followed as we went up the stairs. I had tucked myself under Daniel's shoulder, where I fitted as if measured by a Chinese tailor.

'That was a dangerous thing I did,' said Daniel slowly.

'Hmm?' I was watching Horatio absorbing his evening milk.

'Introducing Georgie into the flat without warning you. I had forgotten what she's like. But she never wanted me before,' he said, a little plaintively.

'Tough,' I replied. 'Perhaps she only wants you now because you are spoken for.'

'Possibly. But I might have lost you,' he said, hugging me closer.

'No, not lost.' I had thought about this and I held him at arm's length while I explained. This was important. 'You might have driven me away, but who is to say that I would have stayed away? Takes more than a six-foot supermodel with blue eyes and golden curls to defeat me. Unless I was sure that you wanted her, not me,' I said, watching him closely. He made a mosquito-banishing gesture with his free hand. Georgie, had she seen it, would have folded her tents and gone to Docklands without further notice.

'Corinna!' He kissed me. 'If you do not yet believe in your superiority over Georgiana Hope in every possible way, I shall have to convince you again.'

'Convince me,' I said, and held out my arms.

He slid forward, unwrapping my shawl, and kissed my bared throat. I shuddered with desire. We shed clothes as we ran for the bedroom, eager and laughing and gasping and laughing again. Tripping over knickers. Tearing off buttons. Oh my sweet Daniel.

The strange thing about sensuality is that it clears the mind. At least, it cleared my mind. Once I had recovered some breath and untangled myself from a sheet which was behaving like an amorous boa constrictor, I laid my cheek against my lover's broad, spice-scented chest and suddenly everything was obvious and bright and the landscape of my mind was illuminated with understanding. Unfortunately, I then fell asleep, exhausted by passion and relief.

Sunday morning announced itself with the scent of coffee and the absence of both my lover and my cat. When I fumbled my way into the parlour I found that the two of them had been sleeping on the couch. Someone had been out and bought crois-sants and the Sunday paper and had put on the coffee. Then, presumably exhausted by all that effort, they had gone back to the couch for one of Horatio's little naps. They were so decorative that I sat doting upon the footstool, watching them sleep. The snuggly cat under the outflung, relaxed hand of the man. Daniel's other long, sensitive hand over his eyes. His bare chest and… mmm…thigh exposed to the cool morning air. Long, smooth, muscular thigh…early sunlight glazing his shiny chestnut hair, growing out of its severe cut. So beautiful.

Today was a day for answering questions. But it was also a day for being happy. I wasn't aware of how unhappy I had been until it was gone. It was like the absence of a backache to which one has become inured by years of ouches. Then one makes an unwary movement and is not immediately punished for it. Takes getting used to. Delightful.

I showered and dressed in a gown and floated out to eat croissants and apricot jam and read the paper until my co-tenants woke up.

The paper was so depressing. Climate change, wars, pollution, logging catchments, using unrefined brown coal, all that stuff we told them about ages ago and only now was it sinking in with Catastrophe not just knocking but kicking the door down—oh, you mean no water? And we need this water stuff to survive? Duh, as Kylie might have said. Not to mention snipers, war in the Middle East looking like it might spread to the Far East, which is us, bombs, cruelty to immigrants, mean penny-pinching grudgingness worthy of the 1834 Poor Law which made Charles Dickens so incandescent, anti-terror laws more terrifying than the terror—aargh! I just want one grown-up in parliament, just one. Or maybe two. I wouldn't want the only one to die of loneliness. One person who will not take a party line of safe in-between wishy-washiness, who will say, this is evil, this is wrong, not only that, this is silly, I won't support it…And since I am not going to get a person like that, I turned to the literary pages and the film reviews instead. If fact wasn't acceptable, what's wrong with good old fiction?

I don't go to films much, preferring to wait for the DVD so I can snuggle up on my own couch with my cat and stop the film when it gets scary or I need a loo break. Or speed it up if it gets boring. Cinemas almost never allow one to do this. Also, I have got into the very bad habit of commenting on the action and plot, and this can get one hissed at in a public place.

I was just wondering whether tickling a sleeping lover came under the heading of improper conduct when Horatio rolled over and yawned in that appealing tongue-curling way which means that a cat is extremely happy, and Daniel opened his eyes. He yawned too, but his tongue did not curl.

'I fell asleep waiting for you to wake up,' he explained drowsily, accepting my kiss and adding a few more for interest.

'Why were you sleeping on the couch with Horatio?' I asked, moving out of his embrace only as the desire for more coffee became paramount.

'In case I had another nightmare,' he said, very seriously. 'I would never forgive myself if I did actually...you know. React badly. Horatio will just scratch me to the bone if I startle him.'

'Isn't it about time that you whispered into my shell-like ear what all this is about?' I asked, handing him a cup.

'Yes, probably,' he agreed. 'All that I can tell you. Some of it is secret, and it isn't my secret.'

'As long as it isn't Georgie's secret,' I muttered.

'Georgie? No, nothing to do with Georgie. Surely you weren't really worried that I might want George rather than you, ketschele?'

'No, why should I think that?' I asked, allowing myself to be scornful now that I knew I was safe. 'Just because I'm short and fat and dumpy and mousy, and she is tall and gorgeous with baby blue eyes and blonde ringlets? The very first time I saw her she was wearing your blue dressing gown and she looked like a *Vogue* cover.'

'Oh,' said Daniel. 'She is tall and glamorous,' he admitted. 'And she does have blue eyes and blonde hair. But she has a heart of pure marble and just as many brains cells as can calculate an expense account to the nearest pfennig, dollar or euro as required. Whereas you are kind and funny and compassionate and witty and acerbic and beautiful and as sweet in my mouth as honey,' he said, and put down his cup to kiss me passionately.

After which I agreed to omit the topic of Georgiana Hope from any future discourse and returned my lover to the matters to be discussed, from which I had been continuously distracted for days by one thing and another.

'Why did we go to see that horrible old man?' I asked.

'Because he was there when Max Mertens stole the treasure from Salonika,' said Daniel.

Well, there was an answer. And just then someone pinged my doorbell and a gruff voice said, 'Police here. Open the door, please.'

Chapter Nine

They sounded like a couple of very unimpressed officers who wanted to come in right now and it seemed only sensible to allow them to do so before they got crosser than they already were. I buzzed them in and Daniel and I met them in the atrium.

'Corinna Chapman,' I said, doing my 'I remind you of your English teacher' impression, which always works on officials. I held out my hand and the primary police officer took it automatically, and then didn't quite know what to do with it. He was a stocky man with a ground-in scowl. His companion was stockier and even more grim. 'How can I help you?'

'You can let us into your bakery,' he replied, moderating his tone.

'Certainly, I'll get my keys,' I said. No point in demanding explanations. Something bad had happened and I could only hope that it hadn't happened in my kitchen.

'You know me,' Daniel told the second policeman. 'What's afoot, Jonesy?'

'Nothing good,' grunted Jonesy. 'You been here all night, Daniel?'

'Except when I went out to get the croissants at about nine,' Daniel replied. 'Why?'

By now I had fetched the keys and led the way down to the street. We got to the corner of Calico Alley, where I was firmly stopped.

'You don't want to go down there, ma'am,' said Jones to me. 'You come and look, Daniel, if you want.'

'Do I want to?' asked Daniel.

'Depends how much you like splatted dead bodies,' said the first officer through his teeth. 'You didn't hear anything this morning?'

'No, not a thing. Splatted, eh? Fallen?'

'From a great height,' said Jones. 'Old lady in this building saw him dancing on the roof of the flats opposite. Then he said, "I'm a bird!" and took off to fly…'

'Except he didn't,' concluded the first policeman. 'Splatted.'

'Like Dusty says,' confirmed Jones, which told me that his fellow officer was called Miller or Rhodes, and also that someone was dead in my alley. I was shaken. Why choose my alley to die in? Plenty of other alleys in the city. I was beginning to feel hunted, or possibly haunted. Did this have anything to do with Meroe's magical revenge?

'Forensics're on their way,' said Miller (or Rhodes). 'But he had a squashed roll or a cake in his hand and we want to know if it came from your bakery.'

'I'll come in through the apartment,' I said. 'I'll be able to tell if anything is missing.'

I ran into Insula and dead-heated them as they came in through my alley door. They looked around at the shining clean, carefully polished machines, the mopped dry floor and the utter absence of anything resembling bread or cakes or rolls or buns.

'I'm closed over the weekend,' I told them. 'I clean up and polish everything on Friday night and I give all the leftovers to Sister Mary for the Soup Run. If your man has a cake, it didn't come from here.'

'We know Sister Mary,' said (provisionally) Miller, thinking about it. 'She doesn't waste a crumb. Leftovers from the Soup Run go to the community farm chooks and ducks. Not that there are many leftovers. The crips, veggies and losers eat most of it.'

I could tell that Constable Miller was not going to make Sister Mary's list of understanding policemen, but at least he was convinced that my bakery had nothing to do with the unfortunate man's fate. I was now fighting down an utterly unworthy urge. Who was making cakes around here? Who was open all weekend? How could I not tell these eager seekers of forensic truth that Best Fresh was their most likely source?

I struggled with my conscience. Then Daniel, with complete inno   nce, said, 'There's a new hot bread shop just down the lane. Be   Fresh. Why not ask them?' and I was relieved of temptation, just as though St. Anthony in the desert had been offered a nice plate of real roast lamb in place of all those visions. Or maybe one of Uncle Solly's salt beef sandwiches.

'Good idea,' grunted Miller.

'Who's the stiff?' asked Daniel as I paused at the top of the steps into my own quarters. I didn't want to go out into the alley.

'Dunno,' said Jones. 'Forensics'll surgically remove our balls if we contaminate the crime scene. If it is a crime scene. You staying here?' he asked Daniel.

'Yes,' he said, consulting me with a glance and correctly interpreting my enthusiastic nod.

'Okay, we might pop up when the scene of the crime officers have gone and have a chat.' And with that invitation or threat, Miller and Jones exited through the Calico Alley door, tossing my keys to Daniel as they left.

We locked all the doors again and retreated, not to the apartment but to the garden, where Trudi's tulips were waving scarlet banners and there might be some comfortable company.

There we found most of the inhabitants of Insula. Mistress Dread was not present, but Mrs. Dawson was there, Professor Monk, Therese Webb, Mrs. Pemberthy and Traddles, Jason and both girls. Cherie Holliday and her father were out. Jon and Kepler were in and clearly wished they were not. Meroe was glowering from the rose bower. Mrs. Dawson, who had brought not only a fine Glasgow picnic rug but a picnic basket to go with it, was dispensing something from her thermos in small cups. I sipped. It was coffee and whisky, hot and unctuous with honey.

'Used to thaw deer-stalkers who get lost in the Highlands,' she explained. 'Or fishermen hauled out of the North Sea. I got the recipe when I was in Mull. Very efficacious for shock. Has everyone got a drink?'

Nothing in the world, not alien invasion, nuclear accident or the sudden arrival of the Duke of Edinburgh, could deflect Mrs. Dawson from being the perfect hostess. She wou d undoubtedly find some suitable refreshment for the a ens—a little more methyl mercaptan in that, my dears? Perhaps a pinch of sulphur?—and the Duke would probably appreciate a glass of the good whisky while she rang the palace to come and collect him. And in the event of the end of the world, then her view would be that we might as well be agreeably occupied while it happened since there was nothing else we could do to avert our fate. A good view, I thought.

Jon sipped and grinned at me. 'Shall I call the meeting to order?' he asked, with gentle irony.

'By all means, my dear chap,' said Professor Monk.

'It's a scandal,' whimpered Mrs. Pemberthy. 'He fell...he fell right past...'

Kylie, of all people, patted her hand. Therese cast a few lengths of good woolly shawl around her. Even Traddles seemed shocked. He did not offer to bite anyone, nor was the sight of Lucifer on Trudi's shoulder enough to rouse him.

'Tell us what happened,' instructed Mrs. Dawson. 'It will make you feel better.'

'I heard someone singing,' said Mrs. Pemberthy, shaking her perm until her earrings rattled. 'Down in the alley.'

'Wassail, wassail?' asked Jason keenly.

'No. Soul cake, a soul cake,' said Mrs. Pemberthy, singing a sad but monotonous little air. Meroe drew in a sharp breath and folded her arms under her breasts. 'So I looked out. Then I heard someone saying, "I'm a bird, I'm a bird", and he was on the roof of the flats opposite. He was dancing,' she said.

Poor old Mrs. P, I found myself thinking. Although she was one of the most genuinely irritating people I had ever met, this was a bit above the odds for anyone over seventy. Or under it, of course. Kylie, Goss and Jason weren't looking very chipper either. Of all of us, Daniel, Mrs. Dawson, Jon and Kepler and Professor Monk were seemingly unaffected. Jon and Kepler because they dealt with disasters every day, Mrs. Dawson and the Professor because of their past, which had been difficult, and Daniel because he had been a soldier, perhaps. Me, I felt faintly sick and faintly drunk. Better not to have any more Hebridean Fisherman Defroster.

Mrs. Pemberthy went on: 'Then I opened the window and screamed at him to get away from the edge, but he didn't listen, or he didn't care, these young people are so careless, and he… jumped. Threw himself into the air. And he fell right past my window. Right past and down and hit the ground.'

'How awful,' said Jon, conventionally. The right thing to say to a conventional person like Mrs. Pemberthy.

Kylie expressed my feelings by saying, 'Euw!'

'What time was this?' asked Daniel.

'Nine,' she said. 'I just put the Sunday service on. I always listen to the Sunday service. Since Mr. P…went away, I don't go to church.'

Mr. Pemberthy was confined in a bin for the incurably loopy, and a good thing too. But we did not mention this.

Professor Monk patted Mrs. Pemberthy on the shoulder. 'Bear up, now, my dear,' he told her. 'I saw him fall too, and it was not a nice experience. But we mustn't give way.'

She sniffed bravely into his best handkerchief. I suspect Mrs. P has a soft spot for the Professor. Kylie and Goss conferred.

'We were asleep,' they said. 'And you can't see into the alley from our place. But we've been hearing that little song around.'

'Around where?' asked Daniel, too quickly. They drew in their tiny horns like affrighted snails.

'Just, you know, like, around,' said Kylie. 'We've got to go,' she said, getting up. 'We've got to learn our lines for tomorrow.'

'We don't know anything about it,' added Goss, and they both scuttled away.

'Damn,' said Daniel. 'My fault. My timing is off,' he added.

'No matter, they'll come around,' said Therese Webb. 'If they've got a story they won't be able to resist telling it in due course.'

'True,' I agreed. 'Jason, did you hear anything?'

'No, or see nothing. I was up here, helping Trudi with the weeding. I never did any garden stuff before. It's sick,' said Jason, Nature Boy. He was, now I noticed, grimy around the edges.

'You never cease to amaze me,' I told him.

'I was here too,' said Therese. 'And Meroe. We are making rose petal cordial, and we came to ask Trudi for some rose petals.'

'And they not get,' said Trudi. 'Not until the roses just start to fall. Then they are at their best for cordials and for oils. Myself, I saw nothing.'

'But Meroe knows something,' I said, tired of all this secrecy. 'And it's time she told us what a soul cake is.'

'It's the spice bread I've been making from that old recipe,' supplied Jason helpfully. 'It says Soaling Cake on the paper.'

Of course. Jason doesn't know how to spell 'soul'. And he was right, it seemed. Soal was the same as soul. Soaling was the same as souling. Whatever souling was. I was still entirely bemused by the whole thing.

'And it's a folk song,' said Mrs. Dawson. 'But there is some other significance to it, is there not, Meroe?'

'Yes,' said Meroe with vast reluctance. 'It's the offering bread for Hallowe'en, Walpurgisnacht, for the feast of Samhain.'

'The feast, as it happens, of the dead,' said Professor Monk without emphasis.

'And someone has profaned it,' said Meroe, and burst into wild, uncontrollable tears.

This was unprecedented. Meroe weeping? For a moment no one moved. Then Daniel gathered our neighbourhood witch into his embrace and rocked her as though she was a child. We all began to tiptoe away.

Therese Webb and I escorted Mrs. Pemberthy to her apartment, made her a warm milk drink and helped her into her fluffy pink gown and comfy sheep's wool slippers. I was obscurely cheered when Traddles nipped at me. He missed, but it was a sporting attempt. Therese donated the shawl, which was a sprightly shade of cerise and matched rather well. We left her tucked up on her sofa with the TV on, her phone to hand so that she could call for help if she felt faint (and also to ring her sister for a long session of complaining) and her faithful, if smelly, companion sitting on her lap. Traddles was a rotten little doggie, but he doted on Mrs. Pemberthy, possibly divining in his minuscule canine brain that if she didn't feed him, no one else was likely to put themselves to any trouble or expense on his account.

We shut the door on Dr. Phil talking about marital tolerance of bondage and discipline—'Would it hurt you to just tie his wrists to the bedhead?'—and looked at each other.

'There is something very wrong,' said Therese. I like Therese. A successful businesswoman for years and years, she retired to Insula to spend her remaining time caring for Carolus and sewing, knitting, tatting, weaving, embroidering and spinning, and here she was in the middle of a black magical farce. I gave her a hug.

'Not to worry,' I said as bracingly as I could. 'Why not take that delightful dog for a nice walk and leave it to me and Daniel and the others?'

'Thank you, dear,' she said, 'but I prefer to go back to my apartment and finish my portrait of Carolus. I'm going to turn it into a tapestry pattern. Those nice young men at Nerds Inc have promised to…now, what was the word? Photoshop it for me? In return for some mending. You'll call me if there's anything I can do?'

I nodded. 'You're a brave woman, to take on the Lone Gunmen's mending,' I told her. 'They subsist entirely on junk food, especially nachos, and everything they own has chili sauce on it.'

'I shall manage, I daresay,' replied Therese stoutly.

I left her at her door.

When I reached the roof garden it contained a reduced cast. The Professor and Mrs. Dawson remained, but the others had faded away on, I have no doubt, important errands ordered by that formidable pair. Trudi, Lucifer and Jason were on the far side of the roof, weeding the peony bed. I could hear Trudi instructing my apprentice on the difference between crocus foliage and grass. Meroe was still weeping and Daniel was still rocking her. Mrs. Dawson had removed herself and her picnic into the temple, to allow Daniel and Meroe private occupation of the rose bower. She beckoned to me to join her and the Professor. Nox sat on his lap, a small jet statue of a contemplative kitten in a red harness. I noticed that Mrs. Dawson was gently caressing her ears, and Nox was allowing this attention. Mrs. Dawson's friendship with the Professor seemed to have gone further than I had thought...

'I've never seen Meroe cry like that,' I said. 'I've never seen Meroe cry at all,' I added, realising this was true. 'What's going on, and do you think there might be any way of stopping it?'

'Have a seat, my dear. I believe this is what the ancients called catharsis,' Professor Monk told me.

I sat down on the warmed marble bench beside his dapper form. He smelt agreeably of tweed. The cloth, not the perfume. And that dangerous Greek coffee to which he is devoted. Mrs. Dawson was wearing her signature scent, Arpège, and the two perfumes blended very nicely. We all smelt of honeyed whisky, and very nice it was too. I drank some more.

'Catharsis?' I asked when I regained my breath.

'Purges the soul with pity and terror,' explained the Professor. 'Poor Meroe has been worrying about this soul cake poisoning for days and now she has to acknowledge it. She recoiled from the shock, and there was Daniel.'

'Very good arms to throw yourself into and an excellent shoulder to lean on,' I confirmed.

'Myself, I have always preferred to rest my weary head on a suitably hospitable bosom, but I take your point,' he replied with a hint of mischief. Mrs. Dawson smiled sweetly.

'You think it is poisoning, then?' I asked.

'What else could it be, dear?' asked Mrs. Dawson, sipping delicately and licking her lips. That heather honey was powerful stuff. 'She says that her ceremony has been profaned. We have heard people singing the soul cake song or the Gower Wassail from the inaccessible dogleg of the alley and since then we have been inundated with maniacs who have lost their senses very unexpectedly, and are not the people one would have thought would be vulnerable.'

'Not your standard drug addicts,' I said.

'Well, no, they all seem to have been well dressed and so on. Even this man who leapt off the building. Did you see him?' she asked.

'No, the police wouldn't let me, for which I am very grateful.'

'There might have been some clue in his attire,' said Mrs. Dawson inflexibly.

I knew what she was suggesting and I didn't intend to do it. 'I'm not going to be allowed to open the back door of my bakery until the scene of the crime officers have been there,' I explained. 'The cops told us that the SOCO would cut off their—I mean, be very upset if anyone even so much as breathed on their crime scene.'

'So I understand,' affirmed the Professor, rescuing me. 'I believe that they work on Locard's principle, and of course opening your door might transfer all sorts of alien matter.'

'Locard's principle?' asked Mrs. Dawson. She might have been at a real picnic. Both of my elderly companions were displaying a sangfroid which ought to have given them frostbitten arteries.

'Every contact leaves a trace,' quoted Professor Monk.

'I see,' said Mrs. Dawson. 'Do go on, Dion.'

'Well, as I understand it, they will come with bottles and vapours and sticky-tape and collect and test every hair, fibre, drop of liquid and crumb.'

'Then they will be there for weeks,' I prophesied gloomily. 'There's everything in that alley from cat fur to pigeon feathers, sparrow droppings, cigarette butts and the remains of the Mouse Police's tuna. Which would add fish scales. They are going to have a really fun time.'

'Grammar,' reproved Professor Monk. 'And there is of course the soul cake itself. Something has been added to it which, I suspect, is not in Jason's recipe.'

'It was Meroe's recipe,' I interjected. 'He only made the connection between soaling and souling because he hasn't completely got the hang of spelling yet.'

'No matter, English spelling is a relatively new invention,' said Professor Monk. 'Until the nineteenth century it was largely voluntary. One spelt it as one heard it. Just look at Chaucer. As long as the dear boy can puzzle out a recipe, it doesn't matter a great deal.'

'I suppose so,' I replied. 'But he has to pass exams if he wants to be a pastry chef.'

'I'm sure that we can manage to teach him,' said Mrs. Dawson. 'I notice, too, that you and Daniel seem to be reconciled,' she said delicately. 'I trust that all is now well between you?'

'It was a misunderstanding,' I said. 'Due to him innocently importing a gorgeous female friend who had designs on him, which he hadn't noticed.'

The Professor chuckled and Nox gave him a reproving look.

'And then she made me a frightful dinner and tried to get me to sell her half my bakery,' I added.

Mrs. Dawson patted my hand. 'And you declined?'

'Very firmly.'

'Good. You do not need a partner. The reason Dion chuckled is that we have both noticed that your Daniel is a very modest person.'

'Chap doesn't know he's handsome,' said the Professor.

'He must have had a very good mother,' added Mrs. Dawson.

'Sylvia, would you take Nox for a moment? Touch of cramp,' said the Professor as he stood up and stretched. Mrs. Dawson accepted Nox and, even more unusual, Nox accepted her.

'Shall we leave Daniel with Meroe?' he asked.

'No, no, dear, we need to talk to her, and she will want to talk too, once she is over this fit of tears. There, see, she is already sitting up and wiping her face. If you would like an errand, perhaps you can return the beautiful kitten to her throne, and bring me back a nice soft towel, some drinking water, and another of your lovely handkerchiefs? I do so approve of your choice of linen, you know. Cats mostly dislike human emotion,' she explained.

Professor Dion allowed Nox to ascend into his arms, where she nestled, looking unbearably poised and disdainful as she was borne away.

Just as he left, Meroe sobbed, caught her breath, and sobbed again. She scrubbed her hands across her eyes and dried her face on her shawl. Daniel kissed her on the cheek. He helped her stand and conducted her over to the temple. She sagged down next to me, shivering as though she was cold. Mrs. Dawson wrapped the Glasgow rug around her, tucking it in at the edges so that she looked like the survivor of a less than successful Highland battle. Culloden, say. Daniel sat on her other side. I caught his eye. He shrugged fluidly.

'I should know?' he said. 'I was just sitting there, suddenly my arms are full of weeping witch. How do you feel, Meroe?' he asked a little anxiously. If Meroe had thought him importunate, he might spend the next few years in a fetching green skin, croaking in the impluvium. In which event I would be happy to kiss him human again, of course.

'Better,' she said thickly. Daniel looked relieved.

'Good. Ah, now here is Dion with a clean hankie and a nice fluffy towel. Wash your face, my dear, dry it, and have a good long drink of water. Crying dries one out so much,' said Mrs. Dawson in a tone which indicated that she knew precisely how much dehydration was caused by tears. She must have cried a lot of them over her dead husband—by all accounts she had loved him dearly. And here she was looking placidly pleased with Professor Monk. Humans.

Meroe did as she was told. The water washed off handfuls of rose petals which had fallen on her as she cried. She drank thirstily. Then she shook herself.

'I need to tell you what has been happening,' she informed us.

'Well yes, dear, I think you do,' replied Mrs. Dawson. 'We have all been caught up in it, whatever it is.'

'The trouble is, I am not at all sure what is going on.' Meroe dabbed at her eyes again. 'All I know is that since Barnabas has come to town, there has been unauthorised and dangerous magic happening. When I was a young witch we did our surveying and asking by nice, safe scrying in water or crystal—though even that presents some dangers to the inexperienced. These followers of Barnabas are taking huge risks. Some of his ritual workings have to do with altered states of consciousness and shamanic journeys.'

'Which were usually induced by fasting and drumming and drugs,' said the Professor.

'Yes. In the US, they use peyote as a ritual poison. In the East they use a concoction of various herbs. I believe that Barnabas is supplying them with mandrake roots, and I know that Barnabas has been researching recipes to open the inner eye.'

'Why?' I asked.

Daniel echoed my question: 'Why now and here?'

'Because he is seeking treasure,' said Meroe. 'We were on the beach when he said he had conjured some.'

'You were on a beach?' asked Daniel, sounding puzzled.

'Williamstown, specifically,' I told him. 'There was a magical mob scene and Barnabas got mugged by men in balaclavas—just when he had found this jewelled plate. Meroe thinks he palmed it.'

'Legerdemain, always a useful skill,' commented the Professor.

'Mugged? Were you hurt?' asked Daniel anxiously.

'No, just tumbled over and scared,' I assured him.

'So, you believe that the Barnabas witches are taking dangerous substances,' pursued Professor Dion. It is hard to deflect a classicist: they have to learn Greek verb mutations and that produces a mind of sprung steel.

'I do,' said Meroe.

'Then how did it get out into the general populace?' he asked. 'And who is singing the soul cake song?'

'That I do not know,' she said.

'Someone needs the money,' I reasoned. 'Everyone needs money. There are clubbers out there who will try anything once. And it looks like you only have to try this stuff once. Perhaps Barnabas is financing his treasure hunt with drug dealing.'

'That is what I am afraid of,' said Meroe on a shuddering breath.

'But it isn't your doing,' said Mrs. Dawson.

'Doesn't matter,' said Daniel. 'I know this one. A bad Christian—he's just a bad man. A bad Jew—he's a sign that all Jews are bad.'

'A bad woman degrades the whole female race,' said Mrs. Dawson. 'Isn't that just like a woman?'

'And a bad witch,' said Meroe, 'brings down oppression on all witches.'

Then there really didn't seem to be a lot else to say. We stared at the roses. They were very pretty. But not informative.

Chapter Ten

Finally Meroe said, 'Well, I can't get out of it any longer. I have to go and talk to Barnabas.'

'Like some company?' I asked as casually as I could. Suddenly I wanted to be out of my lovely garden, away from the white-clad people I could hear scuffling in the alley below, and especially away from the dead man who thought that he could fly. I wondered if he had, just at the last minute, realised that he was falling to his death. 'I might tag along too, if you want me,' offered Daniel. 'In about an hour? Jonesy and his co-ey will be popping up to have a chat any moment, I can tell.'

'All right,' Meroe replied, getting to her feet as if she was very old and wrapping her shawl about her shoulders. 'I'll go and change my clothes, make some preparations. Talk to Belladonna.'

'And Sylvia and I shall remain here for liaison purposes,' Professor Monk told me. 'Do take care, won't you?'

'We shall,' said Meroe grimly.

Daniel and I had only been in my apartment for long enough to put on the kettle when the doorbell sounded and Jonesy and Miller came in. They wanted tea. I supplied it. The Mouse Police, who had been napping on the sofa, removed themselves to the balcony. They were allowed upstairs at weekends. And, like Jason, they didn't seem to take to cops. There were probably warrants out for both Heckle and Jekyll for mouse-molesting, rat-murder and fish-theft. Horatio can take any company as it comes. They did not seem to notice the animals, anyway.

Both looked tired and grimy. Both leaned their elbows on the table and sucked up good lapsang souchong as though the day wasn't expected to bring them anything more pleasant. Which it probably wasn't, at that.

'SOCO say your alley's a biological sink,' grinned Jones.

'Certainly is,' I agreed, topping up the tea cups. 'Would you like a biscuit, perhaps, or a piece of cake?'

'Not for me,' said Miller hastily. Oops. Not tactful, Corinna.

'How about something out of a packet?' asked Daniel.

'There's some of those Dutch ginger bikkies in the tin,' I remembered. 'Trudi gave them to me.'

'Thanks,' said Miller, engulfing three when Daniel produced them. 'No offence, ma'am.'

'None taken,' I said. 'Have the scene of crime people found anything interesting?'

'Not so far as I know,' responded Miller. 'They don't tell us a lot. Ever since all them bloody forensic TV programs got so popular, they've been getting above themselves, SOCO have. Think they're CSI Miami. But we've interviewed all the witnesses and it's clear this bloke was alone. No one pushed him.'

'So, it's an accident,' said Daniel hopefully.

'Not if someone sold him the fairy dust,' said Jones. 'And I'm old enough to remember this happening before, eh, Daniel?'

'Don't look at me,' he protested.

Jones sucked up more tea and I resupplied him and his mate.

'The Summer of Love,' he pronounced with slow relish. 'Only time I ever saw people who thought they could fly was when Timothy Leary brought in LSD. I reckon that's what it is.'

'Acid?' asked Daniel. 'There's always some around, of course. Tiny little doses on blotting paper.'

'This,' said Miller, 'wasn't a tiny little dose. When you went out at nine, the bloke must have been on the roof. You didn't see or hear anything, Daniel?'

'No. I went out the front door into Flinders Lane and straight down towards the station to get the croissants. He must have fallen when I was away and I came in through the front door when I came back. Missed all the excitement—which is good, as I don't like excitement.'

'See anyone around?' asked Jones casually.

'Not that sort of person, no,' replied Daniel. This was clearly a coded conversation.

'Too much to hope,' remarked Miller. 'Ah, there goes the blood-wagon.'

I heard an ambulance crunch and turn, just where the wider-than-usual wheel base always impacts on a slightly raised paving stone.

'We've finished with your alley,' Miller told me politely. 'Body's gone now.'

'Oh, thank you,' I said. There was no way that I was going out there until a heavy shower of rain had fallen and removed the blood and organic material. I am not cut out for crime scenes. I cherish my ignorance of autopsies. The Mouse Police would just have to do without their tuna scraps.

'Do we know who the bloke was?' asked Daniel.

'Yeah, respectable citizen,' said Jones, as though reading from a card. 'No warrants, no criminal record. Wallet and driving licence in his pocket. Allan Morris. Worked for Treasury. Married with two small children. Well, gotta go,' he said, levering himself to his feet. 'Least the widow will be over the poached egg stage by now. Thanks for the tea,' he added, and took himself and his mate away.

'Poached egg?' I asked Daniel.

'The eyes widen with the sudden shock,' he explained gently. 'They don't mean to be callous. It's the job. Now, make another pot of that tea, shall we? And I'm going to have a shower and put on some clean clothes. I feel like I've been wearing these since last week.'

'I feel the same,' I said. 'Bags first shower.'

I beat him to the bathroom by a short half-head and washed myself vigorously with pine-plantation soap, a clean and bracing scent which Daniel also selected when I yielded him the shower. We might not have known what we were doing, but at least we would smell clean.

For her encounter with Barnabas Meroe had dressed not in deep black, which I had expected, but in a drape of fiery red silk with soup-plate sized suns emblazoned on it in gold thread. Huge gold rings hung from her ears. A necklace with the gold reserves of a small European duchy—Mecklenburg-Strelitz, say—encircled her brow and gold coins jingled on her wrists, her neck and around her waist. Meroe was armed against the darkness with pure bright gold. She gleamed.

Feeling very dim ourselves, Daniel and I followed her out into the street, where she summoned a taxi with a flick of the fingers and had us driven to Parkville.

We found that Barnabas and his followers had been accommodated in one block of an undistinguished set of flats built for visiting academics, undoubtedly designed to prod them into either going home or leasing a real house. Nostalgia hit me on the stairs. As a first year accounting student at Melbourne University I had babysat there for a charming American law professor whose child only ate lightly cooked hamburger mince. And thrived on it, as I remembered. The doors were just as ill-fitting as ever and the stairs uneven. Barnabas' search for treasure might have something to do with his living standards. Still, weren't witches supposed to be outdoor creatures, strongly linked to nature and the Powers? Possibly not this one.

Meroe did not knock but thumped the door with her fist and, when it opened, swept in without pause. We followed in her magnificent wake.

The flat was small and crammed with people. Barnabas sat, like Father Christmas, in the big chair by the fire with a couple of girls on his lap. His lap was quite commodious. He saw Meroe, leapt to his feet (spilling both young women, who rolled quite easily, like puppies, onto the floor) and held out both arms.

'Meroe!' he roared. 'Come to me, my sweet witch!'

Meroe threw herself at him, grabbed him around the neck, and swung, both feet off the ground, until he had to bend down. Then she bit his ear. Hard. He grimaced.

Daniel and I looked at each other. Probably better not to intervene, we thought, could be this is some strange Rumanian way of greeting another witch...cultural differences, tolerance, etc. Besides, Meroe looked quite prepared to bite us, too.

On the other hand the victim did appear to be bleeding. The girls sat up. Barnabas was forced to his knees and Meroe came down with him, not releasing her bulldog grip until he was quite under control.

'What are you doing?' she yelled. Her coarse black hair lashed his eyes. Blood ran down his neck. 'You profane the ceremonies! You dare to spit in the face of the Goddess!'

I was, at this moment, not watching the main event but scanning the room for something less bloody to look at. Was this, indeed, that law professor's very flat? I could not remember the number. And all of these buildings looked alike. I thus surprised a gorgeous man wearing an expression of such gleeful malice that I might have gasped, except that I did not want to draw his attention onto me or my lover. He was very goodlooking, perhaps forty with hair as short and plush as a black cat and dark, unfathomable eyes. His chest was bare, with beautifully well defined muscles and little rings in his nipples and belly button. And Meroe's punishment of Barnabas was tickling his fancy, and it was not a nice fancy. Daniel had followed my gaze—he also has no taste for blood sports—and he waded into the mob and drew the man out by the hand.

'Well, well, Rocky, I wondered where you had got to,' he said affably, just loud enough to be heard. 'When did you get out of jail?'

'Daniel,' said Rocky, with little or no pleasure in seeing an old friend again. 'The name is Cypress. Remember that. And this is my mate Cedar.'

A pale youth—no, must have been twenty-five, but as languid as a Gilbertian aesthete—leaned on Cypress' chest and cooed at him. He was beautiful. Cedar was, however, the wrong name. It ought to have been jasmine. Or wisteria. Or even better, ivy, a clinging vine. Cedar's expression, when he looked at Cypress, was one of complete devotion. Cedar had the most beautiful dark brown eyes, like a labrador dog. Cypress went on speaking to Daniel: 'I never expected to see you here. You came with the bitch?'

'Yes, but unless you want me to regale good old Barnabas with highlights of your career, I shouldn't use that term again,' said Daniel, very quietly.

'She bites like a bitch,' said Cypress, and laughed. He was very pretty. But pretty isn't everything. 'All right—' he raised his free hand to ward off revelation—'I won't say it again if she's a pet of yours. I got into Wicca in jail. The others were dumb. Turned Christian. No one ever believes that. But show a parole board a sincere commitment to New Age beliefs and they buy it. Some of them. Some of the time, anyway. There's this big festival so I came along. Lots of magic,' he said hungrily.

'So you wouldn't know anything about the sale of drugs to finance this treasure hunt?' asked Daniel in that same flat tone.

Cypress slid out from under Cedar's hands, ducking his plush head. 'No,' he said quickly. 'I got nothing to do with drugs. I never did. You know that, right?'

'You didn't in the past,' Daniel agreed. 'Theft, yes. Stealing anything that moved including two speedboats and a yacht which you sailed to Tasmania, yes. But drugs, not when I knew you.'

'And I don't now.'

'All right,' said Daniel. 'You know where I am. You probably still know my mobile number. You find out anything, you call me, right, Cypress?'

'Is there a buck in it?' the man asked hopefully.

'I don't know that there mightn't be,' said Daniel. 'And you can go on being Cypress.'

'Okay,' said Cypress, far too tractably, and slipped away, taking Cedar back into the pile of bodies on the floor. Several young women embraced him. Cypress had fallen on, so to speak, his feet.

Meanwhile Meroe was scolding Barnabas. Her mouth was close to his injured ear. His blood was on her lips. She was berating him in a harsh, relentless stream of insults and exhortations which steadily became more, not less, unbearable as they went on. 'You fool, Barnabas, you lead-footed fool, you big jelly-bellied idiot! Do you think gods like being mocked? Do you think they'll forget this because your intentions were pure? What were your intentions? Barnabas! What have you been doing?'

Daniel and I watched, unable to think of a way of helping— indeed, unsure of who might need the help if we gave it. Cypress had escaped Daniel's attention but some of the people on the carpet were getting restless.

'Why's she biting him?' asked one child, pushing a couple of boys aside and crawling to her feet. 'She shouldn't be biting him. Barnabas?'

'It's Meroe,' said an older woman, rubbing her shaved scalp with a narrow, dark palm. 'Best not to interfere with Meroe. Solitary. Powerful. Sibyl's Cave,' she added in a warning tone.

'Oh.' The girl bit her lip. 'I've heard of her.'

'Those Rumanians are feisty,' commented a boy in leather trousers who was almost as decorative as Cypress.

'That means full of beans,' said a woman wearily, shoving a couple of puppy-dog youngsters off her lap. 'I reckon that finishes communion for now. I'm going to slump into a nap. Coming, Celeste?'

'Yes,' said Celeste, a tired forty with red hair looped into a coil.

'Can we talk?' I suggested. The Meroe/Barnabas confrontation showed no signs of slowing down at all. Now he was yelling at Meroe and she was hissing like a Naga to whom an indecent suggestion has just been made by a pit viper of low manners and unpleasant associations.

'Why not?' said the woman. 'I'm Selene. She's Celeste. Come next door. Barnabas wanted a council, but we didn't decide anything.'

'Only because he never lets anyone decide anything,' objected Celeste. 'I don't know what got into us, joining a Goddess-based religion and ending up being pushed around by a man.'

'You have a point,' agreed Selene. 'It was because of Eugenia, really, that we got into it, and when she went to the Goddess, I suppose we just stayed on…she was Barnabas' partner, a wonderful mentor. Oh dear, we have no manners,' she apologised, ushering us into a flat identical to the one we'd just left. 'You came with Meroe, yes? I seem to know you. You're the baker,' she said, her dark face lighting up. 'You're going to make the soul cakes. Your chocolate muffins have frequently saved my sanity. I'm a teacher,' she explained. We sat down and she poured a cool yellowy infusion into small cups. 'Dandelion, want some?'

Daniel and I declined.

'I'm Daniel, this is indeed Corinna Chapman, the baker from Earthly Delights,' Daniel said. 'We came because Meroe might need back-up.'

'If she does, she's got it,' said Celeste. 'She's always been known to be very close to the Goddess.'

'And you've come to town for Samhain?' I asked, talking about a pagan celebration as though I was commenting on the spring racing carnival.

'Celeste lives in Sydney and I live in South Yarra,' said Selene. 'The others come from everywhere—from little covens in Queensland to communes in microclimates in Tasmania. It's always a good feast, because although in Europe it's the autumn, here it's spring. And we are not going to open that debate again,' she added, as though in warning, flapping her hands.

'What debate?' asked Daniel, puzzled.

'Do we reverse the ceremonies' dates because we follow the seasons, or do we follow the seasons and reverse the dates?' asked Selene.

I took a moment to work this out. Autumn in Europe was spring here. Summer in Australia was winter in Europe. The north wind doth blow in England and they shall have snow, and what will the robin do then, poor thing, but sit in the barn and keep himself warm, whereas in Australia the north wind doth blow and we shall be fried to a crisp, and all the robin can do is try to find a drop of water in the bottom of a parched pond somewhere. But presumably in both cases it can hide its head under its wing (poor thing). The common verse of England has always added just another level of confusion to Australian children, plus the sneaking suspicion that they or the robins were living in the wrong country…or someone was…the poets, maybe?

'Oh,' I said. 'Right. What has been decided?'

'Better the communality of all the Craft celebrating the same ceremony all over the world, regardless of seasons,' replied Celeste promptly, 'than halving the celebration just to make it match. Not my view, but I agree to differ. Put on the kettle, Sel? I could do with another cup of tea.'

I liked these women. They seemed very sensible, unlike the lolling young in the other flat. Daniel had found a chair and was absent-mindedly scratching the healing wound on the back of his hand. He was smiling.

'What do you teach?' he asked.

'I teach maths,' said Selene. 'Celeste runs a tea shop.'

'Ah,' said Daniel.

We sat quietly while the kettle heated and tea was made. Through the thin walls we could hear the battle of the witches going on. There was an occasional crash. They were probably throwing things. Things which smashed very satisfactorily. I also heard youthful laughter.

'What is Barnabas doing that Meroe so objects to?' I asked.

'Treasure,' said Celeste. 'He has a plan.'

'I see,' said Daniel, gravely.

'And he did produce some sort of artefact on Williamstown beach the other night,' said Selene.

'Which was then immediately reclaimed by the Dark,' said the redheaded witch. 'Not to blurt out Craft secrets to the uninitiated, but you are friends of Meroe's. We don't like the whole thing, and if it wasn't for having promised to help, we'd be off home. We can always come in for the ceremonies.'

'You see, it's the young ones. They want concrete results from witchcraft. They don't realise that the changes a witch makes are in the universe of her self, not the outer universe. They have been watching *Charmed* and *Buffy* and *Angel* and they want to produce their own demons, preferably really sexy ones. Even the most powerful witches never conjured demons like those girls from *Charmed*.'

'I remember when my shop assistants took up Wicca—Meroe wanted to travel to America to find and assassinate all the script-writers,' I said, laughing.

'Luckily, they forgot about it fast,' said Daniel. 'They were driving Meroe up the wall.'

'These will abandon it as well,' sighed Selene. 'Maybe one or two have the makings. Not more than that. But Barnabas is so charming and jolly and so convincing, and for a lot of them he is the perfect father figure.'

'They need a perfect mother figure,' objected Celeste. 'No one has come forward since Eugenia died. That's almost a year. We call her name in the ceremonies this Samhain. Who will replace her? Urania is not mocked, nor left without an avatar.'

'Well, if she isn't left without an avatar, then she won't be,' argued her friend logically. 'Someone will come forward.'

'We heard that Barnabas is into poisons,' said Daniel, less adroitly than usual. The seamless, sleepy voices of the elder witches were making him drowsy. And in any case, as he said himself, his timing had been off ever since Georgiana had arrived in our lives.

'Poisons?' Selene sat up. 'No!'

'I can't think where you heard that,' said Celeste.

'Perhaps I heard wrong,' Daniel confessed. 'It's been a bad day. A man threw himself off the roof next to us, thinking he could fly.'

'How terrible! Is that what brought Meroe here?'

'Perhaps,' I answered. 'Who can tell with Meroe?'

'Indeed. Really, you must have a glass of the plum tonic and a small working for cleansing. Death is so sticky,' she said, laying out a knife and a pot of cooking salt. 'The contamination hangs around for ages. Especially with a suicide. Such an unfortunate frame of mind…'

We sat as she sprinkled us with salt and drew around our right hands with the knife, and then she and her fellow witch sang a sad, antiphonal song, consisting of the names of the Goddess. Urania, they sang, Artemis and Hecate, Kali and Leucothea. White Queen Sedna of the Snows, Mother Carey with her blizzards and her seabirds, Aphrodite the Stranger scented with roses, the Night Hag and stately Venus, Hebe and Isis, Nepthys, and Egyptian Nut who was, uniquely, the sky goddess, not the earth. And finally the song wound down to the oldest one, the first Goddess, Gaia, who was the earth, wide hipped, big bellied, the womb of the human race, the nurturing breast of all humans, the opulent and voracious beginning of all things female.

It was very effective, beautiful and strange, and when it was over and the salt had been scattered, we felt better. We heard Meroe calling us in the corridor and bade our witches thanks and farewell. We descended into the lobby to wait for Meroe to complete one final blistering opinion on Barnabas' moral character.

'They were lovely women,' I said to Daniel.

He took my hand. 'Yes, they were.'

'And that was a very nice threnody,' I added.

'It was, indeed,' he said.

'Do you believe them about Barnabas?' I asked Daniel as we emerged onto cool, forested Parkville Street, rustling with possums having a day off from mugging commuters for their leftover lunchtime fruit.

'Not a word,' he affirmed.

'Nor me,' I said.

Chapter Eleven

Meroe still wasn't talking, so we went to my own apartment and I decided to do a little light housework—cooking and mending—while Daniel read aloud. I had only just rediscovered the absolute delight of being read to by someone who liked the book and was fluent and easy, and I was awarded an instant understanding of how those Victorian ladies had uncomplainingly crocheted their way through four thousand metres of eyelet lace in a lifetime. The hands move of their own volition while the ears are ravished, though in their case it was probably by Dr. Johnson or Sir Walter Scott, while Daniel was reading Winnie the Pooh.

"'There's a thing called Twicetimes,' he said. "Christopher Robin tried to teach it to me, but it didn't,' he said.

"'Didn't what?' asked Rabbit.

"'It just didn't,' said Pooh sadly.'

Oh, I knew exactly what he meant. None of this soul cake affair made any sense. Well, it did, but the nastiest kind of sense. Why sell lysergic acid so strong that it sent its users instantly insane? Economically, it was silly. The stuff must cost something to synthesise. Why, then, not dilute it to the usual dose and stockpile a lot of it for future demand? Presumably it didn't go off. I knotted the last stitch in a tear I was repairing and bit off the thread. Daniel chuckled.

'Hmm?' I asked.

'I was just thinking how Georgie would see this scene,' he said, now a little warily, even though Georgie was agreed to be a safe subject. 'The perfect Victorian paterfamilias, reading improving literature to the Little Woman. George always said that Jews longed for the good old days of the patriarchy.'

'And do they?' I asked idly.

'No,' he said, very decidedly. 'For a start, if you're the patriarch, it's always your fault. No matter what happens, you get blamed.'

'Then again, you have all those wives and concubines,' I reminded him, rolling up his shirt for later washing and taking up my blue spring jacket, which I had put away clean but buttonless last spring. I had some beautiful ceramic cat buttons to put on it.

'Never did them any good,' murmured Daniel. 'The wives just fought with each other over whose son was going to succeed. More people, less company. Did you ever read the Kipling story about King Solomon?'

I was touched and delighted that we had read the same books as children.

'"The Butterfly That Stamped"? Of course. We might read the *Just So Stories* after we finish *The House at Pooh Corner*. Go on about the disadvantages of patriarchy.'

'Then there's God. You have to have a special relationship with God if you're the patriarch, or how else are you going to produce water from the rock?'

'And what's your relationship with God, then?' I had always wondered.

'Distantly polite,' said Daniel. 'So, George may keep her patriarchy, you can secure your buttons, and I will continue on reading.'

And he did. The afternoon wore on, the massed cats slept, the buttonless became buttoned and the torn was patched. We were just wondering about a little dinner when Jones and Miller announced themselves and stomped up the stairs. I put away the mending and put on the kettle again.

They were, if anything, more grimy. And grim. But they accepted tea and packet biscuits and Daniel engaged them in light banter about what you could catch grubbing about in alleys in this man's city in these degenerate times.

'Oh, I don't know,' I said, having read some very interesting detective stories set in the twenties. 'You probably aren't going to get syphilis.'

'Don't count on it,' growled Jones. 'Got a favour, ma'am,' he said to me.

'Yes,' I said, considerably astonished.

'Wouldn't ask a cleanskin civilian but you're Daniel's lady,' said Miller.

'Yes,' I agreed.

'We went down to that Best Fresh place to check out the cake situation,' said Jones. He was worried, but he was also amused in some not-very-nice way. 'Asked the bloke if he had any cakes to spare so forensics could check 'em out. He was just about to hand over a big bag when some idiot told him about the stiff, and he went right up the wall.'

'And he's still there,' added Miller.

'And what do you expect Corinna to do about that?' asked Daniel, quite reasonably.

'Talk to him,' said Jones. 'She's a baker. He says only a baker can understand and she's the nearest baker.'

'All right,' I responded, before Daniel could argue me out of it. 'But I've never met the man. Best Fresh has only been open for two weeks.'

'Two weeks, eh? About the same time as the nutcases surfaced,' observed Jones. 'Finish your tea, Dusty. We're going to go talk to the bread man.'

'Oh, by the way, there's a couple of uniforms to see you, too,' Miller informed me as we went down to the atrium. There I found the redoubtable Ms. Bray and her cat-loving offsider, notebooks open and pens poised.

'Back again,' Ms. Bray said cheerfully. 'More trouble.'

'Oh, good,' murmured Daniel.

'What are you doing with my interview subject, Mr. Jones?' she asked my escort.

'Gotta go talk to the bread shop man before we end up with a hostage drama and get on the news,' said Jones. 'You know how the boss hates it when we get on the news for being brave and vigilant and that. Might as well come too,' he decided. 'More nice girls around, the less aggro.'

'And that's never been true,' said Miller.

But we all conducted ourselves with great propriety as we went down the lane to Best Fresh. The body was gone but the checked blue and white 'crime scene do not cross' tape remained in Calico Alley, and it offended me.

I was not the only person taking offence in Flinders Lane that late Sunday afternoon. Best Fresh's front door was shut and someone had dragged a long bench and a couple of bread trays across it. A barricade. A scared-witless youth, Eddie, had stuffed himself under the bench and was staring out through the glass like a goldfish watching a cat. Behind him I heard a roaring, and complicated noises suggestive of…things being broken.

'Have you noticed that everyone is yelling at us today?' Daniel slid a hand under my elbow. 'How are we going to talk to this baker if he's inside and we're outside? And if you are thinking of sending an unarmed Corinna into a crime scene alone, you can think again, Jonesy me old mate.'

'Nah, we're using modern and technological methods,' said Jones, producing a mobile. 'Viz, this little machine. The boffins call it a tel-e-phone. It's the latest thing.'

I held it to my ear. Someone was yelling into it so loudly that I could not even make out the words. Jones' laboured irony did not amuse me.

'Hello?' I said into the phone. 'Who's there?'

'Who are you?' came a booming voice.

'I'm Corinna Chapman from Earthly Delights,' I said in my English teacher voice. It is so useful.

'You're a baker,' he said, the volume dropping from 'landing 747' decibels to 'close pass by a news helicopter'.

'That's me. You want to talk to a baker? Here I am. Only I can't get in to talk to you because of all those fallen shelves, and you might let your assistant out. He looks a bit frayed.'

'No!' The voice bellowed out of coherence again. I took the phone away from my mistreated ear.

'This isn't going to work,' I told Jones.

'Keep talking when he gives you a chance,' instructed Ms. Bray. 'That's what they always say about hostage-takers. They want to talk to someone who understands. You just convince him that you understand.'

'Oh, simple,' I said.

She gave me her dimpled smile. 'Go on, then,' she encouraged.

I listened again. The bellow had died away. 'You're a baker,' I began.

'Yes!' boomed the giant.

'Where did you train? I worked in a little Italian bakery in Carlton.'

'In Tassie,' he said, still loudly. 'In Hobart. Made good bread, we did.'

'Not a chain, then?'

'Just a little bakery. Only did a hundred or so. Still had an old bread oven from convict days. You know, with that curved roof?'

'And you light a fire under it. Kiln bread's good bread,' I went on, not sure where the conversation was heading. But if we were going to discuss bread, I could probably talk until whole herds of cows came home. 'Did you test the temperature with butcher's paper?'

'Three seconds to turn brown,' said the baker promptly.

'Two for pasta douro, and spray with water in five minutes.' I chanted the baker's litany, forgotten in this age of thermostats. 'I don't know your name, though you know mine.'

'Wyatt,' said the baker. 'Vincent. You make pasta douro?'

'Yes,' I replied. 'I brought a mother of bread with me from the Italian kitchen.'

'I don't,' boomed Vincent Wyatt sadly, like a mourning apatosaurus. 'They won't let me. It's all pre-made mixes and franchise quality. Quality!'

'I know,' I sympathised.

'And now they're saying that someone is dealing drugs from my shop…'

'I know,' I said again. 'They'd be saying it about me if my shop wasn't closed for the weekend. Come along, Mr. Wyatt, we've got a lot to talk—'

'But they'll close me down!' he wailed. 'I'll lose everything!'

'And making a scene isn't going to help,' I said firmly. 'Come on, I've struck a deal with the police, we leave now and no more will be said. I've got a recipe for—'

'I got to think about this,' said Mr. Wyatt, and the phone went dead. I stared at it for a moment.

'Sorry,' I said to Jones. 'I don't seem to have helped at all.'

'You were great!' said Daniel, hugging me. 'You almost had him. Real life doesn't work out like TV, you know, three minutes of plot, an ad break, five minutes of development, an ad break, and then a resolution with a trailer for next week. He's talking to you. And you gave him something to think about. We'll just sit down on this seat provided by the munificent council and wait for a while.'

'Yeah,' affirmed Jones.

'Meanwhile,' said Ms. Bray, 'there's been a development.'

'Another one?'

'The reports have started to come in from the people who were tested last week. The mad ones,' she elaborated.

I hadn't forgotten them. 'Yes?'

'Forensics are cross,' she told me. 'The agent, whatever it is, eluded them. Metabolised too quickly to be found, but had major central nervous system effects. Eventually they found traces of LSD.'

'I thought as much,' I said. We hadn't told Ms. Bray anything about Barnabas, witches, or ordeal poisons, and we probably should have.

'Far beyond any usual dose,' said Ms. Bray.

'I worked that out myself,' I said. 'And it seems strange.'

'They had crumbs and fruit by-products in their stomachs,' she said.

'Yes.' I saw what was coming.

'So we feel that—'

The mobile phone rang. Jones pressed the receive button and handed it over. It wasn't one of those phones which took pictures or I might have tried to send poor Vincent Wyatt a picture of us, sitting on the iron bench in the lane.

'It's me,' said the apatosaurus.

'And it's me, Corinna, here,' I assured him.

'I can't see any way out,' he said.

'Just come and open the door,' I said. 'It's easy. I'm here.'

'I reckon it must have been that worthless little gum-chewing shoppie Eddie,' he said in a low roar. 'He must've done it. Ruined me by selling drugs.'

'You don't know that,' I urged. That Eddie was earning his weekly wage. I could see his frantic eyes through the window. Terrified eyes, clutching hands. I lost patience abruptly.

'Vincent!' I raised my voice. 'Stop this right now! If it's your assistant, then the cops will arrest him and make him sorry he was born. Now I can't sit out here all day, I've got to go to bed early, I've got baking to do in the morning! You come and open this door. I've got bread to make!'

Silence descended and the phone was cut off again.

'Oops,' I said meekly.

'Possibly not oops,' said Daniel.

Jones rubbed his chin. 'But possibly. Give it another ten and then, if he still won't come out and be nice, we'll have to lay on a negotiator and call out the Sons of God.'

'Sons of God?'

'Special Operations Group,' Ms. Bray told me. 'Otherwise known as Soggies. Snipers. 007s. Licensed to kill.'

'He doesn't seem to be armed,' I said feebly.

'No, but we don't know whether he's armed or not,' said Jones, 'which is why I'd rather wait. Besides, this sort of thing means overtime and the boss hates authorising overtime.'

I was fascinated by this privileged insight into secret police methods. I was also feeling sorry for Vincent. And his shoppie, the wretched Eddie. And for me. I had been plunged without any preparation or training into this and I was sure that I was about to make a fatal mistake.

Ms. Bray captured my attention again. '...so at least you won't have to get up early tomorrow,' she finished. I had missed the start of her discourse.

'What?'

'Because of the search,' she told me again. 'Just a hint, get those Mouse Police out of the bakery before they arrive.'

'They can stay upstairs,' I affirmed. Not open on Monday? My world was shuddering on its axis. I suddenly knew exactly how Vincent Wyatt felt because I felt the same.

Not waiting for a phone call, I went to the barricaded front door of Best Fresh and knocked on it. There was a startled silence inside.

'Come along, Mr. Wyatt,' I said. 'Open the door and come with me. We're in trouble, and bakers must stick together. That's the way, Eddie, you push those racks aside.'

Eddie did as he was bid. There was a piercing scream of metal on metal, then the barricade was gone. Eddie had pressed himself so flat against the window that he seemed to be glued there. Gradually, he sidled along to the door and unlocked it with a subdued clunk.

'Nice,' I heard Jones say.

'There we are. Come on out, Eddie,' I encouraged. Poor Eddie slipped out through the opening door and flung himself into the arms of the attendant police. Then I did something which no hostage negotiator ought to do in a million years of careful negotiations. I heard Daniel behind me protest but it was too late. I shoved aside the remains of the bread racks and went into Best Fresh.

It was no longer the shop it had been. The snazzy plastic chairs had been thrown—one by one, it seemed—into a corner, where some of them had smashed. The blinds hung askew on their rails. Bread racks, rolls, loaves and a whole sack of some sort of pre-mix littered the floor. And in the corner was Mr. Wyatt, huddled close, his hands together and caught between his knees, a picture of misery.

For a moment I didn't know what to do, but clearly this could not go on. Vincent Wyatt was big, with thinning blond hair and a high complexion. He was tending to fat as a lot of bakers do, and was presumably strong enough to take me on in any sort of physical contest. But I did not want to see him running the risk of being shot. People had died enough. Calico Alley was turning into a war zone and I was sick of it.

I crossed the room, kicking loaves out of the way, sank down on my knees in front of him and grabbed his knotted hands.

'Come on,' I said, 'let's get you out of here.'

'Corinna?' The big face was bleared with tears.

'Vincent?'

'Yair,' he agreed. I pulled and he came up out of his crouch. I retained my grip on his hands but he didn't seem to notice. 'Made a hell of a mess,' he grunted as we crunched and waded through the assorted spilt produce.

'Certainly have,' I agreed. 'But it can be cleaned up. Come on. Cup of tea and you'll feel slightly better. Perhaps.'

'It's a scandal,' he muttered.

I kept towing. I brought him to the door and gave him a shrewd shove just as he baulked, and then we were out into the Goddess' good air and the fight totally went out of Mr. Wyatt. He sank down onto the iron bench next to Daniel and started to cry.

'Where did you learn that?' asked Daniel, fascinated.

'Loading unimpressed horses into floats,' I replied.

'Really?' he asked. 'I never saw you as an outdoor girl.'

'I'm not. I had no choice. It was the sort of school I went to, Daniel dear. I had to find an acceptable sport or play hockey and I do not like blood. So I played tennis very badly and they let me take riding. Grandpa Chapman paid for it, bless him. I liked riding,' I remembered. 'Mainly because it's the poor horse who gets all the exercise. You?'

'I can stick on, if nothing surprising happens,' he said, smiling. 'We shall take some equestrian exercise, ma'am, together.'

'A pleasant idea,' I said. It was.

'And what are we to do with our comrade here?' he asked.

Poor Vincent Wyatt was still weeping in a broken fashion. Altogether too many people had been crying at me today. I was suddenly, and despicably, sick of the entire human race (with the exception of Daniel) and wanted nothing more to do with any of them—soppy, soggy, lachrymose creatures. My mind, which sometimes seems to hate me, presented me with a picture of Meroe grasping Barnabas' ear in her teeth. All right, not all of them were soppy—some of them were dangerously violent.

'He's mine for the moment,' said Ms. Bray sweetly, displacing me on the bench with an adroit wriggle of one hip. 'Then I need to talk to you again.'

'All right. I'll go home,' I told her. 'Catch me there in the roof garden. I'll have to rustle up some food, come and eat it with us. Unless you're afraid I'll poison you.'

'No,' she said. 'That is not one of the things I am afraid of. See you in about an hour, then. Ms. Vickery will be delighted to meet the kitty-cats again.'

'Daniel?' I asked as we walked away.

'Ketschele?'

'Kill the next person who wants me to do anything for them.'

'Yes, ma'am,' he said, saluting like Jason in his midshipman role.

Oh, Lord, Jason would be devastated! No shop opening, and what was he to do? Jason had redefined himself as a baker. His previous definition had been heroin addict. This turn of events might set him back—perhaps even cause him to relapse. And he had been doing so well. We had all been doing so well, until that little voice started singing about soul cakes.

I didn't swear, because it occurred to me that Daniel had also put up with quite enough emotion for one day. What we needed was some quiet, some company, and some food.

I was wondering what I could ransack from the nearest 7-Eleven which might make a reasonable repast, and thinking that a few cooked chickens with ginger and honey might meet the bill, as we climbed into Insula and rose towards the garden in the lift. There was a buzz of voices on the roof and my heart sank. I was not in the mood for conversation. I was, in fact, now getting my usual backlash from taking bold action and I just wanted to hide. My head ached. My limbs hurt. And somewhere along the way in the rush of the day's events I had bitten my lip.

But there were all my fellow tenants and there was Daniel and one must bear up, as the Professor says, so I bore up and was richly rewarded. Under the spreading wisteria bower the picnic tables had been set up. Bottles had been opened. Plates were being laid. There was a lovely scent on the air.

'There you are,' said Kylie. 'Like, we were getting so hungry! Come and sit down. Mrs. Dawson said to take this,' she added, passing me two white tablets and a glass of cold water. 'She said you'd have a headache.'

'She was right.' I took the tablets. I sat down on a picnic chair. Kepler, who cannot do anything inelegantly, poured me a glass of white wine.

'We thought that we needed a conference,' said Professor Monk. 'But we also thought we needed some lunch.'

'So we combined them in the ultimate pot luck feast,' said Jon. 'Amazing selection of almost anything you'd like,' he said. 'Kepler's green curry, my stuffed eggplants, muhallabia, and babaganoush, Jason's stash of experimental muffins. We also have cold meat and cheeses from Mrs. Dawson, pickles, condiments and napery from Therese Webb and fruit and various salads from Meroe. Kylie and Goss brought the ice cream, of course. Trudi contributed the sausage which Jason is presently cooking. Mistress Dread brought the beer and the Professor brought the wine. The Pandamuses have invited us all to dinner at eight, because their shop will be closed tomorrow to be tested by the police and Yai Yai just made a new batch of beef stifado and moussaka. Come along, dear Corinna,' he said, smiling his beautiful smile which has made people open their wallets all over Australia. 'What would you like to start with?'

'I would like,' I said, really thinking about it, 'a pickled onion. And cheddar cheese. And a piece of that Scottish oatbread. And isn't there anything I can contribute to the feast?'

'You are contributing,' said Jon. 'By existing. Also Daniel has just gone down to your apartment to fetch that cold frittata he made as a surprise for you.'

I looked around. Everyone was eating and drinking. Jason was forking sausages as to the barbecue born. Mrs. Dawson, who only drank champagne, gin and occasionally whisky, was sipping from a glass of golden bubbles. Goss was nibbling at the very edge of a piece of guaranteed free-of-calories lavash loaded with soft fruit cheese. Jon ate ham, Daniel ate green curry, Kepler tasted his first frittata, Mistress Dread dominated the gentleman's relish. I tasted the chicory and onions, a massively comforting dish.

There was only one thing missing from this consolation feast, and I tried not to mind terribly as I bit into my pickled onion. There was no Earthly Delights bread.

Chapter Twelve

It was such a pleasant lunch and as it drew to an end, it was time for a council of war. I shared with the meeting all I knew or had conjectured about LSD and soul cakes, and Kylie faltered: 'That song, we did hear it about. A bit. Like we said.'

'Yes, you would have if anyone did,' said Jon, as quietly as if he was charming a bird onto his hand. 'You and Goss go to some of the clubs, you live in the city.'

'We never bought any,' said Goss hastily. After an encounter with weight-loss herbs on which they had massively overdosed themselves, both girls were sticking rigidly to a traditional central nervous system depressant called a Mojito. 'Anyway, we never really saw the dealer. If he was a dealer. We just heard the little song.'

'Was it always the same voice?'

'Huh?'

'A high voice or a low voice?' persisted Jon. 'A man or a woman?'

'The same,' said Kylie, chewing a fingernail. 'Yes, the same all the time. A very nice voice. A boy.'

'More like Robbie than Justin,' said Goss helpfully. 'Always seemed to be round a corner.'

'Which clubs?' Daniel was being very careful not to startle our little birds this time.

'Around,' Kylie shrugged. 'Not the rough ones. The groovy ones, where you need good clothes and the door bitch knows how much your shoes cost. You know?'

'I know,' affirmed Daniel. 'No one wearing a dress from Maison de Target is going to get past the guardian.'

'Whatever,' agreed Kylie. 'Thanks for lunch,' she added, and they drifted off to rehearse their lines again. All three of them.

Our little gathering was, at this point, supplemented by Ms. Bray and her co-ey, who had managed to trip over Lucifer's lead and was evidently enraptured. Lucifer, for his part, felt it his duty to personally taste test every single one of her nice silver buttons. She was delighted when he ran out of buttons, scaled her uniform, and perched on her shoulder, patting at her earring with one meditative paw as (being Lucifer) he plotted ambush on the remains of the feast. I could see the little ratbag calculating: one leap across to get onto the back of the bench, another spring onto Jon's lap, then I could land smack in the middle of that large platter of smoked salmon and cream cheese crackers, which have hardly been touched.

The policewoman, who was not without trained forensic instincts, grasped his lead and suppressed him. For the moment.

'Now,' said Ms. Bray, who having been given a chair, a platter of mixed delicacies and a glass of Meroe's lavender and apple punch—and a little time to absorb some nourishment—was looking more cheerful. 'I need to know all the things that you didn't tell Jonesy and his mate.'

'And the reason we should tell you is…?' asked Jon.

'Because I can sneak them into my report, which is incomplete, so no one will know that there was a suspicious delay. His report will have been made by now and you left things out. I know you did.'

'How?' asked Jason.

'Because people always do, especially innocent people,' she told us, perfectly sure of herself. And, as it happens, she was correct. We all looked at one another. Meroe began to speak. Calmly she told Ms. Bray about the gathering of witches, the recipe for soul cake, the suspicions she held of Barnabas and his use of ordeal poisons to reveal treasure. She followed this up with a full disclosure of names, addresses and phone numbers, all of which Ms. Vickery wrote down when Lucifer allowed her the use of her biro. To her credit, Ms. Bray did not laugh, though she blinked a couple of times.

'What's the significance of the soul cake, anyway?' she asked.

'It's a social ceremony,' said Meroe. 'People would go from farm to farm in the old country in autumn, singing, accepting a spiced cake and a drink of wine, and conferring luck on the people within. It was probably a fertility ritual. Almost all of the old ones are.'

'Right,' said Ms. Bray.

'But the song,' said Mrs. Dawson, 'is a compound of several English wassail songs. Same procession, same visit, but beer or cider instead of wine. My point being that the version we are hearing is from England and would be known to people like folk singers and choristers, not to the general public.'

'Not witches?' asked our police person.

'No, that is not the song we sing,' said Meroe, and did not elaborate.

'All righty then,' said Ms. Bray, getting up reluctantly. 'Come along, Constable, detach your puddy-tat and we shall be going, with many thanks. It will take hours to type all this up.'

'What happened to poor old Vincent Wyatt?' I asked.

'They took him off to the hospital for a check-up,' said Ms. Bray. 'Reckon he might have had a brainstorm of some sort. He's got a place to live all right. He'll probably be back to see what they're doing to his shop tomorrow. You did nice work at that hostage scene, you know, Ms. Chapman. It could have gone pear-shaped real fast.'

I assented. By pure luck I had managed to do the right thing. Constable Vickery detached Lucifer, paw by paw, and handed him to Trudi. Ms. Bray surveyed us all and then gave a brisk nod.

She didn't exactly say 'Mind how you go' but she conveyed that impression. I ate a thoughtful salmon cracker or two after they had gone. They were very tasty. Trudi, rewarding Lucifer for not leaping, took one apart and gave him the filling.

'Hey,' said Jason, who had been told that Earthly Delights would not be opening in the morning and had just understood what that meant to him, 'What am I going to do?'

'You aren't sacked or anything,' I told him. 'You can take a day off, like the rest of us.'

'I don't want to take a day off,' he muttered.

'Hey, me neither,' I said feelingly. 'But we're all in this together, Jason. Don't you get any silly ideas about leaving.'

'No,' he protested. 'Course not! I just meant, you know, I've got used to working. I wake up every day at four, I make bread, that's what I do, that's what I am.'

'As well as our Jason,' Jon told him. 'There're a number of things you could be doing tomorrow. I suspect we all have tasks which could be expedited with a little paid help.'

Jason, who had been looking sullen when he thought himself volunteered, brightened up at the mention of payment.

'He can hold the lights for my photographer,' said Mistress Dread. She was in her daytime tweeds and properly known as Pat. She gave Jason an evil grin. 'New catalogue for the leather underwear.'

'Ten an hour for weeding,' offered Trudi.

'Twelve for erecting my insoluble flat-pack bookcase,' said Mrs. Dawson.

'And mine,' said the Professor, who was always short of book space.

'Or you can do a little light cooking for Jon and me,' offered Kepler. 'I have always wanted to learn how to make a cake.'

'Deal,' said Jason to Kepler. Jason was always going to view cooking as far superior to any other activity.

We gathered up the remains of the feast and went severally to our own apartments. I looked in on Mrs. Pemberthy. She seemed much recovered, complained for ten solid minutes without drawing breath, and Traddles nipped at me. So that was all right. I was so tired I could barely drag one foot after the other.

'Bath,' said Daniel, and I ran one lush with violet foam and sank into it while he read more Winnie the Pooh and my nerves, which had been sticking out on wiry protuberances and short-circuiting, sank back into my body and began to assume their proper function. I patted myself dry and dressed in a nightgown, and the last I saw of Daniel, he was placing a cat on my bed and telling me that he would be back as soon as he could.

Then he was gone, Horatio was purring, and I plunged so deeply asleep that I might have been drowned and dead.

I woke at four, slapped the alarm, started to get up, remembered that I didn't have to, breathed a prayer of thankfulness and snuggled down again. 'O Sleep it is a blessed thing beloved from pole to pole! To Mary Queen the praise be given, she sent the gentle sleep from Heaven, which slid into my soul...' Poor Coleridge spent his whole life chasing sleep, which is how he became an opium addict. He knew about its healing powers.

When I woke again at about ten o'clock I felt fine. Until I realised that even at this very moment the SOCO were looking for traces of an LSD trade in my bakery. Still, I was sure they wouldn't find any there.

I let the Mouse Police onto the balcony, where I had set their litter tray. Horatio woke and yawned elaborately. Daniel wasn't back. Moreover, there were croissants in the freezer and the coffee was soon on and I decided to allow myself a slow, comfortable breakfast in the company of the charming animals and the latest Jade Forrester. To get a paper I would have to go all the way down to the atrium, assuming that's where the paper boy might have left mine, and I didn't feel that any news would be good enough to be worth the walk.

Cats snuffled and crunched their way through bowls of kitty dins. I heated my croissant and buttered it without haste. Jade built her plot. The sun sneaked in through the blinds, so that I raised them and revealed a coolish dry late morning. I had missed last night's dinner and I didn't care, though the food would have been excellent. This was not going to be a morning to do anything but pass the time as pleasantly as possible.

At least I was comfortable when the terrible news came. It was announced quite coolly by a man in a white coat, who called me down to my bakery at about noon. The paper clad persons were still pottering around, and the bakery looked a little dishevelled. But it was nothing a good morning's cleaning couldn't cope with.

'I'm Nicholas Timoleon,' he told me, pushing back his glasses. 'I'm afraid that I have some bad news for you, Ms. Chapman.'

'What? Someone has been dealing LSD from my bakery?' I was aghast.

'No,' he said. 'That would count as the good news. The Mass Spec. and other tests are back. What we have, Ms. Chapman, is a biological contamination emergency, and here are the notices which quarantine your shop. If you have any personal possessions you would like to remove, I can allow that if you do it right now. Otherwise I must ask for your keys.'

'Oh, my God.' I almost sank down onto the step, but I needed to stay alert. Personal possessions? Yes, the laptop, the sheaf of bills I had been working on, a book or two and the recipe collections from which Jason had been learning to read. I gathered them into my arms.

'What do you suspect?' I asked. I heard my voice tremble.

'Ergot,' he told me, and conducted me onto the stairs. I heard the door close behind me with a curiously final click. I was shut out of Earthly Delights.

I couldn't think of one sensible thing to say or do when I got back into my own apartment, so I went out onto the balcony and smoked a Gauloise. That occupied some time. Then I went in again, turned on the computer and searched for information on ergot. Some of it I already knew, because it is a flour contaminant. Rye, particularly, though it also affects barley. A wet spring, a cool summer, and voila! Through the soft grains comes the red-purple fungal body called *Claviceps purpurea*. I was told that the indoleamine called ergotamine could be made to yield lysergic acid. Effects of ergotism: mania, paralysis, nausea, gangrene—oh, that poor man with his missing hands! The girl with her feet! Had I done this?

I was horrified to my soul but I kept reading, since lack of knowledge is not comforting either. Dancing manias, St. Anthony's Fire, things which I thought belonged to the Middle Ages, when whole towns went mad. But in 1951 one sack of contaminated flour sent the whole of Pont-Saint-Esprit out on a dreadful, irreparable trip. They had a name for the toxic dough which had poisoned, maddened, killed them. They called it *pain maudit*. Evil bread. I wept. I had been baking evil bread. I wept myself out and sniffled and had another Gauloise.

And then the cats drifted up to me as I sat there. The Mouse Police sprawled at my feet. Horatio occupied my lap. And we all looked out into the lane where the quarantine van disgorged more people and a stream of technicians began to leave my bakery, carrying sacks and bags and boxes, clothes and pieces of flooring, the vacuum bag, the rubbish bin, and even the broom.

Some undefined time later, Daniel came in and stood beside me in silence for a moment. Then he put out a hand. It felt strong and warm. 'Come on,' he said. 'Out of this. Everyone you're responsible for is taken care of. The girls have gone to their rehearsal and Jason is with Jon and Kepler making something called a wonder cake. And, Corinna, you are coming with me,' he said, raising me to my feet. He provided me with clothes and watched as I inserted myself into jeans, boots and jumper and picked up my backpack.

Then we were out of Insula, where I had been so happy, and Timbo was opening the door of his big blue car. He gave me a hug. When hugged by Timbo, you know you've been in a fight. He smelt sweetly of petrol and Darrell Lea Rocky Road, his favourite fruit.

'Willi,' Daniel ordered. 'You know the place.'

And then we were driving down Footscray Road towards the sea. Perhaps Daniel was going to allow me to just throw myself into it. But although my life was ruined and my career destroyed, I leaned on him and noticed that it was a nice day to be outside. The air was cool and the trees were all in blossom. Ornamental cherries in pink and lemon trees in cream and apple trees in white decorated the gardens of Footscray and then Seddon and Yarraville and Newport as we progressed.

Timbo was driving in a stately fashion, as though he was in charge of a hearse. He wasn't even snacking as he drove, though the bag of chocolates was open on the seat beside him, as always. One day, he would reach some critical limit and they would have to disassemble the car to get Timbo out. In fact, since he liked driving so much, it might be easier just to provide some plumbing and an air supply and leave him inside his metal shell, like a large, friendly mud crab.

'Wonder cake?' I murmured, grasping at something Daniel had said.

'Yes, Jason is teaching it to Kepler. What is wonder cake?' asked Daniel.

'It's our charming neighbour Mary Phillipou's recipe. I grabbed it from her when she was teaching it to Mrs. Pandamus for one of those huge family gatherings. Amazingly tolerant cake, you can put berries or dried fruit or chocolate chips into it and it always rises. She also has a boiled chocolate cake which can be assembled in the time between the doorbell ringing and the unexpected relatives dropping in (with their ten assorted children) for tea.'

'Isn't she the good-looking dark-haired woman who came in with all those supplies for Sister Mary's fete?' he asked. 'When that cake shop burned down and we thought there wouldn't be anything for the children?'

Daniel really does pay attention, an awesomely sexy trait.

'The very same,' I confirmed. 'That was wonder cake. Eaten up to the very last crumb. Where are we going?'

'Williamstown,' he told me.

'I can see that,' I informed him as we swept magnificently around into the Esplanade, with its millionaires' houses and astonishing views of the city. I always wanted the one we children called the Admiral's house, which had a widow's walk and a telescope. On the other hand, if I had a view like that I'd never get a moment's work done. Of course, I didn't have an occupation anymore…I dragged my mind away from despair and returned to the subject. 'Why are we in Williamstown?'

'To have lunch,' he said. 'And to meet someone. You'll like her. I think.'

'If she's anything like Georgie, I will personally murder you,' I said. 'I give you fair warning.'

Daniel laughed so hard that he slid helplessly down the seat.

'I'm in no danger,' he said. 'Promise.'

We went on, up a hill and round a corner. I saw the sea. *Thalassa, thalassa*, Xenophon's exhausted soldiery had cried, seeing the end of their dreadful journey. They had fought their way through the whole of Asia Minor and were at last going to shake the dust of the Persian Expedition off their sandals. I knew how they felt.

'Daniel, that is a bathing pavilion,' I objected as the car slowed and stopped. 'An Art Moderne bathing pavilion, such as I didn't know there were any left.'

'A bathing pavilion with food,' he told me. 'Come along, milady.'

'What about Timbo?'

'He's going next door,' said Daniel, 'where they know him and, even as we speak, are putting their biggest pizzas into the oven.'

Timbo grinned, locked the car and lumbered off. I followed Daniel into a, well, a bathing pavilion, all light and glass and glowing napery. We were conducted out into a paved courtyard, open to the sea on most sides. Children were making a sandcastle. People were walking dogs. A few hardy souls were swimming. And we were sitting under an umbrella consulting an impressive menu. Privilege. And nice, too, in a way. I have spent such a lot of my life on the other side of that ornamental rope.

'I don't know,' I said, scanning the available treats. 'They all look delicious.'

'Then we'll have lots of oysters in several ways and a fisherman's platter,' said Daniel, gesturing to a waitress. 'And a bottle of sauv blanc and a bloody Mary to start.'

'All right,' I said.

'And an ouzo, if you please,' Daniel added, as a large, blocky figure lumbered up and took a chair at our table. The chair whimpered, but stood her weight.

'Just bring the bottle,' said the woman.

She was as utterly unlike Georgiana Hope as it was possible to be, sharing nothing but the gender. She was strong and in her robust prime, seeming well able to pick up an ailing donkey and carry it home in her arms. She was clad in a man's flannel shirt, work boots and Yakka trousers which had seen better years. She had a peasant's strong shoulders, wide hips and short legs, but her face was purely classical. Her hair was black, striped with white, as coarse as a horse's tail, dragged back off her face in an untidy bun. Her nose was a beak and her mouth showed a selection of gold teeth. Then she smiled. The last time I had seen that smile I was at Olympia, Greece, and it was on the mouth of the Goddess Athene.

'*Yassus*,' she said. 'Daniel. You Corinna? I'm Chrysoula.'

'The golden one,' I translated.

'All my gold is in my mouth,' she said, and chuckled.

She sat like a manual labourer, knees apart, smoking a hand-rolled cigarette between forefinger and thumb. She was less a female figure than a force of nature and I wished that she and Meroe could meet.

The waitress brought the bottle of ouzo. Chrysoula poured a good slug into the glass, dropped in ice and just enough water, and watched as the spirit clouded. When it was the colour of coconut milk, she drank it off without a gasp. Then she poured another.

'Food?' asked Daniel. Kyria Chrysoula did not disconcert him in the least. I could tell that she admired him for this.

'It's rent this week,' she said, and knocked back another drink.

'My treat,' I said. She gave me a shrewd look.

'Okay,' she said. 'For you. I don't let men buy me dinner,' she said, giving Daniel a wicked wink.

Daniel called the waitress and doubled our order. She was taking Chrysoula in her stride as well. She must have been a local character. I was dying to know what Daniel wanted with this Amazon. But it was not to be thought that we didn't have any manners, so I began the required small talk by commenting on the view.

'Look at the prospect,' I said. 'If this was anywhere on the Mediterranean, you'd have to pawn your watch just to sit here.'

'I tried living away from the sea,' said Chrysoula, doctoring another glass of ouzo. To me the stuff tastes like kerosene, but I was glad that she was enjoying it.

'No good?'

'No good,' she told Daniel. 'Couldn't sleep. Missed the noise of the waves. My girl, she bought me one of those machines which makes tide noises.'

'No good again?'

'All right until the battery died,' she said, snorting with laughter. 'Then I woke up, so we moved. My sister's god-brother Johnnie rents me a house. Costs a fortune. Thieving bastard. But once I get back to work we'll be okay. Hurt my back,' she said, with the astonishment of very strong people when their body has let them down. 'Had to take time off. Government gives me a disability pension until I'm better. This is a good place. Only, sometimes it's either rent or food and I'm too old to sleep on the sand like I used to in Mytilene when I was a girl.'

'And Cassandra, she's all right?' Daniel asked.

'She's a good girl,' said Chrysoula. 'A good girl, my Cassandra. Oysters,' she said scornfully as a platter of delectable shells appeared. 'You eating that stuff when you could have calamari?'

'Yes,' said Daniel, picking up a shell and emptying it into his mouth. 'Your calamari is just coming.'

I ate various oysters, which were kilpatrick and lime and dill and even tequila, which I considered interesting but not wise. I drank an elaborate and lovingly made bloody Mary, nibbling on the celery stirrer. I watched the children flying kites across the sand. The sea sighed and rolled. It was lovely.

Then we tackled a Brobdingnagian fisherman's platter which had bits of every sort of seafood, raw and crumbed and fried and grilled and sauced with three separate sauces, with a huge green salad. Chrysoula ate politely, managing cleanly with her fingers. The food was wonderful, varied and perfectly cooked.

When there was nothing left to eat, Chrysoula cleaned her plate with a piece of bread, poured herself a new ouzo, belched with pleasure, and said to Daniel, 'You want to hear the story now?' and Daniel said, 'Yes, please.'

Chapter Thirteen

'When I was a little girl my father took us north to Thessaloniki, where his mother came from,' Chrysoula said. Her voice assumed the singsong tone of the storyteller. 'This was in the bad old days when there was a war and the Greek government sent all the army away, so when the Germans came there were no brave Greek soldiers to defend us. It fell, that city. For us kids it wasn't too bad to start because the Germans were just ordinary soldiers then and they had chocolate sometimes. We didn't like the Germans as much as the Italians. They just wanted to go home to Mamma, those Italians.'

She paused as she rolled another cigarette. I wondered how old she was. Sixty? Seventy? Surely not older?

'My father was a teacher and in the Resistance, of course, and he had to run. We ran too, and hid, because by then the Germans were taking hostages and we heard that in Crete they had killed the villages of the Amari Valley. Men, women, old people, babies, even the dogs. Everyone dead. And they put up a sign saying "Here stood Kandanos, who defied the orders of the German government". So then we knew what sort of people they were.'

Again she paused, looking back over gulfs of murder.

'Our friends were Cohens. They were Jews. They had to run too. My mother went to see the administrator, a man called Mertens. She took gold with her, her dowry jewellery. She took me with her as well. We knew this Mertens would take money to let people go. We took him money, he gave us permits. This was in the morning and by night we were far away on the train, going south. With us went the Cohens and my friend Rachel. She cried when we made her change her beautiful clothes. Silk, they were, a wrap and an apron and a headdress, and we made her wear my second best dress and an old scarf. And changed her name to Athena.'

'You took the train?' prompted Daniel.

'Yes. Father said, take the train, fast but dangerous, and stay near the doors, and if the Germans board and try to grab you, jump, and maybe some of us will escape. That train was stuffed with people hanging out all over it and on the roof. We did as Father said, though. Stand near the doors and so we did that and the saints held their hands above us. We got all the way to Athens. Then the Gestapo did get on the train and we did jump off and all of us found each other in the bushes and then we set off to walk to Corinth. We had to get across the Corinthian Canal and into the Pelopennesus, where Mother had relatives.

'We weren't alone. There were many many people on the roads. Some of the villages had shut their gates and yelled at us to go round. The Cohen baby was sick and cried all the time. One night we were sleeping in a barn and an old woman came from the house and told us to get out before dawn because we had been betrayed. Mrs. Cohen said that the baby would die, and the old woman took the baby in her arms and kissed him and said, "No, this one will live to be famous," and gave him back, and we went out. She gave us bread and wine and cheese, that old woman. The Germans took her into the main street and shot her when they found us gone.'

I poured her another ouzo. The story was utterly compelling in its simplicity. Still, I wondered why Daniel wanted to hear it.

'So we went on,' said Chrysoula. 'Walking, walking, walking. Took us almost until Easter. Then we got to Kalamata and got a boat down to the village. We were all right then.'

'Were the Cohens still with you?'

'They were family by then,' Chrysoula chuckled. 'The Archmandrite, he told all Greeks to care for their Jews because they were Hellenes like us, not barbarians like the Germans. When we were in Volos there came a man crying, saying, "If you seek for the ghetto of Hania it is two hundred fathoms down". The bishop of Hania was on that boat. And after that the priests never let the Jews go with the Germans. Not from the mainland, not the islands, except those godless bastards on Corfu.' She spat. 'They sent them away and had a festival. But they are corrupt, not true Greeks, it is well known.'

'Where did you end up?' Daniel asked.

'Little village no one has ever heard of,' Chrysoula answered. 'My mother came from there. Called Koroni. Tell you something? One day the Germans ordered all the Jews in Kalamata into trucks and they went and the bishop put a priest in each truck and they sat there in the sun all day. The fear in their eyes, it was terrible. The Germans didn't know what to do. "Where they go, we go", said the bishop. When it got dark we let them out and the Jews ran away. We hid them and in the morning when the Germans asked where are the Jews we said, "There are no Jews here, just Greeks", and he said nothing and forgot about them.'

'But they emptied Thessaloniki,' Daniel prompted.

'We didn't know. The Germans took over and suddenly the Jews were taken away,' she said. 'It was that Mertens. I never forgot him. His eyes were like a snake's eyes. Cold. Then a girl came and said she had gold which belonged to me.'

'And you recognised it?' asked Daniel.

Chrysoula reached around her neck and drew a thick, twined gold chain out into view. It was a thing of great beauty, perhaps Venetian work, with delicate spirals of gold wire all along it and a double clasp composed of lions' heads, locked mouth to mouth. She unfastened it and handed it to me. I nearly dropped it. It was very old and heavy, a much richer alloy than today's.

'Yes,' she told Daniel. 'And I want to know how my mother's dowry necklace came here.'

'Oh, so do I,' said Daniel. 'I want to know that very much indeed. How did you pass the rest of the war?'

'We stayed in Koroni,' said Chrysoula, refastening the necklace and hiding it under her flannel shirt. 'Two of my sisters joined the convent there. The Germans stole all the food but there was still a little to eat, and there are always fish. And we used to glean the rubbish bins for leftovers. I've never been that hungry again,' she said thoughtfully. 'Never will be, while I can work or steal.'

'And the Cohens?'

'The girls went up to the convent. The sisters were hiding a lot of Jews there,' she said. 'He took up fishing, him and his sons and my brothers. Then after the Germans lost the war my father came back and we came to Australia and I never knew what happened to them. But they must have been all right, unless they got on the wrong side of ELAS. There was a civil war,' she explained. 'Greece was not a good place to be after the war. Here is much better. But I always wondered what happened to that baby. Joshua, his name was.'

'Did you ever see Mertens again?' asked Daniel.

'Once I thought I saw him. I had taken the fish into Methoni to market. Not much fish and a lot of seaweed. You can boil seaweed and eat it. I could have sworn I saw that monster, in a fisherman's clothes, on the road ahead of me. I yelled and ran, but I didn't catch him, and maybe it wasn't him. After all, what would he be doing in Methoni? Now, Adelphos Ebraios, I've drunk your ouzo and eaten your food and told my story,' she said, getting up without showing any sign of the huge amount she had eaten and drunk. 'So I'll thank you for my mother's gold, and I will go. *Athios.*'

'*Sto kalo,*' said Daniel. 'Go to the good.'

Chrysoula kissed me on both cheeks, shook Daniel's hand, and went.

'You know what happened to that baby, don't you?' I accused. Daniel poured another glass of wine and smiled a cat-who-has-eaten-not-just-common-goldfish-but-several-imperial-koi smile.

'He's Mr. Justice Joshua Cohen,' he told me. 'And he's been looking for Chrysoula's family all his life.'

'So she needn't worry about next week's rent, then,' I said.

'Not for the forseeable future.'

'Good.' I drank some more wine. 'Where did that gold necklace come from?'

'Thessaloniki.'

'Ta, ta, ta,' I said, making a Greek gesture, brushing one forefinger across the other. 'Po, po, po! You are toying with me. Tell me the whole story.'

'The whole story I do not know,' said Daniel, 'but this is the scenario so far. The Nazis, as you know, kept meticulous records. They filmed concentration camps. They kept the train schedules for Belsen. The Germans are, as someone says in a John Buchan novel, a careful people.'

'Yes,' I encouraged. 'It's Peter Pienaar, by the way.'

'So it is. Max Mertens, the snake-eyed man, kept a register of the jewellery he extorted from Thessaloniki. In it he put the name of the "donor", the weight in gold, and so on. This register still exists.'

'With you so far.'

'So, when the gold necklace was found, it corresponded to an entry in Mertens' ledger and related to Chrysoula's family, and it was, indeed, her mother's dowry gold.'

'Yes.'

'The strange thing is that it was found in the sea off Williamstown,' he said.

'That isn't just strange, that's totally impossible.'

Daniel raised both hands. 'No shit! Kid fell in while feeding the black swans, his father hauled him out and disturbed the bottom of the backwater, and there was the necklace. Being a responsible citizen he took it to the police station.'

'Where someone saw it who just happened to have read Max Mertens' private extortion ledger?' I asked, allowing my extreme scepticism to tint my tone.

'For the moment, that's our story and we are sticking to it.'

'All right. I can believe six impossible things before breakfast if bribed with an enormous meal. And might this have something to do with the ephod that Barnabas palmed and which the forces of darkness immediately stole?'

'It might,' said Daniel.

'Because I bet that a synagogue with such expensive jewellery identifies it in some permanent way,' I went on. 'Even lowly drinking establishments put things like "This pool table stolen from Yackandandah pub" on their property.'

'Indeed,' said Daniel.

'So the ephod would have "This belongs to such and such a place" on the back, wouldn't it?'

'You may be right,' he answered.

'So we go talk to Barnabas?' I asked.

'That is what we do eventually,' he said. 'First we go and talk to someone who can tell us all about Barnabas.'

'How did you cut your hand?' I asked.

'I tripped over,' he said.

'Those wet seaweedy rocks can be very slippery,' I sympathised.

'So I believe.'

We left it at that. I was aware of walking very delicately on the edge of a vast pit of secrets.

We went down the street and past the tennis club, which resounded to the Rolling Stones, and Daniel knocked at a little door in a large door, a set-up which always fascinated me. It opened and we were admitted, bent double in Daniel's case. I felt smug. I was just the right height for a workshop which looked like a heritage museum and smelt like rope and tar and heated metal and wood, very much of wood. Someone was hammering in a calm, measured way which could have been going on for hours. I loved it instantly.

'Daniel,' said the boatbuilder. He was a muscular man with the slightly strained smile of one who depends on unreliable things like boaties and the sea, and the crow's-feet of one who stares into distances against a bright light. He had on a blue sports shirt which a devoted wife must have bought for him.

'Greg,' said Daniel, 'I need your advice.'

'Come into the yard, the boys are just at the tricky bit,' he said.

The boatyard contained nothing but timber boats. They sat down fatly in the water, like ducks, or were hauled out and perched on their keels to have things done to their undersides. I was fascinated.

'If I wanted to sail a boat from Greece to here and sneak in without attracting attention, what sort of boat would I be looking for?' asked Daniel.

'Well, you're going to need at least a forty footer,' said Greg, never taking his eyes off the operation on the scarred, stripped hulk before him. 'An engine of at least eighty horsepower. And sails, of course.'

'Why of course?' I asked, tripping over a cable.

'Because engines don't operate without diesel and it has a habit of running out in the middle of the ocean, where there are few filling stations,' he replied. That made sense.

'How many crew?'

'Three, perhaps. Could do it with two at a pinch.'

'And getting into the harbour?'

'You're supposed to radio customs and tell them you're coming,' he said.

'But if you didn't?'

'No use going to a yacht club, they gossip more than golf clubs. But if you knew someone at a service and repair yard, say mine or my neighbour's, you could just come in and slip the boat. If anyone came asking questions, mind you, there'd be trouble.'

'Your neighbour, I can't help noticing, has a forty foot boat up on the slip. It is painted a bright Greek blue, has eyes painted at the bow, and sails, and an engine of perhaps, say, eighty horsepower?'

'Could be,' said Greg.

'And it's called *Navarino*,' I said. 'So kind of you to show us your yard, Greg.'

We bid our farewells and picked our way out. The man with the hammer was still hammering. I suspected that he might be hammering until the next generation of boatbuilders took over.

'Why hurry us out?' asked Daniel.

'That's the boat,' I said.

'How do you know?'

'Well, apart from the fact that it has eyes like a Greek boat and otherwise fits the admirable Greg's description like a glove, there's the name.'

'*Navarino*? Isn't that an orange?'

'That's what the Western world called the Bay of Messinia.'

'Oh, cheeky,' he replied. 'To celebrate, I think we should have an ice cream.'

I had an exquisite orange and lemon gelato. Daniel had chocolate, with chocolate on top. Navarino. A cheeky boy indeed.

Timbo returned with a sack of leftovers to tide him over the next half-hour. Daniel directed him to drive to a supermarket where he bought Twisties, Cheez-Os, various flavoured crisps, pretzels, tequila, Mexican beer, beef jerky and, in one large bag, corn chips, grated cheese, Tex's Extremely Lethal Total Fire Ban Salsa, a pot of sour cream and a bowl of avocado dip. That, to me, spelt nachos.

And nachos, to me, spelt nerd. Which is a bit rich, considering that the original dish was undoubtedly invented by some of the toughest people in the world and eaten in scorching mouthfuls from movable establishments which put the 'chuck' into the noun 'wagon'. Nachos were meant to be eaten by chili heads and whiffled through those Zapata moustaches by rawhide men who ran steers in deserts. The spices themselves were probably banned under the arms limitations treaties of a dozen nations. But nerds and geeks and dormice people who only came out of their electronic caves when someone tripped over a cord, thus plunging their world into darkness and themselves into traumatic symplegia, had taken to Tex-Mex food. Odd, but there we were.

It was three in the afternoon. I tried not to think of my poor bakery, unloved, alone, deserted, gutted, waiting for the quarantine people to denounce its proprietor as a poisoner and threat to public health. I suspected that Daniel was taking me along with him to get my mind off my grief, and that was kind of him, so I tried to concentrate. It was still a pretty day, and where did I get off mourning my lost business when people like Chrysoula mourned their lost families? Wouldn't Mr. Justice Joshua be pleased to find that the family which had sheltered him as a baby remembered him fondly? And that nice woman would no longer be poor, which would suit her and her girl, Cassandra.

'Nerds ahoy,' said Daniel, as Timbo loaded three green bags full of junk goodies into the boot.

'They will think they have died and gone to heaven,' I commented.

'If they haven't done as I asked,' he replied, handing a spare bag of chicken Twisties to Timbo, 'they will wish they had just died.'

We drove back to the city in silence.

Insula was quiet but Nerds Inc's door was open. Ever since they started making a packet out of research their shop hours have become increasingly erratic. Basically, they open the shop when they feel like it, and the assorted gamers who constitute their clientele appear to have coped with this. I must find out how.

Timbo unloaded the bags of food, gave me a Timbo grin, and went away. The shop was small and stuffed with games, all in bright red packets with exploding trains on the front. Or planes. Though there was one with a lurching mummy, and a lot with demons. I was examining a game which claimed to allow me to pit the might of Caesar's legions against the invading Nazis, and reflected that the trouble with that was Caesar (Julius) was dead when three nerds peeped out from behind machines and squeaked at the sight of me.

Taz, Rat and Gully. Clean enough, except for the whiff of chili sauce and old cheese, because someone's mum comes and takes their clothes for washing every week. Also, they employ a cleaner, a vigorous woman who takes no nonsense about 'don't move that!' but knows enough not to unplug anything. They were unsightly. The waists thickening, the hair washed with soap, their reddened little peepers like startled white mice, the track shoes which had never seen a track. They blinked nervously at me.

'Lunch,' Daniel declared, opening the bags. 'Lead me to your microwave.'

'Daniel,' they said in a relieved chorus. So this wasn't the Invasion of the Woman. They would have coped better with the Invasion of the Body Snatchers. The Lone Gunmen could not, under any circumstances, be called sexy. Or possibly even sexed. 'This way.'

The kitchen was clean. Unused, even. The microwave was large and expensive. Daniel assembled the nachos and I laid out the array of snacks and drinks. My dearest person waited until the heartbreaking scent of cooking cheese, beans and volcanic salsa was wafting through the apartment before he told them: 'Barnabas research, then lunch.'

There was a famished whimper from Taz, and Gully ran into the other room, returning with a pile of printouts.

'I could have emailed all this to you,' he said reproachfully.

'I'm not staying at my flat for a while,' said Daniel, picking up and nibbling a cheese Twistie. 'Talk me through it.'

'I've got all the links here,' said Gully. 'He was born Francis John Markham in Richmond, England. Bit of a scandal about it because his father was a Catholic priest. He's fifty-three years old, an Aries,' said Gully, handing over the papers and receiving a bottle of beer and a packet of crisps in return. He offered me one. I ate it. It tasted like salty stainless steel. Ball-bearing flavour, perhaps?

'Went to school in Richmond and then Cambridge. Married Jane Esperance. Two children. Dumped them and went to Israel,' said Taz, full of cupboard zeal. 'Jerusalem. There he got something called Jerusalem Syndrome and was casevac'd home with a nervous breakdown. Then we lose him for a while until he turns up on the electoral roll in Brisbane.'

Taz dried up and Daniel gave him beer and Cheez-Os. I decided to keep my questions, such as what on earth was Jerusalem Syndrome, until I could ask them in an atmosphere less full of chili.

'Then he set up a website and called himself Barnabas and said he was king of the witches,' offered Rat, his thin plait of hair caught between his teeth. 'The witches didn't like that and shut him down until he stopped calling himself a king.'

'He wouldn't have liked that,' I said.

'No, he didn't, but they outnumbered him, and they're witches, right?' quavered Rat. 'So he got onto LJ and bitched about it but his website doesn't say he's king anymore.'

'What's LJ?' I asked.

They all gave me that look. Actually it's more of a Look. It says, I cannot believe you just said that. It says, your ignorance is unsurpassed. It says, what's the weather like on Venus, anyway?

I refused to cringe and Taz answered through a mouthful of beer.

'LiveJournal,' he enunciated very clearly, as to an idiot or a child. 'People write them, like, what are they called? In little bits. What happens to them every day.'

He appealed to Gully, who shook his head.

'Diaries?' I hazarded.

'Diaries. Online. Every day or so. There are a lot of people who have friends and they all write together on LiveJournal.'

'I see.' I really didn't find the concept too difficult. 'Do you?'

They snickered, sounding like that dastardly dog on *Wacky Races*.

Rat answered for them all: 'Us? We're bloggers. But a lot of mundanes use LiveJournal. It's not hard to use.'

'So can anyone just come along and read whatever you have to say?' I asked. This seemed like insanity to me. The essence of a journal, surely, is its secrecy, a space where you can say anything you like without anyone else knowing about it. I had suffered the humiliations of the damned when that rotten bitch Leanne had read parts of my very own private diary aloud at school. Even now the memory can make me squirm, and I had revenged myself on her by setting fire to her hair ribbon. The idea of baring the soul to an unsympathetic universe was alarming.

'No, there's always a locked part which only friends can access. But the rest of the journal is open to anyone on LJ. We got an LJ persona, just so we can lurk and maybe pick up a flame or so when it's burning,' explained Gully, hardly at all.

'What's your persona's name?' asked Daniel.

'We're Londo,' said Taz, 'otherwise we'd be trolled.'

Who says we all speak the same language? I had understood every word in that sentence and I was no wiser or better informed.

'No, don't tell me,' I said. 'Daniel can translate later. Did you get all the things he asked you for?'

'All of it,' said Taz. 'Except three years where he doesn't seem to have been anywhere. As though the dude dropped off the edge of the world. We're working on it,' he said, salivating.

'Daniel, please?'

'Nachos,' said Daniel, and opened the oven door.

I got out of the way just in time.

'So, how did you do it?' asked Daniel, despite my frantic warning signal. Never ask a nerd how they did something unless you are a fellow geek or have been implanted with the new geek–human universal translator™ (also works on all alien languages of the Western Spiral Arm this side of Barnard's Star). 'Did you hide your tracks?'

'Of course,' said Taz. 'You know that it's very hard to spoof an ISP, even if you use a different number.'

'Though you can do it,' put in Rat. 'Depends if his computer is on.'

'Or if you don't get a TCP reset,' responded Gully.

'Yes, granted,' said Daniel. 'So what did you do?'

'Used an anonymiser,' said Taz.

'Ah,' said Daniel.

'Some ISPs are horribly paranoid,' observed Rat. 'Gimme the nachos, Taz.'

They talked over each other all the time, but since I didn't understand a word of it, this didn't matter. My unruly mind presented me with a thread of G and S: 'This particularly rapid unintelligible patter isn't generally heard and if it is it doesn't matter matter matter...'

'We used a zombie,' said Rat. 'Once you gave us the password we had no need to pretext the ISP for a new one. He'll never know we were there.'

'I believe that,' said Daniel.

'So you can. The zombie's a good servant.'

'Zombie? Isn't that one of the living dead?' I hazarded.

'They aren't dead,' objected Taz. 'They're dudes put into a coma by this toad poison and then dug up again brain damaged.'

'Bullshit,' protested Gully.

'Google,' said Rat.

We prepared another tray of nachos for the starving before we beat a retreat out of the way of all that melted cheese. When we left, they were gathered around an uncompromised machine, absorbing information on Wade Davis and Haiti. Eating Cheez-Os. And arguing about horror movies.

'All right,' I said slowly to Daniel. 'Jerusalem Syndrome?'

'Overwhelmed by the fact of the Holy City. And delusions of grandeur.'

'Trolled?'

'Excluded as a source of spam and banned from the journal.'

'A zombie?'

'Is a computer which has been badly hacked and threaded with viruses, on a bot net. It's close to untraceable.'

'All right.' My head was aching with all these unfamiliar words and concepts. 'How did you get his password? By some strange, even eldritch technological wizardry?'

'No,' said Daniel. 'I stole his wallet.'

We left. Laughing helplessly, in my case.

'Would you mind if we went back to your apartment?' asked Daniel. 'If you really can't bear to stay here we can always go to my place and fling Georgie into the street.'

I smiled at the idea. 'A tempting thought, but no, I have to live here, and worse things have happened to other people. As I was reminded by Chrysoula. We will go in the front way,' I said, and we did.

The atrium contained the entire Pandamus family all protesting loudly, from the smallest child's shrill cry to GreatGrandmamma's croak.

'What's wrong?' I asked.

Seven separate accounts of the outrage followed, so scrambled that I couldn't make sense out of any of it. Everyone was yelling, even the quieter members of the Pandamus family who usually listened. Finally Daniel grabbed Del by the sleeve and the two of them went out onto the steps while I sagged down under a thousand metric tons of righteous indignation.

Daniel finally fought his way to my side with an explanation. 'Health Department closed the cafe like they closed your bakery and Best Fresh.'

This clear statement brought a new wail of anguish. I knew exactly how they all felt, because I felt like that myself, and tears rose to my eyes. Mrs. P grabbed me in a tight embrace and cried down my neck and I damn near joined her.

'It will be all right,' said Daniel, and was instantly denounced by all.

'All right? How can it be all right? We are ruined!' yelled Del Pandamus, throwing his arms wide to demonstrate the extent of his ruin. 'We ruined! Corinna ruined! Even that pig down the lane, he ruined too!'

'But you didn't sell anything poisonous,' Daniel said patiently. I could have told him he was wasting his time. A Greek scene is a significant part of the Sophoclean tradition and not easily interrupted by reason.

'So, they find we didn't poison everyone, they go away, you open again.' Daniel tried reason anyway.

'Who would ever eat with us again, once they thought we were suspected?' wailed Mrs. Pandamus, whom I had always thought so self-possessed. 'Everyone will say, no fire without smoke! There must have been something wrong or the Health would not have shut them down!'

'Daniel, do stop being sensible,' I snapped before he could speak again. 'This is a moment for wailing, so either wail along or go upstairs and find the brandy, there's a dear.'

Daniel hefted the papers he'd collected from Nerds Inc, nodded, patted the nearest pair of heaving Pandamus shoulders, and took his leave. Actually it was more like he 'escaped' up the stairs, not waiting for the lift. I wiped my eyes, blew my nose, blew little Soula's nose, and said, 'We must be strong.'

'Why?' asked Del.

'Because we will find out who has done this to us,' I said. 'And then they will be sorry.'

'Ah,' said Yai Yai. She had not spoken loudly but the little intake of breath had somehow been audible through all those voices. The entire family turned to look at her, tiny and indomitable.

'Yes?' asked Del. The old lady nodded. Her eyes were quite black and as sharp as crewel needles.

'You will find out?' he asked me.

'Trying to do so at this very moment,' I told him.

He engulfed me in a huge tear-stained embrace. 'All right,' he said. 'Then we got something to do. Dinner tonight in the cellar,' he told me. 'Your girls and your boy are getting the food. Eight. Bring wine, much wine.'

'Sounds good,' I agreed. Then I, too, escaped up the stairs to a less fraught atmosphere. Greek scenes can really take it out of you, but the emotional release is wonderful. I felt much, much better. Now that I had something to do.

Chapter Fourteen

What I did next was to sit down and read through reams of Barnabas' diary—sorry, LiveJournal. My view, that putting any diary online was equivalent to publishing it in a newspaper, was confirmed. There might be interesting stuff in the locked away parts. And perhaps they are safe. Unless the Lone Gunmen have been paid to break into them. Even so, email is a trap: it feels private, but it isn't. Like radio. Interviewees occasionally freeze when they imagine how many people might be listening to them talk with the interviewer, but a lot more stray into indiscretion because, in reality, all they can see is the nice insinuating man in front of them and a modicum of technological junk. So they talk freely, and thus we have police reports, scandal sheets, and Royal Commissions. And doesn't the fact that it is in public, that someone else will read it, entirely change the experience of writing a diary? You're writing for an audience, not for yourself. You have to explain things more. You can't just say 'I never forget what she said to me'. Actually that could be an advantage. When I went back and read my school diary, I found that declaration, and I also found that I had entirely forgotten whatever it was that she had said, and even who had said it.

I still write a diary. In ink. By hand. And it's in my dressing table drawer, which is locked. If any burglar wanted to see it, he was not at all welcome. No one was invited. Not even Daniel. Especially not Daniel, when I thought of what I had written about my suspicions of him and Georgie.

Barnabas' website was being accessed by Daniel, who was whistling occasionally. He does this when he is intrigued and it annoys me. I took my sheaf of papers, my notebooks and my cup of coffee onto the balcony, where it was cool. Horatio declined to follow because, as far as he was concerned, a mohair rug was a mohair rug and he had his. If he moved, I could see him thinking, someone human might steal it.

The Mouse Police, not at all bored by being relieved of their hunting duties, formed a warm pool of fur around my ankles as I read and sipped and made notes. I could not hear a sound from the bakery. The quarantine people had obviously gathered their samples and gone back to their laboratory. And Barnabas was proving to be very interesting.

From his Cave in the Holy Mountains Barnabas wrote paragraphs for the enlightenment of his followers, whom he assumed to be female. The more I read, the more I was reminded of someone, but I could not remember who. So I kept reading.

'All nature is beautiful,' said Barnabas. 'All natural processes likewise. Therefore, when the moon demands your blood, bleed freely. Let the issue not be interrupted by padding and cotton and those abominations, tampons, intruding into your sacred flesh.'

I could not see this working for anyone who had to put on clothes and catch a train to Flagstaff every morning. Blood was blood and a contaminant just the same as saliva or urine—not something I want someone to deposit on my bus seat.

'Blood is life,' thus Barnabas. 'To be tasted and revered.'

Euw, as Kylie would have said. I had tasted menstrual blood and it tastes just like any other blood—coppery, salty and, in a word, bloody. I didn't see it as a reverential act, more curiosity. I took a gulp of coffee and read on.

The next five entries, and indeed much of the rest of the oeuvre, were about the Great Rite. Reverence for the Female Principle, conjunction of opposites, and a lot about etheric fluids. I ruffled through my book on Wicca. The Great Rite was the culmination of a ceremony in which the priestess copulates with the priest. Figured. Done in a highly charged, religious state. To balance the energies.

Barnabas sounded like he needed a lot of balancing. And the tone of his pronouncements was getting to me. He was pompous and slithy by turns. I doubted his devotion to the Goddess, but never his devotion to Barnabas. I put down the coffee cup. Perhaps I was just paranoid, but I didn't like Barnabas and the more I read of his LiveJournal the more I felt that clipping his ears would be fun. His advice to young women to wear short skirts and transparent tops was puerile. His offering of private tuition in witchcraft sounded like a come-on. And his influence might well be pernicious amongst the young and inexperienced.

I stood and stretched. The Mouse Police had got cold and gone inside. Seven o'clock, and I was hungry. Time to put Barnabas away and prepare for dinner. Wine, Del had said. What was in the Corinna cellar? Not a lot, actually. Even the chateau collapseau was sloshing emptily. Chateau collapseau would not do for a proper dinner in any case.

Daniel looked up from the computer.

'Going out to get some wine,' I said.

'I'll come with you.' He got up, shutting down his search engine. 'How did you go with Barnabas?'

'He's a sleaze,' I opined, finding my purse under a cat. It was Heckle and he just meowed briefly and fell asleep again. Why he was sleeping on the coffee table was anyone's guess.

'Now that I think of it, I ought to go back to my place, check if George has moved out, and collect some stuff,' said Daniel as we reached the street.

'Back for dinner?' I asked, with hardly a pang at the mention of Georgiana's name. 'The girls and Jason are catering tonight so it should be interesting.'

'Certainly. Don't carry too many bottles,' he said, and went away with his swift, elegant lope, his leather coat floating behind him. God, he was gorgeous. I did not deserve him and I would not doubt him again.

The wine shop sold every possible alcoholic beverage under the sun. I ordered a case of the sauv blanc and a lot of other bottles—this was a time to be extravagant—and Geoff, who was just closing, offered me his shop assistant and the trolley to convey it all to Insula. I accepted with pleasure. I was fine until Geoff, who is a sensitive and charming gay man who spends every Australian summer with his Zurich lover, skiing, pressed my hands and looked sympathetically into my face.

'I'm so sorry about your shop, Corinna,' he told me.

Tears pricked my eyes. 'Thanks,' I said inadequately.

'I know they'll find it had nothing to do with you,' he said. 'There wasn't any hint of trouble until Best Fresh opened. They say the bloke who runs it is spending all his time in Young and Jackson's, sinking whisky by the bottle and making an exhibition of himself.'

Sensitive and charming and had a Presbyterian grandmother, I diagnosed.

'Indeed,' I said.

'So take this as a present from me.' He added a wrapped bottle to the load on the trolley which young James was pushing. 'And don't worry too much. You'll be back behind the counter before long.'

'Thanks,' I said, sniffed, and followed James out of the shop.

He was a nice boy, too. He lugged the trolley up the steps to Insula and into the lift for me. Like all trolleys, it had two unmatching wheels, on one of which the tyre was shredding. James also unloaded the bottles and hauled the metal-wheeled thing away without complaint. And wouldn't accept a tip until I forced the note into the nicely ironed pocket of his uniform shirt.

I unpacked and found that Geoff had given me a bottle of good cognac. That was very kind of him but I had cried quite enough for the moment. I was very lucky in my neighbours.

I washed my face, collected a reasonable sample of bottles, and descended to the cellar.

When Insula was built it was a fully serviced apartment house, so it had an extensive vault where the inhabitants could keep their wine, and a well-equipped kitchen. Recently we had renovated it for parties. Mistress Dread liked it because it reminded her of her dungeon. The apartment dwellers of Insula—the Prof called us the Insulae—ate together once a week or so, on Thursday nights, but I usually excused myself unless I was catering because of having to get up so early. Now I didn't have to get up early. I didn't have to get up at all…

I shook myself. I could smell delicious scents. What on earth had those food-averse maidens and the voracious Jason cooked up between them?

Trudi, with Lucifer on his rightful shoulder, greeted me. She has to take him with her on most occasions because left alone in her flat he finds new and ingenious ways to either destroy something she values or attempt to commit felicide. Eating tulip bulbs, for instance, counted towards both. When she absolutely cannot take him with her she shuts him in a cat cage which now has more chains and locks and latches than Alcatraz. Fortunately he has not yet worked out how to pick a padlock with his claws. While secured he cries piteously the whole time she is away.

'Corinna,' she said. 'Come, sit. Where is Daniel?'

'On his way,' I said. 'I brought wine.'

'I've got the corkscrew,' said Therese Webb.

I noticed that we had a new tablecloth, a heavy dark damask with a fine white cloth spread over the top. Very Victorian. 'Matches the surroundings,' I said as she opened a bottle of red wine and filled glasses. 'Your work?'

'I had a length of cloth left over from another project, and it was just the right size for the table,' she said. 'And the cotton cloth over the top should preserve it from serious stains. Anyway, it's just the colour of red wine.'

'A very canny notion,' I agreed. I sipped. We sat. Most of us were there. Mrs. Pemberthy, Daniel, Mistress Dread, the Hollidays and our cooks were absent and we only had four Pandamuses. I could smell a really enticing aroma. Jon sniffed.

'What is it?' I asked.

'English food,' he said, puzzled but pleased. 'I wonder how Kepler is going to enjoy it. That is definitely steak and kidney I can detect.'

'So it is, how nice. How enterprising,' said Mrs. Dawson. She had dressed for the dungeon in a batwing gown of bitter chocolate wool so fine that it draped like silk. The dress was ornamented with a huge gold brooch from some archaeological dig in Greece.

'Pegasus,' the Professor said. 'And I am not asking who gave it to you—from Golden Mycenae, I'd judge.'

'It was a gift,' said Mrs. Dawson.

Trudi poured more wine for me and a short shot of gin for herself. Jason and the girls entered, carrying dishes. He was wearing his cook's whites, and Kylie and Goss were not wearing very much of anything. What they did have on glittered.

'Fortunately this cellar is very warm,' murmured Therese.

The feast was laid out. They had made pies and pasties of all varieties. Jason had recently been fascinated by pastry and annoyed that his first attempts had turned out to have the consistency of teak and the taste of cardboard. Clearly he had been perfecting his skills. I surveyed the table: steak and kidney pies, chicken pies, Greek spanakopita, pissaladière, quiche (both Lorraine and cheese), ratatouille pie made with filo pastry, a vegetable pastie especially for Meroe, and a huge green salad. It was a feast. We applauded, the cooks blushed, and we picked up cutlery and watched as the crusts were cut. Steam gushed.

'We made fillings all day yesterday,' Kylie told me. 'Out of Jason's pie book. Used up every saucepan in our flat and most of Jason's. It was fun.'

'And I did the pastry today,' said Jason. 'Got a tip from that old book. Kept sticking my hands into iced water. And we get to put the pastry in the fridge to keep it cold. But it's still a bit iffy. I don't think I want to be a pastry chef.'

'No matter, dear boy, these look excellent,' said the Professor, passing his plate for a piece of Cornish pastie. He tasted and smiled. 'Perfect,' he said. 'When I was a child we used to go to Cornwall for the holidays and the pasties tasted just like this.'

'It's the oldest recipe,' Jason told him. 'Just turnip, potato, meat, onion and parsley. The new books put a lot of other stuff in.'

'This was lunch for a Cornish sailor,' said the Professor. 'Or a ploughman or shepherd. He would be cold and miserable— even in Cornwall it gets cold and miserable—and then he would think, aha, a pastie for lunch, it's been six hours since breakfast, and a pint of cider to go with it, a feast for a king. He wouldn't have known any other vegetables except the ones you've used. That was good judgment, Jason.'

'Thanks,' said Jason. Meroe dissected her ratatouille pie and complimented the girls on the even consistency of the vegetables.

'You have to cook them in order,' Kylie said, as pleased as if she had just been awarded a date with the male lead of *The OC*. 'Jason explained it. They cook at different rates. But I'm having a piece of the fish pie,' she said, and passed it along.

Lucifer, reduced to a famine-struck shadow, made a sad little meow and Trudi put him on the floor with some of the delectable salmon filling. She tied his leash around her ankle. Lucifer was quite capable of going foraging on his own account and people have this odd prejudice about kittens' feet in their food.

It was all delicious. The Pandamus family, after a couple of suspicious sniffs, tucked into the spanakopita and the pissaladière, which is a strong tart made with olives and anchovies. I personally had never eaten enough steak and kidney pie in my life. I remedied this. Daniel came in late and was regaled with some of everything.

'A feast!' he exclaimed. 'In whose honour?'

'All of us,' said the Professor. 'We needed a treat and Jason, Kylie and Gossamer have amply provided it. Have some of this quiche Lorraine, it's first rate.'

'Thank you,' said Daniel, and picked up the nearest fork.

There were some leftovers, though not many, when the cooks brought in dessert. It was an apple pie of massive proportions, to be eaten with cream. Jason had also made a variety of little biscotti to have with coffee. I was eating very well since my ruin. I wasn't going to think about that. I was determined to stay in Insula. I would just have to get a job, doing something other than baking. Assuming I didn't go to jail for murder…

The apple pie had an unusual flavour. Instead of the clove and cinnamon I was expecting, it tasted sweetly but unmistakably of…

'Roses?' I asked.

Kylie and Goss giggled. 'We had to steal a few when Trudi wasn't looking,' they confessed. 'Jason found this old recipe. The Romans—'

'Cooked apples and roses together,' said the Professor, delighted. 'It's in Apicius! I always wondered what that combination tasted like. Wonderful! I could come round to reconstructive archaeology if it tastes this good.'

'So, you steal my roses,' growled Trudi.

Jason flinched. 'Just a few,' he said. 'And it's a nice pie, isn't it?'

'You can steal them any time you like,' she said, patting him. 'Just not the tulips.'

'No one cooks with tulips,' Jason said, crossing his heart.

Dinner concluded in a general slackening of belts. Mrs. Dawson had shown great forethought in wearing that loose dress. I was very impressed by the quality of the food and the fact that Kylie, Goss and Jason had managed to work together without major tantrums.

Therese and I rose to clear away while the cooks were toasted and regaled with wine and biscotti (vanilla Coke, in Jason's case). We collected the leftovers into plastic containers and scraped plates and stacked them for the sink. When Insula was built, the dishwasher had not been invented. And I quite like washing dishes. We had pooled our resources and bought a set of plain cheap crockery for the cellar so it did not greatly matter if a fumble-fingered servitor dropped a few.

We had stacked, rinsed and washed most of them as the party outside began to wind down and our fellow tenants came to collect their particular scraps. The Professor got the rest of the fish pie, though I suspected that Nox would be the major beneficiary of the filling. Mrs. Dawson had apple pie, the Pandamuses the rest of the spanakopita, Meroe her vegetables and the Professor the pastie. I had almost half of a steak and kidney pie, which I was intending to devour cold. Cold steak and kidney pie is a wonderful thing. Jon and Kepler joined us to do the drying and putting away.

'So, how did you like the English cuisine?' I asked Kepler.

'Very interesting,' he said diplomatically. 'I liked that anchovy tart.'

'He still hasn't got over the revolting concept of sausages,' confided Jon affectionately.

'And steak and kidney,' added Kepler. 'But they did very well, very well indeed. You can see that it was a lot of work.'

'Must have taken most of yesterday and today,' I said. 'Look out for that carving knife, it's—'

'Sharp?' asked Kepler, closing his fist on the cut on his palm.

'Stick your hand under that tap, it's cold,' I said, pulling him to an empty sink.

Meroe came in at this point and took over the first aid. She seemed subdued. She had eaten well but hardly spoken during dinner. She grabbed Kepler's wrist and soused the wound, then wiped it clean with a piece of kitchen paper. Then she gripped it hard between both of her own palms.

Kepler, who had been looking as though he wished he was somewhere else—Laos, perhaps, in a monsoon—said, 'Wah!' I had never heard him exclaim in Chinese unless he was actually speaking the language.

'Does it hurt?' asked Jon anxiously.

'Yes,' said Kepler. 'No.'

Meroe was pressing his hand hard enough, I would have thought, to flatten it like a paper doll. But there was no pain on Kepler's smooth, shapely face though he had paled to the colour of old ivory. His expression, in fact, bordered on astonishment.

'Meroe, what are you doing?' I finished the washing-up, since there didn't seem to be any need for my help, and Jon automatically dried and stacked the last of the dishes. The others had gone. Daniel, me, Jon, Kepler, Therese and Meroe were alone together in the scullery. It smelt of wet stone and soap and seemed a strange place to find a miracle.

Because when Meroe released Kepler's hand, the cut was closed. Of course, the pressure might have done it, but I did not believe this for a moment. I am something of an expert on culinary injuries and that had been a deep cut across the soft part of the palm. Usually it would take a week to heal, and only then if you kept it out of water. And Sister Mary always said the thing about miracles is, they are miraculous. Inexplicable. And happen in ordinary places, like the kitchen of an apartment house. In front of at least one sceptical witness.

'Nice work,' commented Daniel.

'How did it feel?' asked Jon.

'Like being stung by insects,' said Kepler, flexing his hand. 'Thank you,' he said, and bowed deeply, hands to forehead. Meroe returned the bow.

'At least I can still do some things,' said Meroe, pleased. 'You have an interesting hand,' she said to Kepler. 'You have the line which says that you will fall in love with only one person in your life.'

'Already have,' replied Kepler. He collected Jon and they went upstairs.

'Well, that was a most agreeable evening,' said Therese, who seemed shaken. 'And I believe that I might have an early night.'

'And if you can spare a few minutes, Meroe?' I asked her. 'I want to talk about—'

'Barnabas,' she anticipated. 'All right. I'll just go up to Leucothea for a while.'

'If you're too tired,' said Daniel gently, 'it can wait. I imagine that healing people is fairly exhausting.'

'Actually I am a little drained,' she admitted.

'Tomorrow will do fine,' I told her.

Then Daniel and I were alone in the scullery. It was still a very ordinary little chamber, with the salad bowls wiped clean and the scent of past and gone meals lingering on the still air.

'Well,' he said.

'Well,' I agreed.

We went up to Hebe, drank a little cognac, and went to bed.

At four in the morning I woke. The alarm hadn't gone off! I was late! Reason returned. Then I tried to go back to sleep and couldn't. My eyes kept springing open. What was worrying me? I got up properly and closed the bedroom door on the sleeping Daniel.

The Mouse Police, who were used to being fed at this hour, welcomed me without their usual pile of deceased rodentia, but I fed them anyway, along with Horatio, who even abandoned his mohair rug for kitty dins. I made myself a cup of hot chocolate. No effect. I was just wondering whether to take a sleeping pill, which would mean that I would sleep half the day, when I realised what it was.

That flour. That sack of rye flour mix which had been conveyed to my bakery by mistake. It had smelt funny. And I had sent it back to Best Fresh and retrieved my own pure organic rye. I had sent it on, even though I knew that there was something wrong with it. How could Eddie, a gormless unskilled worker, distinguish between good flour and bad flour? That idiot who worked nights in Best Fresh could barely distinguish between his arse and his elbow. The boss would have known, but it would have been in the mixer before he arrived. It was all my fault. That boy who thought he was a bird, that girl with the missing feet, they were all my fault. And I had even gloated that Best Fresh would have a ruined batch of bread. I had laughed. I couldn't stand the thought.

I couldn't sit here, either. I couldn't bear staying in the safe quiet with such emotions burning a hole in my mind and heart. I sneaked into my bedroom and found my clothes, shoved them on and crept out into the atrium and thence into the street. Where was I to go with a load of guilt on me like Mount Atlas?

I wavered. Never a wise thing to do in the pre-dawn hours in a big city.

Someone grabbed me by the arm. I turned on him so fast that he stumbled. I was in the mood to beat something to a pulp and a chance woman-groper would do just fine. I wouldn't even mind if he beat me to a pulp. I deserved it.

I nearly fell over, pulling my punch, and I did hit him a tidy clip over the ear. He didn't even wince. It was Jason.

'Corinna, I've remembered about that sack of rye flour,' he said. His eyes were pools of dread and horror. I knew just how he felt.

I sat down on the steps and pulled him down with me. 'I know,' I said. 'First thing today we tell the cops. But this isn't down to you, Jason. You just did as I said. You're my apprentice. It's my fault.'

'I thought it was funny,' he whispered.

'So did I.'

'But I could have argued with you. I could have dumped the stuff in the alley. It's my fault too,' he insisted.

We sat still, looking at the street. A small, bitter wind blew into my face. It was getting on for dawn. Jason shivered. He was only wearing jeans and a t-shirt. His feet were bare. He must have done as I did, dragged on some clothes and run out into the open as though he could flee his guilt. But guilt runs faster than any human ever could.

'No point in dividing the blame,' I said at length. 'Not much point in sitting here grieving, either. Can I come up to your flat? I don't want to wake Daniel.'

'Okay,' he agreed. We stood up. I brushed at the seat of my trousers, which were dusty.

Then someone groaned in Calico Alley.

Chapter Fifteen

'No, I can't stand it,' said Jason wildly.

'Yes, you can.' I walked to the corner. A man was slumped near my back door. The police tape was gone, I noticed. I knelt down next to him, fending off Jason, who was pulling at my arm. The face turned to me.

It was Mr. Vincent Wyatt from Best Fresh, and he was as drunk as several skunks. I was almost stifled by the wash of raw alcohol as he breathed out.

'Pissed,' said Jason with infinite relief.

'As a newt. Slip inside and get me a bottle of water and some paper towels, will you? After we haul him up onto the step.'

It took both of us. Mr. Wyatt was in that boneless state of inebriation which means that a drunk can fall down an embankment, tumble across a couple of broken bottles and collide with a tree without bruising or cutting himself. We finally managed to gather all his limbs into a fireman's lift and sat him with his back against the Insula wall and his head inclined, rather fortuitously, over a handy gutter. Into which, joggled by our moving him, he began to throw up his last bottle of whisky.

A fairly disgusting ten minutes later, he was drinking water and throwing it up, which was an improvement. Ten minutes after that he was retaining water and wiping his face with the paper towels. There was no one about in our part of the city. Still too early for the office workers.

'You're killing yourself,' I told Mr. Wyatt. 'If you want to kill yourself, go and do it somewhere else. And by some neater method.'

'Like jumping off the roof?' he sobbed. 'I poisoned that boy. It's all my fault. I did it. It was all my fault!'

'What?' asked Jason, taken aback.

'Gimme a drink,' he demanded. 'Do I know you?'

'Jason. I'm the apprentice at Corinna's bakery. This is Corinna,' he added, in case Mr. Wyatt's alcoholic amnesia had progressed.

'Nice woman,' said Mr. Wyatt owlishly. 'Don't deserve to be ruined. But me. I deserve it.'

'We both do. Now, where do you live, eh?' I asked.

Vincent Wyatt made a complex gesture with both arms which conveyed that he lived somewhere north of where he was presently sitting. Moving made him sick again. Jason lunged while Mr. Wyatt was occupied and came back up with a wallet.

'They lose their sense of direction,' he explained to me. 'The really old blokes do, too. Now, he must have a driving licence or something.'

'I'm not even going to ask how you got so good at picking pockets,' I said, inspecting the wallet.

'I might have to go back to it,' said Jason. His eyes searched my face for signs of hope. 'If I get back on the gear.'

'And why should you get back on the gear?' I demanded.

'It hurts,' said Jason simply. 'And junk makes it better.'

This was no time for a lecture. I gathered him into my arms and hugged him hard. Even if he didn't want to be hugged, I wanted to hug him. He didn't struggle.

'Junk makes it better for a little while,' I said. 'Then it makes it worse. You remember. We'll get through this, Jason. If we can't be bakers anymore we can be something else. I'm not going to lose you, you hear me?'

'You're a nice lady,' blurred Mr. Wyatt.

'I hear,' said Jason into my shoulder. Wonder of wonders, he actually put his arms around me and hugged me back. Then he kissed me loudly on the cheek.

'You and me, eh, Corinna?' he said, almost smiling.

'You got it, Midshipman Jason.'

'Cap'n,' he said. He drew away from me, stood up and saluted. 'Orders, sir?'

'Let's find out where this poor sodden wreck lives and take him home. Then we can cook ourselves some breakfast. And him, too.'

'He's got one of the apartments in Cathedral Lane,' said Jason, holding a card up to the streetlight. 'Come on, mate, you can't stay out here all night. Cops'll be along any minute.'

He was right. The patrol passed us as we rounded into Swanston Street. What we were doing was clear, however, especially as Mr. Wyatt had started to cry again. They let us past without comment. Jason managed the outer lock and the lift. Luckily Vincent didn't have any contents in his stomach so there was no mess, and we got to the apartment in fair order. It was five thirty in the morning.

The flat was small and unbelievably messy, though not downright sordid, by which I mean there were no old condoms, pizza boxes or sour cartons of fulminating milk. There were clothes all over the floor and the bed had not been made. Jason lowered Mr. Wyatt into a chair while I hastily reassembled his bed and then we put him into it.

'Place is a real mess,' said Jason. 'What say we clean it up for him?'

'And possibly learn interesting things while we do so?'

He didn't even lower his eyes, much less blush. 'Yeah, maybe,' answered Jason the Shameless. But he was also Midshipman Jason the Efficient. He had entered my employ as a cleaner and he still wielded a mean mop. And it wasn't as though we had anything else to do.

There was a bedroom and a parlour, but apart from a kitchen in which one could not even twirl a highly cooperative kitten and a bathroom suited only to anorexic midgets, that was it for the Cathedral Place apartment. I started collecting bottles. There were a lot of bottles. I was sorry to see that Mr. Wyatt had blotted himself out with the cheapest fortified port and the worst Genuine Old Whisky made in Collingwood. He was going to have a hangover to which the term 'exploding cranium' would be appropriate. Jason commented as he handed me another cardboard box: 'I know this stuff. They used to say it had ten thousand dead brain cells in every bottle. Only derros drink it.'

'We're used to a better class of drunk in Insula,' I said, thinking of Cherie Holliday's father, Andy, who only drank Absolut or Laphroig and was now confining himself to one bottle every three days, which was an improvement on two a night. And he now drank it mixed with things like water or orange juice instead of straight from the freezer. Jason stuffed an armload of soiled clothes into an empty laundry basket.

'You know, he's pretty organised,' he said. 'I mean, most drunks don't have a laundry hamper, or a desk.'

'He was probably fine until that rye flour arrived on his doorstep,' I said bitterly, straightening out a pile of papers, separating the newspapers and the correspondence and the junk mail. 'Tie this into a bale for the recyclers, will you, Mr. Midshipman?'

'I been thinking about that,' said Jason slowly, doing as I had ordered.

'And?' I put a towel and several t-shirts into the laundry basket.

'It can't have been just that rye flour,' he said, 'cos it was going on too long. There was only one sack of dodgy mix, and it would all have gone in one batch. Not like our pure rye, which lasts us a week. That was a mix and that fuckwit Eddie just emptied it into the mixer.'

'You are right,' I agreed, struck by his excellent logic. 'And the soul cake song…'

'Was going on before the courier gave us the bodgy sack.'

'So it was.'

We had cleared the lounge. The bedroom contained more soiled clothes and more bottles. The kitchen was grimy but not filthy and Jason turned on the hot tap and found the detergent. Bubbles foamed over a collection of dirty dishes.

'So it wasn't us,' he said. I gave him another hug and he still didn't fight me.

'Maybe not,' I agreed. 'Maybe not, indeed.'

No flat was ever cleaned with such diligence by two such superstitious people attempting to buy off Fate. I opened windows to let in the cold breeze. We found a broom and swept the flat clean. We stacked and rattled bottles and papers and Jason slid seven loads of rubbish down the chute. We carried all the recyclables down to the basement, where we found a bank of washing machines and dryers. It seemed a bit much to do the man's laundry after invading his life so comprehensively.

'He can sit here and recover,' I told Jason. 'Nothing like watching the socks go round to soothe the mind.'

'Really?' asked Jason. 'I always got bored and fell asleep.'

'That, too, might be useful. Here's some money, go and buy him bread and milk and some coffee, he's out of coffee. Eggs, bacon, that sort of thing. We might as well make ourselves some breakfast. And whatever you are having yourself, of course.'

'Sir!' Jason took the purse and ran off towards the all-night supermarket. He ran lightly like the boy he was, heels springing. Suddenly, we were all right. For that I was willing to resurrect any number of drunks, from the dead if necessary. Though for that I was going to need Meroe and I hoped that she was sleeping soundly in her satiny lilac and purple bed with her black cat curled up in the small of her back as usual.

The little flat looked and smelled much better as I came in again. Vin Wyatt was asleep rather than passed out. I filled a clean mineral water bottle with tap water to supply his dehydrated body as soon as he woke and set it next to his bed. The furnishings had come with the flat, that was clear. They were easy minimalism, IKEA chic. Which made them easy to clean as well. Though hell to assemble. The lounge room carpet, now visible, was going to need a vacuum cleaner and there was nothing to do immediately but fill the kettle and find the cafetiere and some clean cups, so I did that, and then sat down to thoroughly invade Mr. Wyatt's business privacy.

Best Fresh was a franchise, which meant that he had to pay franchise fees, as well as all his operating expenses and rent. He had put up an initial fifty thousand dollars, which was now almost gone, and he was making a small profit, just enough to service his debt. He employed two part time workers at dirt poor rates, Janelle Richards and Eddie Ramsgate. Not surprising that the gum-chewing girl showed little enthusiasm for her tasks and that Eddie had spotted Jason ten dollars for not telling on him about the flour.

Mr. Wyatt needed to transform his business into a success, and having dedicated workers, and paying for them, was the key. He should get up and do his own baking and employ someone during the day who liked bread. Then he could double the assistant's wage and get someone with more presence than poor Janelle. Also, getting up and doing his own baking might keep him off the booze. Of course, maybe he had just taken to it lately. Which might explain his choice of poisons.

I scanned the list of permitted breads which Best Fresh supplied to its franchisees. Not a lot of room to improvise. None, in fact. The essential thing about a franchise is that wherever you buy, it will taste exactly the same, whether it's Kentucky Fried Chicken with its identical mix of the Colonel's secret herbs and spices, or Coca-Cola, which sold the essential cordial to be diluted with local water. This reliability promotes brand loyalty and explains the state of perpetual war between, as it might be, Coke and Pepsi. However, it means that a franchisee can't go off on his own and start inventing new chicken dishes or innovative hamburgers. It's not wrong or right, it's just the way that these things work. What had persuaded Mr. Wyatt, who seemed to be a good baker from what he had told me when we had met before his plunge into the bottle, to accept restrictions like these? The idea of an inspector coming into my bakery and telling me that my cream buns had too much cream in them and therefore must be altered would have made my blood boil. Or at least simmer.

His personal finances were sound enough, though stretched. He had a nice little share portfolio, though lately he had plunged on Navarino Gold, the company about which Mr. Benson, the muffin-appreciating wunderkind, had had doubts. Still, it wasn't expensive, and he didn't have a large number of shares. The others were sound enough. He owned a small house in Templestowe. His divorce had just been finalised. His driving licence was going to expire in a week. His insurance premiums were due. He had a couple of photographs of a dark-haired woman with a small child at the beach under his blotter. And if he didn't get a wriggle on with his BAS, he was going to be fined.

I didn't discover anything more enlightening in the papers and I was slotting them into their folder when Jason came in with bulging bags.

'I went a bit OTT,' he confessed, piling them on the little kitchen bench. 'But I'm—'

'Starving?' I guessed.

The glaze of pink donut icing on his chin was a bit of a dead giveaway. He nodded. We set out Jason's food on the coffee table and the couch—more donuts, cheese rolls, those sad, limp microwave hot dogs, several packets of biscuits and a huge bottle of vanilla Coke. I made coffee and toast, found a frying pan and cooked myself some eggs and bacon.

The scent of coffee woke Mr. Wyatt, who drank his bottle of water and a double fizzy Berocca with puzzled docility and went obediently back to sleep. He did not seem surprised that his flat had been augmented by me and Jason. His eyes shut as he hit the pillow.

'Eggs?' asked Jason hungrily, having polished off more junk food than a science fiction convention in a little under twenty minutes.

'And bacon.' I yielded him the kitchen and took his place on the couch.

I felt so much better. Yes, that might have been a contaminated sack of flour and it might have been the cause of one freak-out, but not all of them. The freak-outs both preceded and followed the sack of contaminated flour, so where, I wondered, were the soul cakes coming from? Who was making them? The police report said that the victims all had the remains of cakes in their stomachs. It was reasonable to assume that the soul cakes were indeed cakes. They hadn't come from my bakery, of that I was positive. Where, then, was the devil's baker who was making *pain maudit* on my territory?

Nothing sprang to mind. I was tired. I closed my eyes. Jason woke me after he had demolished the remaining toast and bacon and eggs and done the washing-up.

'I reckon we'd be better leaving the old bloke to sleep it off,' he told me.

'And we'd better get back to Insula before everyone misses us.' I sat up. 'What's the time?'

'Gone seven thirty,' he said. I wrote a note, leaving my phone number. Jason put the Berocca on the clean kitchen bench with a glass next to it and we took our leave of our slumbering colleague.

Daniel was waiting at the front door of Hebe when I came up in the lift.

'Ah, Corinna,' he said airily, concealing what I thought might have been a sigh of relief. 'There you are.'

'Here I am,' I said. 'I went out on an errand of mercy to rescue a fellow baker from delirium tremens,' I explained.

'I thought it might be something like that,' said Daniel. 'I assumed that Jason was with you.'

'He was, and he ate a breakfast which would have stunned a Gorgon. Sorry, I should have left you a note. Have you eaten?'

'Yes, and I have to go and see to a few errands myself. A box was delivered, I left it on the coffee table. Back for lunch,' he said, kissed me, and went.

The box contained a gorgeous florist's arrangement of flaming parrot tulips. The note said 'Sweet Corinna, let's go a-Maying'. More cavalier poets. Darling Daniel. He must have put in a weekly order and not wanted to stop it even though we were reconciled. I placed the tulips on the coffee table and they glowed in the early sun, slashed with scarlet and white like medieval doublets.

I was feeling so relieved that I didn't even jump when Senior Constable Bray and her offsider Constable Vickery rang the bell and demanded entry. Helen Vickery was instantly mobbed by the Mouse Police, who had fond memories of her ear-scratching ability. She dropped to her heels and began to demonstrate it to massed purring.

'Sit down, have some coffee, maybe a piece of apple pie?' I asked.

'Nice,' said Ms. Bray approvingly. 'Do you want the good news or the bad news?'

'Both,' I said. 'Tell me the bad news first.'

'Traces of ergot detected in spilt flour on a bakery floor,' she said crisply, accepting a cup of coffee and a fork. I put two plates of pie and the pot of cream on the coffee table. Constable Vickery helped herself, and allowed Heckle and then Jekyll to lick a glob of cream off the end of her forefinger.

'And the good news?'

'It's in Best Fresh. Nothing in yours at all. Earthly Delights came out as clean as a whistle, except for some cat fur. About which you might get a stiff note.'

'Oof.' I let out a breath abruptly.

'As you say,' agreed Senior Constable Bray. 'This is good pie. Your apprentice?'

'He's a good boy,' I said proudly.

'But he used to be a bad boy,' said Ms. Bray.

'I know. He was a junkie.'

'And a thief,' she said keenly.

'As you say.'

'This doesn't worry you?'

'No,' I said with perfect truth. I got up and fetched myself some pie and a new cup of coffee. 'If he steals from me I'll sack him and bang goes his career. He goes to a drug counsellor every Saturday.'

'Yes, I know.'

Horatio had awoken and was requesting a dab of cream. Ms. Bray looked at him coolly. He looked back. I wondered who would win. There was a pause. Then she dipped a finger into the cream on her plate and offered it to him. In a formal, marked manner, Horatio condescended to lick it. Honour was satisfied. Ms. Bray and Horatio then withdrew their mutual regard. Horatio sat down for a wash. Ms. Bray returned to her subject. 'I suppose if he hasn't got back on the gear with all this upset, he's not going to. Where's Daniel?'

'He went out to do some errands. He said he'd be back for lunch.'

'Patrol said you were carrying Best Fresh's Vincent Wyatt back to his flat this morning. How is he?'

'About now, he is waking to the hangover of the century,' I replied.

'What did you learn about him? You were in his flat for hours and Jason went out to buy food.'

'Ms. Bray, do you know everything about me?' I demanded, trying to be offended and not really succeeding.

'Most things,' she chuckled. 'But not all. Bit vague on your shoe size. And the situation still has enough puzzles to stop us getting bored. For instance, I don't know what connection this soul cake thing has with this magic convention which hit town at the same time as the cakes did, which may be a coincidence or may not.'

'So they are definitely cakes?' I said. This information exchange was going to work both ways if I had anything to do with it.

'Yes, every person examined had cake in their insides, and the path lab managed to find the ergot actually in some of it. Massive doses, massive.'

'What else was in the mix?'

She stared at me. Horatio nudged her very gently and she began to stroke him, almost without noticing. He has the best subliminal moves of any cat I have ever met.

'What do you mean?'

'I mean, was there fruit, cinnamon, was it yeast dough or made with baking powder?'

'I don't know. Why would it help to know?'

'Well, the traditional soul cake which the witches require is made of bread dough with extra sugar and dried fruit and spices. Jason made some up from an old recipe written in Middle English. It would be interesting to know whether whoever made the lethal ones was using that recipe and might be a witch, or was just making poisonous rock cakes.'

'I see. We can ask. Make a note, Helen.'

Ms. Vickery found her notebook, which was under Heckle, and made a note. Then she spoke for the first time.

'You were asking about Mr. Wyatt,' she reminded Ms. Bray.

'So I was. Helen is my memory. What did you find out about him?'

'Not a lot.' I detailed what I had discovered. Ms. Bray smiled. She had a hidden dimple, which flashed when she was pleased. She was very attractive when she smiled.

'That's a bundle,' she said admiringly.

'And what do you know about him?'

There was a pause, in which Ms. Bray realised that she was stroking a cat, stopped, and continued to stroke. 'It was an amicable divorce, as divorces go,' she told me. 'Wife happy with new bloke and not asking for too much in settlement. Little daughter, Tamsin, aged seven. He has access every weekend and half the school holidays. They stay in the Templestowe house. No criminal record. Six driving offences in twenty years, all speeding. Did a bread-making course at RMIT, passed top of the class. Ordinary sort of bloke, really.'

'What about his employees?' I pressed my luck. Ms. Bray put down her empty plate and sipped her coffee, looking at her own notebook.

'Edward Ramsgate. Aged nineteen. Born in Kent, England. Parents came here when he was a baby. Father went off ten years ago. Didn't finish Year Eleven. Dim lad, works the night shift. Not a mental case, just not too bright. Couple of children's court offences, no ticket on a train, drunk in a public place and minor with.'

I looked at her. Jargon was jargon the world over. She dimpled again and explained.

'Sorry, minor in possession of intoxicating liquor. Got a bond. They all do in the children's court for anything short of arson or murder. No further offending. Lives with his mum in Abbotsford. She's on the pension. Two sisters, both younger, still at school, nothing on LEAP. This is his first job.'

'Nothing there connected to witches or drugs?'

'No,' she said sadly. 'Janelle Richards, aged eighteen. Eldest daughter in a family of five. Child of complete losers. Mother an alcoholic. Every child has a different father and only one of them pays any child support. They manage in transitional housing on benefits. Every now and again Mum goes on the booze and the children get sent to foster homes. Janelle's supposed to be the most stable of all of them according to her social worker. Mum's a shrew, suspected of beating the kids, always gets into violent relationships and has to keep running away from awful partners.'

'Thus the transitional housing,' I commented.

'Yeah, they've worn out several social service agencies. The only one which keeps on trying is the Salvos and they're supported by God.'

'Poor Janelle,' I said.

'Yeah, life's tough sometimes,' said Ms. Bray without noticeable sympathy. 'Some religious sect is looking after them at the moment. The whole family's moved out to Bendigo, staying on some sort of communal farm. Lots of prayer and good country food. They're safe for the time. Until Mum fucks up again and they get thrown out for moral turpitude.'

'So is Janelle travelling from Bendigo every day? Surely not.'

'No, I've got an address for her. She's staying in Carlton. She might have a chance if she ditches her family. Nothing known, by the way. So that's the state of play at the moment. Quarantine has cleared your bakery and you're free to start trading whenever you like.'

'I think I might leave it for the rest of the week.' I had considered this. 'I haven't had any time off since I started Earthly Delights. Until we find out what's going on with the soul cakes. No point in starting up and having to stop again.'

'And give the punters time to forget about those headlines,' said Ms. Bray. 'Well, better get on. Say farewell to your puddy-tats, Helen. We have to talk to Corinna's witch. She'll probably turn us into frogs.'

'I think she does toads,' I told her. 'Just loose Ms. Vickery on Belladonna and Meroe will be fine. She trusts Belladonna's judgment.'

'So, who's Belladonna?' asked Ms. Bray, getting up and brushing cat fur and crumbs off her blue skirt.

'Her cat,' I said, a little surprised. 'Her black cat.'

I shut the door on her astonished face and went to have a bath. I hoped Meroe wouldn't find it necessary to turn Ms. Bray into a toad. I liked her.

Chapter Sixteen

When your day is not planned, it structures itself around tasks and meals, I found. I hadn't had a holiday since I opened the shop, and now that I was free of suspicion, I was elated and felt like doing something just for fun. I rang Jason and told him we were clean.

He whooped. He was going to be employed assembling Mrs. Dawson's flat-pack bookcase. 'I've got my own allen keys,' he said proudly. I just hoped that by the end of the day he would still have (1) all his fingers and (2) his temper intact.

I bathed in lush vanilla foam. I washed my hair. I sat out on the balcony to dry it as the day warmed towards summery temperatures. The tall green indestructible plants which Trudi had put into the blue glazed pots appeared to be thriving. The city hummed around me, busy and self absorbed. People went into Heavenly Pleasures, the chocolate shop, and came out with tiny wrapped parcels full of delight. I reminded myself that I must buy a small selection of their treasure. Daniel came in just as I was thinking that I ought to go for a nice brisk walk to make room for lunch.

'Ketschele,' he said, kissing the top of my head. 'I love the scent of your hair.'

'Darling,' I replied, 'thank you for the flowers.'

'Flowers?'

'The tulips. They are beautiful.'

'They are beautiful,' he agreed, 'but they aren't from me.'

'No?'

'No.'

'Or the croissants?'

'Not them either. It seems,' said Daniel, with a gratifying edge to his voice, 'that you have a secret admirer.'

'And one who knows me very well,' I said. I could not feel threatened by parrot tulips. 'I have good news. Earthly Delights has been inspected and declared free of any contaminant whatsoever.'

'Wonderful!' Daniel hugged me.

'And I am taking the rest of the week off, because I've not had a holiday, and because the soul cake mystery still isn't solved,' I told him. 'Now, how about you?'

'When I woke and found you gone without a note,' he said, 'I feared that something awful had happened. I was just going to scour the city for you when you came home.'

'Yes,' I said, and explained. He listened intelligently.

'I see,' he replied. 'And you took Mr. Wyatt home. That was kind of you.'

'Not entirely,' I said, and detailed what I had found out about him, and for good measure threw in all of Ms. Bray's information. Which was what the techno geeks call an info dump, and had to be digested slowly, with a bracing pot of chai and a few biscotti. While he was thinking about it, he produced from his pocket the jewelled plate I had last seen in Barnabas' hands and gave it to me.

'*Ephod* means "shield",' he said. He had unshipped his laptop and was typing into it, recording all this new information.

I examined the ephod. It was beautiful. Solid. Studded with all the stones which the Bible had required. I could see that it was meant to hang in the middle of someone's chest, suspended by heavy chains from both top corners. It felt very old, though possibly not as old as Mrs. Dawson's Mycenaean brooch. I turned it over and found that Hebrew letters had been engraved on the back, which was otherwise unfigured.

'What does this say?' I asked Daniel

'*Rechoosho Shel Beit Kneset Kal Yashan,*' he said, still typing.
'Which means?'
'Property of the Kal Yashan Synagogue.'
'And the Kal Yashan Synagogue was in Salonika?'
'Yes, *metuka.*'
'What does *metuka* mean?'
'Sweetheart.'

He kept typing. I thought about it. Chrysoula's chain, extorted from a Greek family in Thessaloniki. The ephod, stolen from a synagogue in Thessaloniki. Both stolen by the Nazi administrator, Max Mertens. In, as it happened, Thessaloniki. What had happened to the treasure subsequently? Old Spiro had been Mertens' translator, the old beast. If he knew, it was too late to ask him without a specially equipped fireproof medium. What had Max Mertens done with his treasure? Had it been stolen from him? Had Chrysoula indeed seen him in sailor's clothes, near her home village late in the war?

As if in answer Daniel, still typing with one hand, reached into his pocket with the other and gave me a small bundle of papers. I set them on the table and pinned them under Horatio's tail, always a useful paperweight.

I had photographs. Black and white, blown up from old ones. A clean-cut man in a uniform. Max Mertens. I always stared into the faces of known monsters, trying to find something in the shape of the face, the expression, the eyes, which told me that this was a man who had shoved the Jews of Salonika into trains and sent them off to dreadful death. Every day, for weeks, until he ran out of Jews. I had never found it in Nazis. They just looked like people. It was the most frightening thing about them. Mertens looked like a moderately well-groomed, self-important man in a uniform, and that was all you could say about him from the outside.

Then I had a photo of a ledger, which I could read because it was in German. Underlined was 'Temple jewellery from Kal Yashan'—*Tempel schatz aus Kal Yashan*—and under that *Goldene kette mit lowenkopf aus Karamboulis, Mary, Venezianisch,* meaning a gold chain figured with lions' heads, Venetian, from Mary Karamboulis. Chrysoula's mother's dowry chain and the ephod on the same page. This must have been Mertens' capital acquisitions journal.

Under that was another photo, a blurry face blown up from a smaller picture. It might have been Mertens. He was wearing a Greek fisherman's cap, which one should not wear unless one is both Greek and a fisherman. He was standing on the deck of a small boat, grinning and holding up a big fish. The sign over the pier read Faneromeni in English and Greek and someone had written 1935 on the back. So Max, if this was Max, had been to Greece before the war and knew Faneromeni well. Wherever that was. I could look it up later. I had a Jet Lag guide to Greece somewhere.

Next I found a copy of a bill or account, I thought, but it was in Greek and I couldn't read it. There followed several other accounts, and then a newspaper cutting from the *Hellenic Times*, a newspaper published in Greece for a while to educate English speakers as to events in Greece, much like the *South China Morning Post*. I had always loved it for its flexible interpretation of the language. I was rather sorry when Greece got all modern and the *Hellenic Times* started employing people who really spoke English, and even proofreaders, which much diminished its Grauniad charm. Then, of course, it went out of business. The exact date was missing but the year was 1957. There was a large black headline: 'Startling Event in Kalamata Yesterday!' The article went on:

In the main market of Kalamata, which is famed for its olives which everyone in the world knows are the best, Mr. George Hammadis (72), well known and respected grandfather of seven and proprietor of Hammadis Fishing Tours You Will Enjoy, was making some small purchases in the market from Mrs. Ariadne Loukas (71), widow, whose stall carries the best broad beans in their season from the farm of her son, Vasi (32). Imagine what was Mr. Hammadis' surprise when he saw in that market a man who he had never expected to show his guilty face in Greece again, scared as he must be of the righteous vengeance of the brave Hellenes!

Mr. Hammadis was taken aback. His heart beat faster. His face went white. Mrs. Loukas offered to fetch him a chair. But, old man as he was, he went straight up to the villain. 'Thou art the man!' he declared fearlessly, pointing the recreant out to the policeman present, who was Constable Costas Elounda (31), son of Mr. Petros Elounda (53) of the Post Office. The man thus denounced attempted to get away but was seized by the growing crowd, who had also recognised him as Max Mertens, Nazi administrator of Thessaloniki, thief and murderer.

Mertens protested his identity but Mr. Hammadis was honest and sure. He had often seen the villain Mertens in Thessaloniki during the war, when he managed the extinction of the Hebrew Hellenes and also extorted much valuable treasure from the hapless Jews and the Greeks trying to escape Nazi butchers. Constable Costas Elounda (31) arrested the monster forthwith and sent his assistant, Probationary Constable Fillipo Pangrati (19), only son of the widow Pangrati (39) of Koroni, to the Post Office to make an urgent telephone message to the police chief in Kalamata.

Then Constable Elounda removed the rascal to the cells in the police station as the people of the market were increasing their protests. We are told that the Godless beast Mertens will be sent to Kalamata and thence to Athens for trial. Readers of the *Hellenic Times* will be informed of all new developments in this case as they happen.

Well, well. There ought to be a record of the trial of the Godless beast Mertens, if indeed he was tried. Wasn't 1957 a bit late for war crimes trials? Then again, when had Mossad kidnapped Eichmann? I found my copy of *The House on Garibaldi Street*. 1957. Well, well, not too late at all.

It was time I got dressed. With a nice walk in mind, I put on jeans and suitable walking shoes and my favourite t-shirt. It was emblazoned with medieval ladies on horseback and the legend said 'Well-behaved women seldom make history'. I put on my woolly jacket and checked the pockets for emergency money and tissues.

Daniel was still typing. I had more bits of paper. Another picture. An account of an earthquake in Kalamata in 1986. Calamitous Kalamata, they called it. That whole sea is ringed with faults, but this one sounded like a particularly bad earthquake, toppling houses, felling sea-walls, killing twenty-two people and injuring hundreds.

The last bits of paper were addresses and phone numbers, written in a variety of inks and crossed out, one after another. Pages from someone's address book, it seemed. They all related to someone called Yanni.

Just as I laid down the last piece of crumpled paper, Daniel pressed save and closed the laptop.

'You were with the raiders who took this ephod from Barnabas, weren't you?' I asked. 'That's how you cut your hand.'

'Yes,' he said. 'I was with them.'

'And you can't tell me who your fellow raiders were?'

'No, I can't.'

'But there's nothing to stop me guessing,' I told him.

'Nothing in the world,' he responded.

I took a good look at him. He looked tired but excited. His eyes were smudged underneath but bright. He was one day unshaven, his jaw darkened. A very attractive combination.

'I've read all the papers you gave me. I love that *Hellenic Times*. The style is inimitable. Was Max Mertens actually tried in Athens?'

'He was. That's a matter of public record. They found him guilty and sentenced him to twenty-five years in jail.'

'Good for them! But, hang on, 1957, isn't that the time of the troubles?'

'Yes, and Max Mertens was sold back to Germany for a huge load of aid. The Germans nailed the money for Greece to the floor and wouldn't release it until they had their Max back. Don't hold it against them too harshly.'

'I don't,' I said. 'Putting Mertens in jail was a nice gesture, though. But what was he doing in Greece? That was bold. There was a picture in your pile that showed he had been to Greece before the war—someone was bound to recognise him.'

'Bold. Or desperate.'

'Why did he want to go back so badly?'

'For that,' said Daniel, 'we first have to see an elderly German and then another elderly Greek. Can you cope?'

'If you can,' I said. 'Though I'm not feeling very pro-German at present. Is the Greek likely to be as bad as Old Spiro?'

'God, I hope not.'

'This would be Yanni of the many addresses?'

'It would.'

'First,' I answered, 'I must see how poor Mr. Wyatt is.'

'He's ruined,' said Daniel. 'According to you, someone in his bakery made the soul cakes.'

'No, there's ergot on his floor, that's all we know,' I said. 'It might have come from that contaminated sack of rye mix, if that was what was wrong with it, and we don't know that. Damn, I forgot to make a note of his phone number. But I left him mine.'

'He'll call if he needs you,' said Daniel. 'Now, what about this secret admirer of yours? What else has he sent you?'

'Oh, this and that,' I said coyly. To my own surprise. I didn't know that I did coy. 'All perfect little things, to make me feel better. I felt sure that it was you,' I said truthfully.

'Why did you need to be made to feel better?' demanded Daniel.

'Because of Georgie, of course. And the contamination of my shop and the ruin of my life. Not important at the time, perhaps, but it upset me.'

'Of course,' he said, not taking offence at my tone. 'I'm really sorry about Georgiana. I just didn't notice.'

'No, you didn't.'

He slid an arm around my shoulders and I leaned into his embrace. Sweet Daniel. Now, what was my new Hebrew word?

'*Metuka*,' I said into his chest, 'let's not worry about it. Where do we find your elderly Nazi?'

'In a nursing home,' said Daniel with a sly grin. 'How's your German?'

'Pretty average,' I replied. My girls' school had been good at languages and they offered outings and cultural evenings as well. Though that had introduced me to Wagner, of course. And Caspar David Friedrich.

'Helmut wasn't a Nazi,' Daniel told me. 'He was only a sailor.'

'Oh, good. I'll just call Meroe and see how she got on with the cops.'

'And I'll call up Timbo,' said Daniel, and reached for his mobile phone.

Meroe answered the shop phone, which meant that she had not been arrested. I listened for background croaking but couldn't hear anything except the pacific tinkle of wind chimes.

'I told them everything,' she said listlessly. 'All I knew about all of it. They attended politely and made notes. Belladonna liked that young woman, Helen. So they won't misuse what I said.'

'Earthly Delights is off the hook,' I told her. 'But I'm going to take the rest of the week off. I'm just out with Daniel, unless you need me?'

'No, thank you, I am looking forward to a nice soothing day stacking boxes and selling herbs. Quarantine didn't find anything here either. I should think not. Ergot, indeed. There are enough ordeal poisons in the world without coming to look for them in the Sibyl's Cave.'

'There are a lot of ordeal poisons?'

'Certainly. Damiana, acacia bark, mandrake, morning glory seeds, any number of mushrooms taken by the acolyte in a devout spirit so he can see the ancestors. Or by the drug-crazed lunatic, of course…and that's only what comes to mind instantly. Madness. There is a lot of it about.'

'I know,' I agreed wholeheartedly. 'See you later then.'

'Blessed part,' she said, and hung up.

'Madame?' asked Daniel, holding out his elbow. 'The gracious lady's carriage awaits.'

I picked up my backpack, slid a hand into the crook of his arm, and we walked out together.

I wondered what our driver was going to find to eat as we moved into the polite and tree-lined suburbs. Camberwell, Caulfield, they wouldn't be ready for Timbo. Somewhere in Kew we stopped. Expensive place. Nice rose garden. High walls. Daniel directed Timbo to open the boot, where he had previously stashed a picnic hamper, and we went up the carefully graded path into a spacious reception area more suited to a five star hotel. But there it was, the old age smell: urine and eau-de-cologne and wet washing. It was very faint, almost undetectable, but it was there. Inadvertently, I wrinkled my nose, thus insulting the starched woman at the desk.

'Yes?' she asked in a voice which was designed to frighten poor people and freeze rich people. She was a thin blonde on her fiftieth botox or her first facelift.

'We've come to see Mr. Helmut Schwartz,' said Daniel. 'I'm sure that we have an appointment.'

She made a show of consulting a ledger on her desk. No newfangled computers for this refuge of the well-heeled antique. She pressed a button, a sweet chime sounded and a nurse appeared.

'Take these…' there was the faintest pause before she said '…visitors to Mr. Schwartz, please.' The 'please' was also infinitesimally delayed.

The nurse, a cheerful, strapping young woman, conducted us at a very fast walk along a corridor painted chrome green with ivory highlights. Very Martha Stewart. Before the jail sentence, of course.

'How is Mr. Schwartz,' asked Daniel, 'Nurse—' he bent to read her nametag—'Simmonds?'

'He's all right,' she replied, slowing down a little. This was a relief. I was getting out of breath. 'He's losing his English, but his German is still pretty good and his memory otherwise is good enough. People do that, you know, shed languages in the reverse order they learned them. He doesn't have a lot of visitors, though. His granddaughter comes in every week. Poor old buggers mostly outlive everyone they knew in the old days.'

'I didn't take to your boss,' I commented. She flashed me a happy grin.

'She's not my boss, thank God! She's just the receptionist, and one day someone will surgically remove it.'

'What?' I asked.

'The broom up her arse. Here we are.' She opened a chrome green door on my laugh. 'Herr Schwartz?'

'*Ja,*' said an old voice, and we went in.

Helmut Schwartz had been a big man. He must have stood six feet tall in his prime, and he had been blond, to judge by his pale blue eyes. A fine specimen of Aryan manhood. Now he was shrunken, crumpled, very, very old. He was sitting in an easy chair, binoculars in hand and bird book in lap, looking out the window. He did not start with surprise.

'Daniel?' he asked. '*Sie Sind* Daniel?'

'*Ja, ich bin* Daniel,' said the love of my life, sitting down on his heels.

'They told me you would come,' he said, in German. 'That you want to hear the tale of Mertens' treasure.'

'*Ja,*' said Daniel.

'Wheel me over to the table, if you would. Then you can have a chair each. *Gnädige Frau*—' he gave me a formal little nod—'if you would be so kind.'

We did as he asked. He gathered his thoughts together and began to speak, and I made notes as unobtrusively as I could. But after a while I don't think he noticed me at all, or Daniel, or the old body he was trapped in. He was back in 1943, a twenty

year old sailor, presented by the Nazi administrator of Salonika
with an offer he couldn't refuse.

'I had been smuggling them out for months,' he said. 'Those
that wanted to go to Palestine. We got them into boats and off
to Turkey. Though the U-boats got some and the English got
others, most of them landed safe. I already had enough money,
deposited in the bank in the Great Bazaar, to prosper if I ran,
and I was going to run, taking the last boat myself, for what we
were doing in Thessaloniki was filthy, not a fair war, just theft and
murder. But I let greed rule me. I waited for one more journey.
A fatal error; I never made it again, not in my whole life. Also
there was a girl—you understand?'

Daniel nodded. We understood.

'Mertens, he came to me and said, I know about your treason—he called it treason—to the Fatherland, to Herr Hitler, to
Germany. I will denounce you to the Gestapo unless you find
me a boat, have it loaded in secret, and take me away. You have
five nights until the dark of the moon. I sweated to find that
boat! He gave me money to buy her and finally I found one I
could handle with only a couple of hands. I warned my network
and we never saw each other again. But with me I took my girl,
dressed as a boy in overalls and cap, and my brother Hans. I had
plans which Max Mertens knew nothing of. He sent slaves to
load the boat—I called her *Pandora*—and we left in the dark of
the moon and slipped out of Salonika like a ghost ship.'

Nurse Simmonds came in at this moment escorting a tea
trolley. She flapped a huge white napkin and it settled on Herr
Schwartz like a bedsheet. Then she poured his tea, strong Indian
tea with a lot of milk and sugar, and indicated to me that I could
be mother for Daniel and myself. The plate on the old man's
tray contained crisp ginger biscuits. Not general nursing home
issue. This was a high class establishment.

'I learned to drink tea like this in Australia,' commented
Herr Schwartz when he had sipped his cup empty and eaten
two biscuits. 'On the Snowy River. It was a great enterprise, now

forgotten. I only hope that men shall forget our wicked deeds as fast as they forget our good ones.'

'You will be forgiven,' said Daniel gently. 'The people who escaped to Palestine have not forgotten you.'

The old man made a pleased grunt. I took his cup and dusted him with the napkin. He patted my hand.

'Hmm! If God is good. Where was I? I am old, I forget.'

'Mertens' treasure,' I prompted. 'You took the *Pandora* out of Salonika harbour in the dark of the moon.'

'So we did,' he said, tapping his fingers on the binoculars. 'It seemed to be fated to be a good journey. We flew down the coast of Greece with a fine fast wind behind us, not stopping for five days. I still did not know where Mertens meant to go. He did not speak to me, except to give me orders. And we were busy with the ship, there being only three of us. She was heavy, too, being ballasted with gold coins. They shift sometimes. He might have been heading for Italy, though that would be strange as it was held by Germany. Bari, perhaps. Lawless place. Anyway, his plan was to go almost to Crete and then across and up the west coast of Greece, and that was as far as I understood. So we did as he ordered. The seas were calm but the moon was ever waxing and we could only travel at night. I never knew why he had no forged papers. Papers were easy enough to come by in Salonika. I could have made him a nice set myself, if he had asked.'

The old man chuckled. His pale blue eyes were twinkling. I could understand a girl deciding to run away with him, even if it meant dressing in overalls and cap and working as a deckhand.

'But our luck ran out, as luck always does. *Ja*, it ran out.' He sighed. 'We were off the bay of Messinia when an English submarine saw us, rose and challenged us in Greek. I couldn't speak Greek, neither could Mary, she was Turkish. Mertens was below, asleep. So they attacked. We fled. *Pandora* was between two low islands when the torpedo got her and we were all plunged into the sea. Luckily we were blown clean out of the boat, not trapped and sunk inside, and the English boat picked me up, and Mary and Hans, and took us to Alex to a prisoner-of-war camp. It

wasn't too bad. They freed Mary after the Turks vouched for her
and they let Hans and me loose in the town once they found
we were not Nazis. I decided that the destiny of the world was
in England and America and therefore I learned English. Hans
was homesick and couldn't concentrate. And Mary and I...'

'Married?' I asked. He gave me a sad smile.

'She found she could not leave Turkey,' he said. 'Or her family.
She went back, when they allowed her. Then the war was over,
the world sane again, and I went to Australia and worked on the
Snowy River scheme. That was a great work. That taught me
about water, and I became a hydraulic engineer with the money
I collected from the Istanbul bank. I married, I had children,
I had a good life. I grew old and came here after my wife died.
They look after me and I like being looked after, and I watch
the birds. And all that time, all that time, I never knew that Max
Mertens survived the wreck. I thought him sunk and drowned
in the remains of the boat.'

'*Zo*,' said Daniel, and he told Herr Schwartz how Mertens'
story had continued.

'He came back looking for it?' swore Helmut Schwartz. 'The
villain! But he did not find it?'

'No,' said Daniel. 'He went back to Germany, became a
lawyer, and died in 1976.'

'And all the time he knew that a fortune lay under the waves
and he had to work for his living like all of us. Oh, that is nice,'
said the old man appreciatively. 'That is a very good joke.'

'So, can you tell me where the *Pandora* went down?'

'Certainly. Between the islands of Schiza and Sapientza, at
the outflow of the bay of Messinia. Nearest sighting mark was
a little Venetian castro on the shore and the big rock shaped
like a dragon, streaked white by the seabirds. There you will
find the wreck of *Pandora*, if the sea hasn't eaten her altogether.
That bay is carpeted with wrecks. The Turkish fleet were sunk
there by the British in 1834. And they say even Roman ships
are there. It is dangerous water. I am tired. Have I told you what
you need to know?'

'*Ja*,' said Daniel. '*Besten dank*, Herr Schwartz. Here is a little present from those who sent me.'

He unwrapped a bottle. 'Schnapps,' said the old man. 'And my favourite brand. You will give my fond regards to Saba? Now, can you wheel me back to the window? They throw out the bread from tea, and the birds come down for it. Don't look sad, lovely lady,' he said to me as he picked up his binoculars and began to focus them. 'I am so old now that I have only one question left, apart from the eternal one.'

'What is that?' I asked, dropping a kiss on his cheek.

'Why do wattlebirds hate pigeons?' he said, and chuckled.

Timbo had cleared the picnic and was sitting on the kerb, smoking a Winfield and, simply by his presence, bringing down the property value of the whole neighbourhood. We got into the car. I handed over my notebook.

'The boat sank,' I said, 'in what sounds like an inaccessible place, and in the dark. How could anyone find it again?'

'Ah, there's the mystery,' said Daniel. 'What's more, that island is used by the Greek navy to test weapons, so no one is allowed near it. Poor Mertens, sitting in his law office and slaving away, how he must have hated knowing that all that gold was just lying there and he dared not try to get it, or send anyone, because no one can sneak in under a bombardment to do a bit of illegal diving.'

'But he must have tried. He could have blackmailed someone, that's what he did with Helmut Schwartz.'

'Ah,' said Daniel, 'but even if he did, he could not trust them to come home with the bikkies. Too perilous. That ship was carrying about four million pounds sterling worth of treasure. In 1943 prices.'

'Served him right,' I said.

'A good joke,' agreed Daniel.

We went back to Insula in silence. We had a lot to think about. And when we got there, who was waiting for us but Georgiana Hope, in a camel and dark brown ensemble the cost of which might have given Mertens' treasure a run for its money.

'I need to speak to you,' she said.

To me. Not to Daniel. I did not want to let her into my house. Some sort of instinctive revulsion. Heavenly Pleasures had recently added a few pavement tables to their set-up, where they served hot chocolate of the gods. I led her there and we sat down.

'I want you to sell me your bakery,' she said.

Chapter Seventeen

I ordered hot chocolate for three from the apprentice and tried not to gape. George's hair dye had obviously damaged her brain.

'No,' I said. 'How much more clear can I be?'

'But consider,' she urged. 'This quarantine will have destroyed your niche customers. Being shut for this length of time, they'll find bread elsewhere as good as yours. And they won't come back. A poisoning scare lasts for ages.'

'George!' remonstrated Daniel. She gave him a full-face one thousand watt smile. Which had no effect on him, I was pleased to note.

'Sorry, Danny, but I'm telling the truth. They call this a commercial reality. You'll need to start again and you'll need capital, even if you don't go to jail. So, what do you say, take up my offer?'

'No,' I said. 'I might add, no, no, never. Not ever. You will get your hands on Earthly Delights only if I and all my heirs are dead. No.'

'She means it,' said Daniel. 'Drink your chocolate and digest your spleen, George. You are not going to get Earthly Delights. Why do you want it so badly?'

Georgiana stared at him. For a moment, she had no words. 'A…fancy,' she said at last. 'Just a fancy. I'm at the Hilton, if you come to your senses,' she added. She got up and walked away.

Daniel and I shared the extra cup of chocolate between us. It does not do to waste food.

'That was strange,' I said.

'Come to your senses? Where does she get off saying things like that?' fumed Daniel. 'The woman's lost her marbles. At least she's moved out of my flat.'

'She did make you buy a set of real plates and clean the windows,' I comforted him. Hot chocolate has a mellowing effect on my temper.

'There's that, I suppose.'

'Why does she want Earthly Delights so much?' I wondered aloud.

'Because it's yours? And she can't have me?' guessed Daniel. 'Because I'm yours, as well?'

'Are you?'

'Oh, yes,' said Daniel with the rich satisfaction I always associate with sunshine and peace and chocolate. I took his hand. The gash on the back had almost healed.

'Well, Sherlock, what now?'

'There's my elderly Greek,' he said.

'And here's my colleague,' I told him, seeing Vin Wyatt wavering along the lane.

'He doesn't look well,' commented Daniel.

'Better than this morning. Then again, dead would be better than he looked this morning. Hello, Vincent. How do you feel?'

'Better than I deserve,' he said ruefully. 'Can you do me a favour, Corinna? A couple of favours. The cops say I can't leave the flat, they'll need to talk to me again. I must contact my workers. Poor buggers. Janelle and Eddie. Can you do it for me? Only I don't want them to feel that I'm ditching them. I'll think of something for them. A good reference at least.'

'I might,' I said, deeply conscious of Vin's business being ruined and mine rescued. 'Can't you phone?'

'No one's answering. Eddie's just in Abbotsford, you might drop over there? Janelle's in Carlton. Here're the addresses. Just

give them this note from me and tell them not to worry, it isn't
their fault.'

'All right,' I said, catching Daniel's nod. If he wanted us to
do this we could do it easily enough. 'I'll get around to it today.
You drink some more water, Vincent, and get some rest. I'll let
you know how I go.'

'Thanks,' he said. Clutching his forehead, he staggered away.
You don't spring back from a three-day drunk on one Berocca
and half a night's sleep.

'Shall I summon Timbo again?'

'After a nap,' I said, sliding a hand down his arm to his wrist.
'I think we could do with a siesta.'

'Yes,' agreed Daniel, and followed me like a lamb.

We woke at about two, slowly and lazily. So lovely, so very
lovely, my beautiful Daniel. I stretched in complete luxury. And
kissed him again, just because I could.

We rose and dressed slowly, relishing the feeling of being
thoroughly loved. I was never going to get used to this. I said so,
locating my knickers where I had flung them over the mirror.

'Me neither. I keep wondering if I made you up,' he confessed,
donning a sock. Daniel can make putting on socks sexy. Which
probably says something about my blissed-out state of mind.
'Then you astonish me and I know you're real,' he added.

If he went on like this I would have to tear his socks off again
and we had work to do. I contented myself with kissing his bared
shoulder and then his ear, which reminded me of Meroe biting
Barnabas. Why had she bitten him? Just righteous Rumanian
rage, or was there some magical reason? I offered this question
to Daniel.

'Isn't there something about scoring a witch above the breath?
And if you have to draw blood with your teeth, an ear is a good
place to bite. Human teeth aren't very sharp,' he said, pulling on
trousers and then shirt, dammit. 'It's quite hard to draw blood.
Mostly you just bruise.'

'I almost don't want to know how you know that.'

'But you do want to know?'

'Yes, of course.'

'I've been in my share of pub fights, but the reason I know about drawing blood was an art installation in London many years ago. There were things which had to be done in order: cough, smile, laugh, urinate, dance—you know the sort of thing. It was very popular, active art. One of the instructions was "Bite a friend. Until there is blood." It was a Mistress Dread moment, or meant to be. But the artist—'

'Artist?' I objected.

He shrugged. 'Whatever. The actor chose a shoulder and tried to bite through the skin, and couldn't. The poor subject was shaking with pain, and still all there was to show was a huge bruise. I was watching this. With complete disbelief, I might add. And I thought about it. You'd either have to nip up a fold of skin and use a pre-sharpened tooth, or try for a soft part, and the lobe of the ear is probably the most accessible soft part. Of course if you miscalculate you might bite it off.'

'Erk,' I commented. 'Too much information, as Kylie would say.'

'Quite.'

'Where shall we go first?' I pulled my seatbelt down to fasten it.

'My Greek is in Footscray. Janelle in Carlton is closest,' he said. Timbo started the car.

'Aren't you sick of driving us around, Timbo?' I asked, feeling a little conscience stricken.

'I'm never tired of driving, Corinna,' he replied. 'I could drive all day and all night. Nothing to do when I'm not driving but watch TV. You can get real sick of watching TV real fast. And Mum says I clutter up the house.'

'Don't you go out or anything?' I asked.

'I go to the Grand Prix every year,' he replied. 'And to Phillip Island. And out to Sandown. And Daniel got me a job once a week teaching defensive driving to kids. That's fun.'

Since there was no one I would rather have had in charge of an out-of-control car than Timbo, who had a deep spiritual connection with all engines, I just murmured an agreement.

Janelle's address was not actually in Carlton but in Parkville, the same block of flats we had come to with Meroe.

'Are you getting a bad feeling about this?' asked Daniel.

'Meaning that there is a connection now between Vin Wyatt's ergot and Barnabas and his treasure hunt?'

'Yes, something like that.'

'Could be a coincidence. They happen a lot in the real world. I'm always noticing them.'

'You're just sorry for Janelle.'

'That, too.'

We rang, but there was no one at home. I didn't want to leave Mr. Wyatt's note in case Janelle was no longer with the witches, or perhaps (though that would be stretching coincidence to Fortean proportions) had never been aware of them at all, being lent the flat by some academic acquaintance. Janelle didn't seem to be the sort of girl to have academic acquaintances.

Daniel rang the bell for the apartment of the witches we had met on our first visit and we were answered. The security door didn't open, but after a while Celeste came out to us.

'Janelle? Mousy, droopy girl? They're at the tattoo place this afternoon.'

'Who are?' I asked.

'The girls,' she said. 'The younger ones.'

'Barnabas' acolytes?'

Celeste pursed her lips. 'You could call them that. And the boys, Cypress and Cedar. Hang on, someone said Janelle wasn't coming back here, she was off to Bendigo, was it, to see her sisters? Have to ring her later, they ought to be back after five. Blessed part.'

We thanked her and went on to our next appointment.

Abbotsford had been gentrified but retained its working class feel. You could buy sourdough at the local shop, but it also stocked sliced white bread in its plastic wrapper. The Ramsgate family lived in a small brick house which had not been renovated.

We rang the doorbell and were admitted by a worried woman in the very last pinny in captivity. It had improbable blue roses on it. They matched her rinse and perm. She had to be fifty and an old fifty at that.

'Eddie? He's real upset,' she said. 'Thinks he's lost his job, thinks it's all his fault. Come in,' she invited, and we were conducted into a cosy dark lounge room where a vacant youth was eating crisps and staring at a car race of some sort on the TV. The high performance engines went whizzing round with a noise like a Scooby Doo monster-sized mosquito. At any moment I expected someone to pull off a mask and say, 'Professor Jones! So it was you!' 'Yes, and I would have got away with it, if it wasn't for you meddling kids!'

'Eddie?' said his mother. 'People from your boss to see you.'

Eddie looked up. He was the same pimply and gormless youth that I recalled, with an added gloom which had settled around him like fog.

'What does Mr. Wyatt say?' he demanded. 'That I'm sacked?'

'No,' I said. 'Here's a note.'

I gave it to him and he unfolded it, but his eyes just seemed to skim over the surface.

'Hasn't got his glasses,' said his mother. She took the piece of paper from him and read it aloud. '"Dear Eddie, don't worry, if it looks like I can't open again I will find you something else. Vincent Wyatt." Well, that's nice,' she said in a tone of rising indignation. 'Gets my boy involved in a poisoning, and all he can say is he'll find him another job! When Eddie's been getting up at four every morning! Do you know what that's like?' she demanded of me.

'Believe me when I tell you that I know,' I said in return. 'Don't be too hard on Mr. Wyatt, he's in big trouble himself.'

'Deserves it, carrying on with that young girl,' snarled Mrs. Ramsgate.

My mind boggled. What would a young woman like Janelle see in a red-faced older man like Vin Wyatt? But then what, I supposed, did her mother see in all those brutes to whom she kept attaching herself? The ways of the heart are inscrutable, as the Professor would say. Or possibly the ways of the wallet, of course.

'Really?' asked Daniel.

Eddie took another crisp. 'Oh,' he said. 'P'raps. But he's all right, Vin is. That was nice of him. To think of me. Yeah, Mum, I know what you're gonna say, but no one else wanted to give me a job. Paid all right too, more than Jobsearch. Tell him, thanks.'

'Why couldn't you answer your phone?' asked Daniel.

'They cut it off,' said Eddie solemnly.

'Who did?'

'The government. They only let you keep a phone for three months. I have to get another one soon. Only now they want Mum to sign for me.'

'Oh, right,' said Daniel, who apparently understood this. 'And what are you doing with yourself?'

'Gotta go down Centrelink tomorrow.'

'And he's been out every night with his rotten friends,' snarled Mrs. Ramsgate.

'Mum,' protested Eddie.

'Wasting his money!'

'They pay for me,' whined Eddie.

'Well, nice to meet you.' I didn't want to stay for the argument.

Mrs. Ramsgate conducted us to the door, apologising. 'Sorry, it was kind of you to bring the note,' she said. 'He's a good boy really, my Eddie, he just gets into bad company. Goodbye,' she said, and I waited until we were en route to Footscray and the elderly Greek on our list before I asked: 'The government takes your phone away?'

'He signs up for a free mobile phone and a contract, and then he doesn't pay for the calls, so they cut him off,' said Daniel. 'The kids can run through two or three companies before someone gets wise and cuts off their credit. Now they ask him to get a guarantor. His mum, in fact. And she's bright enough not to sign. A chatty kid can find himself with a bill for thousands of dollars if he can't SMS.'

'And Eddie can't SMS?' I asked.

'No, ketschele, he can't text because he can't read,' said Daniel. 'He shows no signs of having ever owned spectacles. It's a common excuse.'

'Oh,' I said. 'Listen, we left consideration of Barnabas where it lay because we got distracted. Shouldn't we be investigating him further? He had the ephod, after all.'

'We're seeing the Lone Gunmen tonight,' said Daniel. 'They've got some more information.'

'Right.'

We tootled off to Footscray, in the scent of mystery and chicken Twisties, and I wondered what it would be like not to understand the multiple essential signals of the world: not to be able to read or write. I couldn't remember not being able to read. It would be like trying to travel in a world without maps.

The elderly Greek lived in what, at school, we always unkindly called a wog palace: a two storey brick building with white stone pilasters, and, in this case, lions regardant supporting shields on the gateposts. Such houses usually had a vegetable garden in front, as did this one: tomatoes, chilis, zucchini, basil and peppers. They all looked extremely healthy. As a concession to Western taste someone had planted two daisy bushes on either side of the gate. The name on the letterbox was Nikopoulos.

'I'm here to see Uncle Yanni,' Daniel told the gaggle of children who fountained out the front door when he rang the bell. They all raced back into the house, yelling, 'Uncle Yanni! There's a lady!' and we were ushered inside by a middle-aged woman, presumably Kyria Nikopoulos, who resembled Mrs. Pappas so closely that I had to look hard to distinguish between them. This lady had brown hair and was wiping her hands on a blue checked tea towel.

'Hello,' said Daniel. 'I'm Daniel. Saba sent me.'

'He's in the garden,' she told us. 'Come through.'

She was not overly welcoming, especially for a Greek. She seemed wary. The children picked this up and stopped dancing around us, falling back into a defensive huddle with the smallest and the boom box in the middle.

'I haven't come to cause him any trouble,' said Daniel gently.

Mrs. Nikopoulos' face darkened and she wrung the dishcloth between strong hands. 'He's always brought trouble,' she said bitterly. 'Ever since he was born. He broke my mother's heart with his criminal ways. But come along,' she said. 'Maybe he can make up for some of his sins before the devil comes to claim him.' This sounded very promising.

The house was cool but the garden bright. An old man was sitting under a grapevine, smoking a Papadimistrou and drinking what smelt like either expensive oven cleaner or cheap homemade wine. He looked up and smiled at me.

Oh, my. All he needed was a bandana and a cutlass to join the crew of Captain Jack Sparrow's latest ship without need for interview. He was bald, brown, skinny and charismatic, with a thick gold ring on one finger and gold rings in his ears. Someone had tattooed a full rigged ship on his chest. The blue was faded under a scribble of pale chest hair but I could still see all the details. He waved at us to sit down in a couple of unravelling cane chairs and said to the woman, 'Ouzo, coffee, Lydia! Have you no manners?' She sniffed and bridled but whisked herself back into the house.

He looked at the children and grinned. 'Later,' he promised. 'Later, there will be ice cream.' They vanished like little mice. This was a man with power.

'Are all those children yours?' asked Daniel.

'Some of them. I live here with my brother-in-law. He's an accountant.' He dragged out the word with infinite scorn. So the harassed Lydia was his sister, not his wife. He caught me thinking this and gave me a flash of teeth.

'My last wife died ten years ago. They wear out too fast, women. Well. *Shalom*, Christ killer.'

'*Yassus*, Pirate,' returned Daniel, stretching his legs. 'Nice place you've got here. Vines bearing well?'

'Too dry this year,' said the pirate. 'Good for olives, though. How are things in the spy business?'

Daniel did not look at me. 'Fine,' he said. 'And how are things in the treasure business?'

'Dead,' said Yanni Nikopoulos. 'Saba sent you to hear the story,' he said. 'How much?'

'The good of your soul,' said Daniel evenly. They stared at each other as Lydia clashed things in the kitchen. A standard female way of expressing dissent or requesting assistance, depending on the context. I almost got up to join her, but did not want to miss a word of the story.

'Might be worth it,' mused Yanni, stubbing out the cigarette on the concrete. 'Who's your beautiful woman? I never saw you with a woman in tow before.'

'Corinna,' said Daniel. 'This is Kyrie Yanni Nikopoulos, a well known and respected buccaneer.'

'Delighted,' I said, giving him my hand. He kissed it. His grip was firm and his lips, strangely enough, soft.

'You hang on to her or I'll take her away from you,' Yanni threatened.

'No, not this one,' said Daniel. I smiled at him and Yanni gave me back my hand, laying it in my lap with a pat.

'No,' he said slowly. 'Not this one. *Mazel tov, adelphos.* A good woman is above rubies.'

'But rubies are also useful,' hinted Daniel.

Lydia came into the garden with a tray on which reposed ouzo, water, coffee, and a little plate of those Greek doughnuts which are dipped in syrup. We sipped and munched and I tried not to drip onto my nice shirt, and did not succeed. Yanni watched me with a grin.

'A good woman is one who enjoys her food,' he said. 'The generous type. I always liked them generous. All right. You want to know about Inousires Nisia, eh?'

'I do,' said Daniel. 'With special regard to secrets and treasure.'

'Ah,' said Yanni. 'That was a bad year, a bad year for me, the year that Kalamata fell down.'

'1986,' I said.

'So it was. I came here with my parents, a long time ago, I am an Australian, but my distant family, they were in trouble, and I went to rescue them.'

I heard a loud 'Ha!' of disbelief from the kitchen, where his sister was listening through the window. 'You tell the truth,' she warned. 'You old devil. Lies are no use to you where you're going!'

'All right, there was maybe a little profit to be made by the right man,' responded Yanni. 'My son had got into a little business with a fishing combine. They fished for all sorts of things, you understand? Around and about in the Bay of Messinia.'

'Antiquities?' asked Daniel. 'Lot of wrecks down there.'

'And no one is allowed to scuba dive,' said the old man. How old was he? He could have been forty or seventy.

'Eh...' he said, allowing the syllable to draw out and opening both hands. 'Well, anyway, at the foot of Messinia are the Inousis islands, Sapientza and Schiza. Little rubbish islands, no water even for goats, no fish, only rocks and birds. Useless. But perhaps useful if a man knew the right place.'

'Where a boat called *Pandora* was torpedoed in 1943?' asked Daniel.

'Maybe. Maybe so. I never knew its name. In 1960, on holiday, fishing around there in a lawful *ploio psareme*—licensed,' he added proudly, 'a certain man came upon a rotten sack caught on his anchor, and when he pulled it up it had gold coins in it, so he...'

'Marked the place and said nothing?' guessed Daniel.

'What do you think?'

'That's what I think,' confirmed Daniel. 'And came back the next dark of the moon for another dip?'

'Indeed. That man might have been someone like me, you see. That man was not greedy. He took what I needed and went home and bought this house and brought my sister and her man and my children and my wife and then...I left it.'

I had noticed the segue between 'that man' and 'I' and didn't say a word. I sipped my cold water.

'Then I heard that my son had made a mistake,' he said. 'I went to him. He was in jail. He had been smuggling cigarettes. I needed the money to get him out and so...' He shrugged.

'You went back to *Pandora*.'

'In the dark, in the wind,' he said. 'Only time the patrols would miss us was in the middle of winter. I sent my partner down and he said, the wreck's gone, the seabed's shifted, let me search a bit further, and then it got darker and colder and when I hauled him up he was blue and nearly broke his teeth shivering. But we had enough again and went ashore. He knew where the wreck was, I didn't. The big earthquake broke all the seabed there, a wooden ship would slide and fall. I didn't need no more, I got my son out and brought him here, but later I heard that my partner was arrested too. Jailed three years. A wild boy, that one. Albanian father,' he said, shrugging again. 'What can you expect?'

'Did they catch him with treasure?' asked Daniel.

'No, drugs,' said Yanni, spitting. 'Filthy things. I never smuggled drugs.'

'What was your partner's name?'

'Petros,' evaded the old man.

'Petros who? Come on, Saba said you'd help,' coaxed Daniel.

'That Saba of yours knows too much already,' muttered Yanni.

'You tell him!' shrieked Lydia from the kitchen.

'All right. Petros Ioannides.' Yanni dug into his pocket and came out with a piece of paper folded small. He gave it to Daniel, who spread it on his knee.

'Very good,' he said, giving it to me to copy into my note-book. I managed an exact copy, Greek letters and English and rows of numbers. Apart from some loose tobacco and a coffee smudge, that was it.

'You be careful,' said Yanni suddenly, leaning forward and taking Daniel's wrist in both his hands. 'That Petros, he is a wild one. An *andarte*. A gambler. Never go back for the fourth bucket, that's the rule. I got the house and the son and the rescue because I never went back to the well for the fourth time. He would. And the fifth and the sixth.'

'I hear you, pirate. I'll take care. By the way,' said Daniel, standing up, 'ever hear the name Barnabas?'

'Only in the Bible,' responded Yanni.

'Which you ought to be reading!' screamed his sister.

He insisted on conducting us to the door, where a ring of children waited tensely, like leashed greyhounds.

'Here,' said Yanni, handing over a note. 'Ice cream for all. Even your mother,' he added, raising his voice so that he could be clearly heard by unimpressed ears in the kitchen. 'She likes butterscotch.'

Timbo started the car again. 'Home?'

'Home,' said Daniel.

'I liked your pirate,' I said.

'Most women say that,' he smiled.

'So he found the wreck by chance?'

'Possibly. Yanni will only tell us what he thinks we can find out by other means anyway.'

'And now we need to find his wild Petros Ioannides?'

'Yes.'

'And what does "Saba" mean?'

'Grandfather. In Hebrew.'

We were playing a game, I knew. Daniel wouldn't tell me anything outright, but he would answer yes or no if I asked the right questions.

'Is Saba your actual biological grandfather?'

'No, he's dead. Both of them.'

'But Saba is your client?'

'In a manner of speaking.'

'And he's asking the questions?'

'Yes,' he agreed.

'In order to retrieve the treasure, which has somehow got from the Inousis islands to here, even after the Kalamata earthquake shifted the seabed?'

'Yes, because Petros found it again,' said Daniel. 'And we need to retrieve it.'

'Why?'

'Because it was stolen from the murdered,' said Daniel fiercely. 'And it must go back to their children.'

'Ah. Yes, of course. But, look here, what use are a lot of gold coins and jewellery, even if they are fished up? It can't be sold. You said there were millions of pounds' worth. That's a lot of gold. Someone would notice. You can't just flood the market with highly identifiable coins and hallmarked religious treasures. And why on earth bring it to Australia when Europe or even South America is so much closer? It's insane.'

'I know,' he said. 'But how else to explain the ephod and the dowry necklace?'

I thought about this. He was right.

'Coincidence doesn't cut it, does it?'

'No.'

Chapter Eighteen

Insula was quiet and we made coffee and sat down for a recap. Daniel and I puzzled over the pirate's piece of paper.

'Looks like a phone number,' I said.

'Not enough digits.'

'Would be if it was an old one,' I said. 'Put a nine in front of it and see what happens.'

'An idea,' said Daniel, and stabbed out the numbers. He held out the phone. The 'this number is not connected' message was telling him to check the directory and try again. 'So much for that,' said Daniel. 'Some sort of code, perhaps?'

'What does it say in Greek?'

'Petros is a man's name, but it also means rock.'

'On this rock I shall found my church.'

'Eh?' he asked, not knowing the reference.

'Sorry, New Testament. After your time.'

'Funny. No, unless the numbers are meant to be divided into groups of four…thus.' We looked at the groups of four: 2125 3729 1450 8381 0. 'No, doesn't mean a thing to me.'

'Nor me. When are we seeing the Lone Gunmen?'

'About now-ish,' said Daniel. 'We'd better go down. They'll never come up here.'

'You go, and I'll start some late lunch or early dinner,' I offered. 'How about a nice ratatouille?'

'Too healthy. The vitamin Q in my blood has sunk to critical depths. Make me a London cabby's fry-up of tomatoes, mushrooms, eggs and bacon,' he said, grinning. 'Kosher bacon, of course.'

'Kosher bacon?' I called after him as he left the flat. I had never heard of kosher bacon. Surely a contradiction in terms?

'You just sprinkle it with water and call it lamb,' I heard him say as the door closed.

'Cheeky boy,' I said to all three felines, who now presented themselves for food and caresses, but food first, before they collapsed. What they got was carefully sectioned coils of bacon rind, which were well appreciated. I left them in a heap on the balcony, washing their greasy paws and whiskers.

We now had a pile of information, but not a lot of analysis or even synthesis. Janelle worked in the peccant bakery, assuming that Mr. Wyatt's Best Fresh was the source of the soul cakes. This was reasonable only in that no other source had been found and someone was selling them in the dogleg alley right behind the shop. All those people in white wrappers had tested everything they could possibly test and the only ergot, hence LSD, had been found in the spilt flour on the floor of Best Fresh. That looked like a fact.

I am an accountant. I like facts. My hands continued to prepare a fry-up which no London cabby could refuse while I stacked, examined, polished and set aside facts as I came to them. When I had been through them all, I would be able to try and make sense of them.

So. The soul cakes had been made in Best Fresh and sold in the clubs and had driven people mad. That might have been what they were intended to do, or it might have been seen as an unfortunate side effect by people who wanted the money and didn't care what effect their wares had on the consumer. People who weren't intending to stay in the business long, because even a plague organism knows that if it kills off too many hosts it will itself die. Someone in the slash-and-burn school of marketing, in fact. Another fact. I polished it with my tea towel and piled it on the other.

Who was making the soul cakes? Not Mr. Wyatt, he was too distressed, too straight, and too unimaginative. That left Eddie, a dim bulb who had no other interests and greatly valued his job, and Janelle, who had contacts with the witches and was one of Barnabas' acolytes. Along with, come to think of it, those two vicious boys, Cedar and Cypress. Or Rocky, as Daniel had named the prettiest one. Mrs. Ramsgate had said that Janelle was carrying on with Mr. Wyatt, but Eddie didn't seem to think so, though it was hard to tell with Eddie. And why would Janelle be doing that if she was within enthusiastic hugging range of the jovial and charming Barnabas, the father every mistreated girl thought she should have had?

Fact, and I didn't care for it at all: the person who seemed most likely to be making the soul cakes was Janelle, and she might—might!—be making them for Barnabas. Who would want them made because...? Money, of course. Or possibly— and here I dropped an egg, luckily into a dish—to sabotage the samhain celebrations? I remembered Meroe talking about how much witches disliked one another. Did Barnabas hate the conservative witches so much that he would try to poison them? I wouldn't have put anything past the big fat crook. But if that was the case something had slipped. He should have been keeping them for the actual ceremony, thus sending all of the participants on an involuntary trip. Perhaps someone else had intervened at this point. Sort of a fact, and I dusted it.

That concluded my consideration of the soul cake problem, because it now crossed with the mission on which Daniel had been engaged for the last week. The treasure of Salonika. We knew more about this one. Stolen by Max Mertens, who black-mailed Helmut the sailor into escaping down the coast of Greece in 1943 in a boat called *Pandora* which was ballasted with gold coins and other treasure. The boat was sunk by a British subma-rine and the crew rescued, except for Mertens, whom Helmut Schwartz had considered drowned. Helmut comes to Australia and becomes a successful hydraulic engineer and now lives in a nursing home. So far so good.

Mertens escapes and comes back to Greece in 1957, an act of extreme boldness. He is recognised in Kalamata and denounced and tried for war crimes and jailed, all without being able to get to the wreck of the *Pandora*, because it is now in a place where the Greek navy test their missiles and is under constant patrol. Germany gets their Max back but he dies in 1976 without any sign of prosperity except that earned by his own efforts. Facts.

And no one is allowed to go scuba diving in the Messinian gulf, where the battle of Navarino took place, because of the theft of antiquities. Fact. But a pirate called Yanni went fishing there, probably on or between some nefarious errands, and he, possibly by chance, catches an anchor in a soft cloth bag full of coins. He draws on this bank three times. Twice to finance his big house and his family in Australia. The third time to buy his son out of jail. And there Yanni leaves it, a cunning man who does not ride his luck. Fact.

But according to Yanni, his partner Petros is the only person who now knows where the wreck of the *Pandora* lies, somewhere other than where it was before the great earthquake of 1986 hit calamitous Kalamata. A map or sighting marks, such as we had from Helmut, would not help anyone find the treasure now. Petros of the Albanian father, a wild man. A dangerous man. So was this Petros the person who had brought all that gold to Australia?

And in the name of all the gods and goddesses, why here, and why now? Because at least some of the Salonika treasure was definitely here. The child had found Chrysoula's mother's dowry chain in the salt mud under a lot of black swans. The ephod, likewise, in the shallows of the sea. Both of those things had come from Max Mertens' original stash and nowhere else. They were last seen in a sinking boat off Schiza, and now they were in Williamstown. Fact.

Weird. At this point Daniel came back with another sheaf of papers and I started dishing up his fried eggs, tomatoes, mushrooms and kosher bacon. With it there was toasted sourdough, a good sourdough but not as good as mine. My mother of bread was sulking in its bucket in my bakery. I had dropped in and fed it this morning. Which now seemed to be a long time ago.

This might explain why, after eating a portion of the eggs and bacon, I made myself a small orange blossom—gin, orange juice and Cointreau—sat down on the couch, sipped it, and fell asleep. Too many facts and an early awakening really take it out of you.

I woke to the scent of coffee. Daniel was offering me a cup. I drank. Outside, it was getting dark. The table and floor were littered with sheets of paper, and the wastepaper basket was full of screwed-up balls of the same stuff.

'I hate to wake you, but I need some help here,' said Daniel.

'I'll just go and wash my face,' I blurred.

I had fallen deeply asleep. I felt like someone had hit me on the head with one of those Wodehouse stuffed eelskins. When I returned I drank the rest of the coffee and looked at Daniel's work. He had been doing exactly the same as me, though I hadn't made notes. Facts were piled on one side of the couch. Things which might be true were on the other side of the couch, under Horatio. Surmises were all over the floor.

'The trouble is that we have lots of connections but they don't make any sense,' he complained. 'Why, for example, should Barnabas have the ephod? Or, indeed, how did he get it? Who gave it to him? And if he knows what it is and where it came from, how dare he flourish it about in the company of people who might be expected to be able to read Hebrew—the kabbalah being fashionable at the moment—and who are bound to ask how it came into his hands? It's mad. Is the whole of the Salonika treasure here? Perhaps the ephod was stolen by one of the slaves who loaded the boat and brought it to Australia after the war.'

'Along with Chrysoula's mother's Venetian chain?' I quibbled.

'Well, yes, maybe.'

'Or maybe not…'

'And if the whole of the treasure is here, where is it, who brought it, and why?'

'And other questions,' I sighed. 'Anything more about Barnabas?'

'Yes, here…' Daniel scrabbled through his notes. 'The missing three years are accounted for—he was in the army. He was married too, or did we know that? Oh, yes, we did. Two children, long deserted. His wife filed for divorce and had no trouble losing him. She never remarried. Always a bad sign.'

'Maybe. Why did he leave the army?'

'Discharged honourably. Weak heart. Overweight. Flat feet. Short sighted. God knows how they let him in in the first place. He is not my idea of a soldier.'

'No,' I agreed. 'Where was he stationed?'

'Germany,' said Daniel.

'Aha,' I said, rather as a ploy to see if something occurred to me. Nothing did.

'Well, yes, he might have met Mertens there,' said Daniel. 'But whatever Mertens told him or didn't tell him about the wreck of the *Pandora*, she wasn't there…oh, yes, she would have been. Mertens died in 1976 and the earthquake wasn't until 1986. Does that help?'

'Not really. Even if Mertens told Barnabas where the *Pandora* was, and she was still there in 1976, she was gone by 1986, and even that pirate Yanni's partner only found her by chance. And only Petros, I hope you realise, knows where *Pandora* is now. Assuming he took careful notes of his position while he was being buffeted about in freezing water and hauled in blue with cold.'

'Yes, assuming that. We have to lay hands on Petros,' said Daniel. 'And we don't know where he comes from, or where he might be.'

'Other than that, we're laughing. His father was an Albanian, Yanni said. What's the most common Albanian surname?'

'No idea,' said Daniel promptly. 'But I can find out. Let's look at Barnabas again. Does he know where the treasure is?'

'Could be,' I answered. 'Could also be that he didn't know anything about it, and the ephod either came to his hand by chance or was summoned by his treasure ritual. If Luna, there is silver, he said. And there was, before you and your balaclava'd friends pinched it.'

'And you believe in magic,' scoffed Daniel gently.

'You stay around Meroe for too long, you believe against your will,' I told him. 'Remember Kepler's hand?'

'Yes,' said Daniel. 'Yes, that was certainly...unusual. Magical.'

Intellectual honesty is the rarest thing in the world, and my darling Daniel has it. Daniel did not want to believe in anything supernatural, but he had seen Meroe heal Kepler with his own eyes, and he had always believed them, so he did not try to lie or evade. I adored him, completely and suddenly. A blush mounted my breast and made my cheeks flush red. He leaned over and kissed me.

'I love you too,' he said.

'Barnabas as a dupe I can believe,' I said, when I had got some breath back. 'Barnabas as a magician is harder to believe, but I can do it. Barnabas as a crook is easy. All possibles.'

'So,' said Daniel. He set me gently aside and got up. 'I had better go and check out my flat,' he said. 'Get some searches going on my own computers.'

'Report to Saba,' I said.

'Yes,' he agreed. 'He will want to know what we have found out.'

'Give him my best wishes,' I said. I stretched. I was pooped. An hour's nap had just informed me how tired I really was, what with excitement and pirates and car journeys and puzzles.

'Why don't you have an early night,' he suggested. 'I'll be back before you know it. And I'll bring breakfast.'

'If you see Georgie, tell her I haven't come to my senses,' I said to him, and waited until the door shut before I shucked my clothes, bathed my weary bones, and took myself and the cats off for a nice long nap. I had had an exciting day, but now it was over.

I woke knowing that there was more research to do. It was four am and it couldn't be done until the government offices opened so I turned over and went back to sleep, Horatio aiding me in this by lying very close and breathing in my ear. This might have been why I dreamed of lions and goddesses and woke abruptly when someone dropped a cup and said, 'Damn!'

Fortunately it was Daniel. I am not good at mornings and if a burglar dropped in at seven am on a non-working day I could easily just offer him tea and go back to sleep. This might even prove to be a good strategy, of course. It would certainly unbalance the burglar.

But it was coffee and good croissants and cherry jam which awaited me in the complete silence which makes my morning experience golden. Daniel slipped into the bathroom for a shower and a change of clothes; he had certainly not gone to bed. I hoped his flat was free of Georgianas. On the table in front of me was a strange little electronic sort of plug thing. I asked the shaggy wet Daniel who emerged about it.

'It's a bug,' he said. 'It was on my phone. I am about to check yours as soon as I can get that Heckle to give me back my towel.'

'Give the nice man the towel, Heckle,' I said to the cat, who had been dragged bodily out of the bathroom, all claws entangled in it. He then decided that he didn't want the lousy towel anyway and where was the breakfast which was his right under section 34 of the Domestic Animals Treaty 1876?

I laid out food in bowls for everyone and went back to my croissant. Peace reigned once more.

'The animals are getting bored.' Daniel scrubbed at his wet hair with the retrieved towel.

'True, and they can go back to the bakery now,' I realised out loud. I opened the locked door onto my own stairs and both Heckle and Jekyll bolted their breakfast and collided in a furry scrum as they galloped for the magic portal.

'There's a mouse down there with my name on it, says prominent local hunter,' I mused.

'Rat,' said Daniel, listening to clanging and growling. Something tipped over with a crash.

'Rat, hell, that sounds like a full scale hippopotamus. Heckle? What's going on down there?'

Horatio raised an eyebrow, looking interested. I went to the head of the stairs, but all I could locate was Heckle's fluffed-out tail. I descended and saw what he had bailed up against a mixer.

'Daniel?' I said quietly.

'Corinna?'

'There's a snake in my kitchen.'

'So there is,' he said.

'I hate snakes,' I said, frozen to the spot. It wasn't a very big snake, but then it didn't have to be. It had dropped flat and was weaving to and fro, hissing like a kettle. It was patterned in a diamond design of grey and taupe and might have been beautiful if I had been in any state to appreciate it.

'What do we do?' I asked through numb lips.

'We do nothing to interrupt Heckle's concentration,' he told me.

Do nothing, fine, I could do that. I might never move again. I could see that Heckle had all the snake's attention, and I could also see Jekyll sneaking up on it from the side. This was a bit much to ask of the poor moggies. Tough back alley fighters as they were, they might have had to outface dobermans and cranky brushtail possums and cars and (in the case of Jekyll) a street sweeping machine but snakes were surely above the odds. But they seemed to know what they were doing…

With a fast, very violent stroke, Jekyll knocked the snake aside as it struck at Heckle. Heckle leapt on its back and bit down on its neck. I heard a crack.

It wriggled for while, but it was dead. The two fighters batted at the corpse for a few minutes, but lost interest and wandered off to seek for their more usual prey. I unfroze slowly.

'Did you ever read *The Case of the Speckled Band*?' asked Daniel.

'Came between me and sleep for six months.'

'Right. I'll just go and collect the body. Poor snake.'

'Poor snake?' I gasped.

'Yes. It didn't get here on its own ribs, you know. Someone must have brought it here. Someone who doesn't like you,' added Daniel.

'Ribs?' I was bewildered. It was too early in the morning for this sort of thing. I called the cats and rewarded them with extra good green French cat treats, *pour le minou charmant*. They gobbled them down, a little puzzled by my largesse. As far as they were concerned, they had finally managed to get that sneaky thing which had been annoying them, possibly for days. Goddess alone knew how long the snake had been there.

And when Daniel showed me the body, laid out on the dustpan, I was sorry, too, in a way. It had been a lithe, muscular creature with a right to live and very pretty eyes, and now it was belt material.

'Scales on the letterbox opening in the door,' he told me. 'Someone slipped it in from outside in Calico Alley. It's a tiger snake. They get cross.'

'Do you think there was only one?'

'Heckle and Jekyll would know if there was another,' he assured me, which was correct. 'I'll just put it in a bag and we'll show it to the nice policewoman. This is a murder attempt, Corinna, or at least malicious mischief.'

'Oh, come now…' I temporised. Then I considered how I felt about snakes. 'All right. God, I went down this morning to feed the mother of bread…There's some plastic zip-lock bags in the drawer. What's this?'

'Your warning,' guessed Daniel as I picked up a sheet of paper from the floor.

'How do you know? Have you read it?'

'I don't need to,' he told me, sacking the snake. 'No one would send a snake through the letterbox and not a warning.'

'Right. It says "leave us alone bitch". Not very imaginative and short on information. Leave who alone? There are so many contenders.'

'Anything on the back?'

'Just a couple of smears.' I sniffed. 'Smells vaguely eucalyp-tussy. An athlete, perhaps, or someone with a really bad cold. Damn it,' I said to Daniel, 'I'm going to make some bread. Just for Insula. Just because I can. And because whoever sent this poor doomed reptile doesn't want me to.'

'Good,' he said. 'I'll join you when I've made a few phone calls.'

I put on the smallest mixer and began to make my special favourite bread, seven seeds. This requires the baker to sit and pour seeds through her fingers to ensure a perfect mix. It is a picky, finicky job, just perfect for the aftermath of a shock. This was what I was made for, I thought, measuring poppy seed and fennel and caraway and coriander and cracked wheat. I am a baker. Not an investigator. Not an accountant anymore. Just someone with a feeling for yeast and silence.

Squeaks announced that the rats had seen our little holiday as a chance to recolonise. They were now being evicted. Also heading for a dreadful doom, for everyone else in the alley used poison. But there were a lot of dreadful dooms around and the mixer was throbbing, the dough waiting, and I thrust all philosophy aside and began to make bread. Then I was hit with a revelation.

I knew what I had to do to make some sense out of the Salonika treasure problem. If I was right, the scheme was so clever that it took my breath away. Someone with serious commercial sense had devised it. I could not see Barnabas as a businessman. Really not. A guru, yes, a con man, yes, a bad influence, certainly. But a capitalist? He didn't have the right kind of mind. Who, amongst the cast, did? I thought idly about people as I added the oats and the rye berries. There was a lovely scent of warm meadows from my sacks. Scottish meadows, I thought, purple heavens with larks, fields of raffish barley running down to the salmon river. When I made olive bread I thought of cerulean Greek skies and white churches and olive trees with their roots in the sea. Bread is as romantic as I get.

Then it was time to leave everything to rise. I took up the phone and rang Jason. He arrived quickly. I noticed that his hands were ornamented with a lot of bandaids.

'Carpentry went well, then?' I asked.

'Got it together in the end,' he replied ruefully. 'Bloody thing! I reckon Mrs. Dawson's right, the instructions were in Hindi. Though the Prof reckoned it was Chaldean. But I'm not going to tackle another one of those things any time soon, since I got away with all my fingers. What's up? We trading again?'

'Special order,' I told him. 'I want you to do a few trays of your absolutely best muffins.'

'Sure,' he said affably. He changed into his best overalls, and lit the oven.

I went off an hour later, leaving him to mind the bread. I needed information and I knew just where to get it. On the doorstep I encountered Kylie and Gossamer. They were dressed for the street, meaning they had on several garments, however skimpy. They looked tired.

'Corinna! Jason said it was all right about the bakery!' they exclaimed.

I hefted my box. 'Yes, everything's fine now,' I said, suppressing all news about snakes and treasure.

'We can come back next week,' Kylie informed me.

'Because our bit of the soap is finished,' added Goss.

'But they've got us on their list now and the casting director said he'd call us again.'

'Wonderful!' I congratulated them.

'When we put on a little weight,' said Kylie. 'Is Jason cooking muffins?'

I laughed as I went down Flinders Lane. It was going to be an interesting day.

Chapter Nineteen

I obtained my information and walked back, past Best Fresh, which was still festooned with quarantine tape, thinking. Tonight was Hallowe'en, All Hallow's Eve, Soaling Night, and Jason was, on Meroe's orders, making soul cakes which would be free of any ingredients except spice, sugar, dried fruit, flour and yeast. Tonight we ought to be able to clear up the mystery of the Salonika treasure. I just needed a few more bits of information, and I was reasonably sure that between them the witches and Daniel could provide them.

The bakery was redolent with spices. Jason was just breaking open a soul cake and examining the crumb.

'Pretty good,' he said critically, handing me half.

It was a flattish bun about the size of my palm. The crumb was perfect, moist but not soggy. I bit and chewed. Terrific. 'Wonderful,' I told him.

'Rest of them along in a couple of hours,' he said, and I left to seek out Daniel. He had gathered all his papers together into one heap and was looking as if what he really wanted was a flame-thrower.

'Fear not, I think I've worked most of it out,' I said. 'Has the lovely Ms. Bray left me a message about the drugged cakes?'

'Yes,' he said. 'They're baking powder, not yeast.'

'Good. Jason is making the soul cakes, the real ones,' I said. 'The ceremony for Samhain is tonight. I am going to see to a few other things—can you mind the phone? By the way, is mine tapped?'

'No,' he told me.

'Right.'

'Where are you going?' he asked.

'To see Janelle.'

'But she's in Bendigo.'

'I think she'll be back by now.'

'Ah,' he said.

And, being Daniel, he didn't ask me any questions. He just shuffled the papers, sighed, extracted his mobile from under Horatio, and began making calls.

I took a tram. I wasn't in a hurry. The witches were all partaking of a picnic in the park when I found them. It was a beautiful, warm, smoky day. Perfect for lazing about on a suitable lawn and watching someone more energetic play.

The acolytes were engaged in a game which involved standing in a moving double ring and flinging a bean bag at someone on the other side. You then kissed the target person to massed giggles. Most of the players were girls, but I noticed the dark and dangerous Cypress there, with his slimmer, paler friend Cedar. All of them showed signs of recent illumination, a Celtic bracelet around one upper arm. It didn't look too bad, actually. I wondered how much it hurt.

Lying in state under a tree was Barnabas, attended by three maidens. One was combing his beard. One was kissing his mouth. One was tickling his belly, and if that wasn't what she was doing, I did not intend to carry my observation any further. He lifted his eyes and saw me. Beautiful brown eyes, soft as a deer's. Sensitive eyes. I dragged myself out of them.

'Hello, Barnabas,' I said cheerily. 'Preparing for the big event tonight?'

'Indeed,' he said, freeing one hand and reaching it out to me. 'You will be there?'

'Wouldn't miss it,' I answered.

The maidens were dressed just as his website required: transparent blouses and short skirts. They looked curiously dated. And their eyes were not clear. They were dazed or fogged, drugged perhaps with real chemicals or else blissed out on Barnabas, and either way I did not envy them. He gave me a smile which hovered next to cruel as he contemplated them. Not a nice man, that Barnabas…

The dancers moved, throwing their bean bag. It whizzed through the ranks and I caught it by reflex.

'Choose! Choose!' they chorused, and Barnabas rose like a grampus on one elbow. I would rather have kissed that poor dead snake. I didn't want to cause a scene and I needed someone else to kiss. Male, for preference.

'You,' I said to Cedar, and he approached me. He was half naked. His bare chest was almost hairless and a little plasma trickled from his new tattoo. The boy surrendered his mouth willingly. It was soft and pliable and warm. He tasted very young. His eyes were brown and unfocused. I felt suddenly revolted, as though I had taken advantage of him. I pushed him gently away.

And flinched as I intercepted a full strength glare of hatred from Cypress which ought to have acid-etched his name on my retinas. I did not like these games.

I found Janelle, cut her out from the herd, and the interview went much as I expected. Then I caught a tram home.

Daniel was pacing. He did this very elegantly, but he was pacing nonetheless.

'There you are! Jason says that all the soul cakes are made and Meroe is asking you to call.'

'Then let's call,' I said, taking his hand. 'Your Saba, he needs to know that the matter will come to a head tonight, on the foreshore. At the Samhain ceremony.'

'I think he might have guessed that,' said Daniel, 'but I'll convey the message.'

'And you might have a few of your fellow raiders lounging around looking inconspicuous.'

'That, too, can be managed.'

We were both preserving a straight face. I wasn't going to share any information and neither was he.

'Well, then,' I said meaninglessly, and we went down the stairs to the Sibyl's Cave.

There we met Selene, Celeste, Belladonna and Meroe, which was the full complement for such a small shop. They were all sampling soul cakes and seemed more cheerful.

'Just tonight, then it will all be over,' I heard Serena say, poking at her straggling bun. 'And those idiots will be going back to their lairs, and we can go home to ours.'

'Blessed be,' sighed Meroe, and caught sight of me. 'Corinna! These cakes are wonderful.'

'Jason is a very good baker,' I said. 'Meroe, whose idea was it to hold the ceremony on the foreshore at Williamstown?'

'Barnabas,' she told me. 'But it's a good idea. It's wilder there than any part of the bay nearer the city, and fewer houses overlook it. I don't fancy taking off my clothes on Elwood beach.'

'No,' I agreed. 'Do you, in fact, have to take off your clothes?'

'Not for Samhain, no,' she said. 'Stands to reason. Back in the old country, it's autumn. No sense in having one's whole coven contracting pneumonia. But here it's spring.'

'And there are midges. And sandflies. I'd keep my skirt on.'

'A hint?' she asked, eyes very bright.

'Just a little one. What did you want with me? Daniel said you sent a message?'

'Yes, I did. Have you solved the soul cake mystery?'

'Yes,' I said. 'Well, sort of solved.'

'Is it safe to go on with the ceremony?'

'Probably,' I temporised.

'Oh, very definite,' said Daniel.

'So you have done better?' Meroe asked him.

He looked down through his fringed lashes. 'No. Probably is the best I could say, too.'

'Then we shall trust in the Goddess, and proceed,' said Meroe.

'See you tonight,' I said, and we went out.

Then we put ourselves to bed and made love and slept and made love, because there was nothing else that the world needed us for, which was wonderful.

It was darkening and cooling and we put on dark warm garments. Whatever the witches did, I wasn't going to be taking off any clothes unless I had to. Daniel and I both wore jeans and a dark blue pullover. I went down to the shop and noticed that the admirable Jason had cleaned up after his muffin making. The Mouse Police were asleep on their old flour sacks again. They had enjoyed their foray into gracious living but they clearly didn't want to stay there. I stuffed a lot of things which might become useful into my backpack and we went out into the street where Timbo waited to convey us back to Williamstown.

'Strange little place, Williamstown,' commented Daniel. 'It was the first settlement in Melbourne, you know, but they moved to the Yarra bank because there wasn't enough fresh water here. It's always been an odd backwater, very sure of itself, very superior. A little island of civilisation in the industrial west.'

'Gentility, you mean. Civilisation is a lot to boast of, even for as pretty a place as this.'

'So it is,' he agreed amicably.

I was keyed up and snappy. Facts and semi-facts were whirling around in my head and I was grumpy with possibilities. We arrived far too soon at a park which ran down to a flattish rocky prominence. Through it ran a bicycle path. It was very plain and ordinary.

Except that it was populated with witches. I tried to recall what Meroe had told me about Samhain. Descent into darkness, she had said. The beginning of winter. A time to reflect, to consider, to put all things in order for the contemplations and endurance of the long cold. And a time to play games, sing songs, play tricks, the last light-hearted chaos before the sobriety of the cold. In this hemisphere, of course, it was spring, but I had enough to think about without bothering my head about philosophy. Time, also, to talk to the dead. So how was this picnic going to go?

'Into rings!' exclaimed one woman, and the crowd began to move, forming into fairy rings like I had when I had unwisely ventured on folk dancing. There was a drummer, a fiddle player and a harp, and they all began to play a jolly, bouncy tune.

And round and round and round they went, hand in hand, hair flying, skirts floating. Barnabas and his girls danced. Selene and Celeste danced. Old women danced. Even Cypress and Cedar danced. Daniel and I crept under a thrawn tree to be out of the way.

The music went on, the dances continued. It grew fully dark and a bonfire was lit, and the strings of women began to circle it. I was watching the sky for the rising moon when I became aware of a change in the music. It became slower, sadder, a dirge. A lone voice called out a name: Alice! Then another—Jeanette— and another. Eugenia. Bindi. Isabel. Lizbeth. Agnes. Running under the names was a prayer.

'We commend unto the Goddess of many names these our sisters who have left us, and beg that they may speak one more time, here in the darkness before the descent, here on the grass by the sea which estranges us, here in the dark: speak, speak, speak.'

My job was to watch, and I watched, but I felt the longing pulling at me, the loss, the desire to hear just once more a loved voice which was now stilled forever. On the light salt wind they pleaded, the witches, for one word, one breath, from beyond, and called the names of the dead into the gathering darkness, their words going up like showers of sparks from the bonfire. Now, just on the cusp of the year, when the veils between the worlds were thin, the ghosts might reach through with their cold fingers and touch the world of the living once more.

'Hear now the names of the Goddess, she who is all, Hecate Queen of Witches, Great Mother, Isis, Artemis, Aphrodite, Diana, Melusine, Arianrhod,' announced Meroe. 'We gather here to dance and sing in her honour and remember our dead. If there is a spirit here, speak to your sisters! For now we dance the great circle, and any who will may come to us.'

She followed the next witch, and they snaked into a circle around the fire, and as they moved they shed garments and took hands again. Firelight glinted on their sweating skin, hot on shoulders, gilding breasts and arms. Daniel gasped and drew back under the tree. I leaned forward, fascinated. I was being dragged into the dance. He put a hand on my thigh, and it seemed as heavy and cold as a toad.

There were my sisters, free in the darkness, and I could feel their power building. Between the dancers and the fire two figures now appeared. One was crowned with the moon, tall and masked, bare breasted and female. The other was huge and male and he wore a horned mask.

'Cernunnos!' the witches named him. 'Hail Cernunnos! Hail the horned man!'

The music stopped. The dancers slumped down in their circle. Around them came servers carrying baskets of soul cakes and cups of wine. I took one of each. The wine was good red chateau collapseau. The soul cakes were just as Jason had made them. The witches feasted and wiped their faces with their flying hair. The circle was, however, unbroken. No one left it. They rested and feasted for perhaps half an hour while the figures in the centre stood unmoving.

They were dressed, I noted, as witches, with the witch's tools: cup, wand, cords and athame. I knew that this was a knife, though it was customarily blunt, used for ceremonial cutting only. Cernunnos was Barnabas. I knew that belly. He was very dominant with his horn-crowned head and jutting beard. If anything else was jutting, I didn't care to discover. Beside him the Goddess was masked in silver paint. Her breasts were perfect, neither a girl's nor a woman's, beautiful and somehow unreal. The music continued, thumping and ringing, as the witches feasted and their gods stood motionless, awaiting their worship.

The witches then got up, shaking off sand and crumbs, and the circle began to move again. The moment I had been expecting came. The Goddess turned to the God and they, too, began to dance around each other. It was awful in the proper sense:

creating awe. But there was something wrong. I strained my eyes. That knife—wasn't it rather shiny for an athame? Shiny not as to the jewelled hilt, but as to the flame along the blade? Wasn't it, rather, as sharp as a razor? And wasn't this the culmination of the ceremony? A dreadful premonition hit me like a blow. I shook Daniel's hand off my thigh and leapt to my feet. I wanted to scream but I didn't seem to have any breath and no one would have heard me over the music and the chanting. I was about to see murder done and I had to prevent it. There was death on the wind tonight.

I saw the flash of steel, dived through the dance and brought the Queen of Witches down with as good a rugby tackle as any All Black could have boasted of. We hit the ground hard, fighting.

The dance halted. I knelt on the woman and pried at the knife in her hands, and she fought like a maddened beast. Meroe came to us, wrenched the knife from her and threw it away, then slung her by main force of outrage out of the circle, harvesting her crown and mask as the assailant flew. Then she put them on and grabbed the horned man by the shoulders and shook him.

'Dance!' she ordered in a penetrating voice. I was still struggling with a shrieking, scratching fury. 'The rite shall not be broken by unbelievers. We call on our dead to protect us, our Goddess to stand by us, her law is love of all things! We shall sing and dance and make music, for all is joy in the presence of the Mother, and her power is in the earth and the sea!'

And the music started again, and the great circle moved, and Meroe stood proud as Queen of Witches, her crown on her shiny black hair, her face transformed by the rising moon into a silver mask of uncommon beauty and power.

Meanwhile I had managed to drag my captive to the tree, where Daniel sat on her and I searched her for any more weapons. Black clad figures had flitted through the servers, arresting various persons. We put our prisoner into a hard armlock and stumbled her away to the waiting house where all was to be revealed, and as I went I was pleased that it had worked, and that I had been right, but oh, the music and the singing and the dance, it dragged at my heart.

Someone—Saba, I supposed—had borrowed quite a large house on the hill overlooking the ceremonial ground. We shoved our swearing captive inside and three young men took her away from us, which was a mercy, because her long nails had ripped furrows in my ribs and she had made a spirited attempt to gouge one of my eyes out. Daniel had been kicked and was limping.

Inside was a large hall, full of people and lights, and I felt bewildered—I had been down in the Samhain dark so recently. A door opened into a cosy library where a large man was sitting in an easy chair, a cigar in his mouth, a small glass of port in his hand.

'In here, dollink,' said a familiar voice. I should have known.

'You're Saba?'

'Three times over,' said Uncle Solly, grinning. 'You did good! Now Sarah will get you some first aid and some clothes and maybe a drink and we will sit down with the bad guys and make them tell us all about it. You did good, *metuka*,' he said gently, touching a finger to my bloodied brow. 'You too, Daniel. You're a good boy. I'll tell your mother, if you like.'

'Please don't,' Daniel begged. 'She'd only think I have been doing something dangerous.'

Sarah was a short plump cheerful girl with a full first aid kit and very sure hands. 'You're shocked,' she told me. 'Here's sweet tea. Drink it while I have a look at these scratches. She must have had steel reinforced claws. Still, not too deep, no need for a stitch and she missed your eye.'

I drank the tea while she cleaned and patched my wounds and gave me a new blue windcheater to wear, in just my size, which argues that someone had done some good staff work. I was ushered back into the library where Uncle Solly held court. The nephews and cousins were there, all dressed in black. There was Janelle, and Eddie, and our captive, who had been tied to a convenient chair. There was Cypress and Cedar, sneering. Uncle Solly gave me a small glass of neat cognac and I sat down next to Daniel, who was looking as though someone had roughly scrubbed him and dressed him again without drying him. He was ruffled and gorgeous.

'It was such a good idea,' said Solly, in his warm, delighted voice. 'So clever, *nu*? Find the treasure, yes, the good Petros did that, out with that old pirate Yanni. He could find it again, too. Grease enough palms and play the weather right and a clever diver could salvage the treasure. Ballast a boat with gold coins, yes, and the stolen gems.'

'Petros?' I asked.

'Rocky,' groaned Daniel. Cypress lifted a lip in his direction.

'Cypress,' he said. Cedar pressed closer to him, wondering what was happening, shivering. Cypress put an arm around him. 'All right. I found the treasure that the old man didn't dare go back for. I dragged it up off the seabed.'

'Brave,' said Solly admiringly. 'Then what?'

'Barnabas came and talked to me about it. I don't know how he knew. He was looking for the treasure too, had an old map. I bought a boat in Greece and Cedar and me and a student sailed her here—took us three months but we brought it here,' he said, trying to look at the bound prisoner's face. 'I slid her into a boatyard in the dark, between two bright lights, when even the seabirds were sleeping and the sea was as flat as a plate. No one saw us. Then we scooped the gold out from under the ballast leads, a handful at a time, and Cedar took it to Bendigo in his backpack. That's all she said we had to do. We did it. One-third of it is ours.'

'No,' said Solly. 'It belongs to the dead, Cypress. The murdered ones who died in despair, calling on God. Who did not answer. Can't you hear their voices wailing on the wind?'

Cedar shuddered and clung to Cypress. Their naked skin slid together.

Solly considered them. 'I got an offer for you,' he said, 'because you didn't hurt anyone, you just brought the treasure home. I'll give you money—not a third of the treasure, but enough. You go north, eh? Where you have always wanted to go. Set up a little diving school in Cairns, say?'

'And in return?' the strong face twisted.

'In return, you say nothing, eh? I let you go, you say nothing, you take your friend out of here, this is not a good place for him, and go home and pack. *Navarino* isn't yours, it's not a good boat anyway, you can buy better in the tropics. I got tickets,' said Solly, taking them from a table and fanning them out. 'Tickets, travelling money, settlement. You leave tomorrow. What say?'

There was a pause. Cypress looked at the sum offered. Yossi coughed. I scratched my sticking plaster. Then Cypress grinned, a wild, bold, flashing grin. 'Deal,' he said.

He took the documents, hefted Cedar, and Yossi led them out. We heard the front door close and a car drive away. Then the silence crept back. I could hear the sea again. I thought of Chrysoula, who could not sleep without hearing the sea.

'You, Corinna,' Saba said. 'Tell us about the soul cakes.'

'They were *pain maudit*,' I said. 'Meant to send people mad. They were never meant to be loosed on the streets. Someone thought they'd make a little extra money. They weren't made with yeast, which takes time and skill. They were made with baking powder and ready after half an hour's work with an unoccupied oven. They were meant to cover up a murder, and it was a really good idea, if unbelievably ruthless.'

'Janelle?' asked Uncle Solly.

'No, it wasn't Janelle,' I said. My head ached. I extended my glass for another cognac. 'Janelle knows all about manipulative men. It suited her to hang out with Barnabas' girls, but she was never taken in by him.'

'The witches were nice to me,' stated Janelle firmly. 'After all those years with Mum, do you think I am going to go with a big fat crook like Barnabas? Not a chance,' she said. I could have applauded.

'And what about Mr. Wyatt?' Daniel asked.

'Or him,' she said. 'I'm going to Sydney with Celeste. She says she can give me a job and there's a spare room in her house. She runs a tea shop. I'll be all right,' she said.

'So you will,' said Uncle Solly, nodding at Sarah, who escorted Janelle out. 'Go back to the festival now, and the Goddess bless you—sorry, Lord,' he addressed the heavens. 'So was it you, then?'

Eddie Ramsgate was pushed forward. He hung his head. His pimples glowed like traffic lights.

'She gave me the recipe and told me to bake them,' he said. 'I did as she said. She kissed me,' he added. I was suddenly very sorry for Eddie. Beautiful women wouldn't have kissed him a lot. And never would again, unless he won Tattslotto.

'Eddie didn't mean any harm,' said Daniel. 'At least, he didn't know he was going to do any harm. He's sorry.'

'And he wanted the money for…?' asked Uncle Solly.

'His mum,' I said.

'It was her,' protested Eddie, pointing to the prisoner. 'She gave me the mix and told me to make cakes with it. I didn't know there was any harm in them. She said they would be drugged, and Mum says people buy drugs at nightclubs, so I went along and sang the soul song.'

'You sang it?' I demanded.

He looked hurt. 'My mum's got all Fairport's records, and Pentangle, and the others,' he said, and began to sing: 'Soul cake, a soul cake, please kind missus a soul cake, an apple, a pear, a plum or a cherry, any fine thing to make us all merry, one for Peter, one for Paul, one for him as made us all,' in a fine, clear tenor.

'Well, blow me down,' said Daniel.

'Me, too,' I commented.

'Eddie, you did the wrong thing,' said Uncle Solly, 'but you're a good boy and we'll say no more about it. Now off you go to your mum, and stay away from bad company.'

'Okay,' said Eddie. He left. I had no idea whether he had understood any of the proceedings.

Uncle Solly poured himself another glass of port and relit his cigar. 'Tell us more, *metuka*,' he said to me.

'About the soul cakes? She must have been here for weeks. They were meant to drive the Samhain ceremony mad,' I said.

'They were meant to send everyone out on a trip, and cover up the murder of Barnabas by his—'

'Daughter,' shrieked the prisoner.

Georgiana Hope, nee Esperance, had not taken defeat well. Her eyes were wild, her hair torn, her face scratched. She was still beautiful, but beautiful like a mannequin, not like a human. The bones were perfect. The animating spirit was evil. It was Samhain, and some of the cold reek of death seemed to rise from Georgiana. Of course, we might have just dragged her through some stagnant marsh. I clung to the view that it was swamp water.

'Barnabas is your father?' asked Daniel.

'He deserted us,' she said. 'He left us in utter poverty. My mother worked herself to death to keep me and my little brother. And you've let Cedar go with that pirate! I'll never see him again!'

'The fate of many,' said Uncle Solly. 'You decided to kill him? When did you find him again?'

'Years and years ago,' she said sullenly. 'I found him on the web. Him and his acolytes and his girls, and my mother wearing her hands to the bone scrubbing floors so that I could go to school in one good dress! I worked hard, I won scholarships, I ran businesses, but she was never happy with me, she always said it should have been Cedric that had the business mind and he could rescue our fortunes. Even after I rescued them she was never content...'

'So when Cedar met Cypress...?' I hinted

'He told me about the treasure. Barnabas had been in Germany and got some sort of map from the original thief. But Cypress had actually found the gold. Idiots. They were thinking of trying to sell it in Europe, where every transaction is supervised by some Jew. They would have been caught instantly.'

She sat up against her bonds and Yossi pushed the ragged hair back from her face. The goddess' silver make-up was smeared across her shoulders and neck and fanned into her ears. She looked lopsided, grotesque.

'A drink, maybe?' asked Solly.

'I won't drink with you, filthy Jew,' she spat at him.

'Ah well, then, you can go thirsty,' he shrugged.

'Drink with me,' I said. 'I am in awe of your commercial acumen.'

She snarled at me, the rosebud mouth twisting over white canines. But she accepted water from me and sipped at it without actually trying to bite my hands.

'What commercial acumen?' asked Uncle Solly.

'Uncle, give me one of your cigars.' I had been off cigarettes for a long time but the scent of that Cuban cigar was more than I could bear. I took it and lit it and blew out a stream of smoke. Wonderful. I was immediately dizzy. 'The soul cakes were just personal revenge. But we had the same problem—didn't we, Daniel?—thinking why bring the treasure to Australia, and how is it to be sold? And the answer was so clever. What is Australia known for? Minerals. You set up a mining company in, as it might be, Bendigo, where there is still plenty of gold under the ground, and then you set up a nice little smelter and...'

'Melt it down,' said Sarah, clasping her hands in front of her bosom. 'Oh, that is clever.'

'It's exactly the same as laundering money,' I said. 'But heavier and harder, of course.'

'How did you find out?' asked Daniel.

'I asked the Benson wunderkind on the stock exchange to swap me some names of directors for Jason's muffins.'

'Nice,' Uncle Solly approved. '*Nu*, what are we to do with you, eh? You have killed one person and injured others, though that was not your intention. You have corrupted several people. You have tried to kill Corinna's business.'

'Why did you want Earthly Delights so much?' I asked.

'Because it's yours and you love it,' she snapped.

'And the snake?'

'What snake?'

'I know you sent it,' I told her. 'There was a smudge of bush spices on the back of the threatening letter. And your signature scent. Poison.'

'A little present,' she sneered, giving up.

Solly sipped his port and spoke again: 'But you didn't actually do too much harm, and you have been instrumental in retrieving most of the treasure of Salonika. We have seized the office of the company in Bendigo and the boat, and of course the stash in Williamstown. Pity that clumsy Cedar dropped things like the ephod out of his backpack while he was unloading, eh?'

'Idiots,' muttered Georgiana Hope.

'We could call the cops,' said Uncle Solly.

'And I could tell all about you and Mossad,' said Georgie.

'No you couldn't, because it is well known that Mossad does not exist,' said Uncle Solly. 'I run a deli. All of the local policemen eat there. I do not think you would be believed. But here is a problem,' he appealed to the room. 'What do we do with her, eh?'

'I know a real deep pool,' said Yossi.

This idea, I had to admit, had great appeal to me. This bitch of a woman had tried to ruin my business, steal my Daniel, had corrupted poor Eddie and been responsible for one death and several irreparable injuries. I had not forgotten the young man with no hands.

'I like that idea,' I said.

'You would,' she said, cold as venom. 'You've got it all, haven't you? You've got Daniel.'

'You could have had him too, you saw him first,' I told her. 'You only wanted him because I had him.'

'I never wanted him at all,' she said slowly.

'No?' I arched an eyebrow. It hurt. I stopped arching it.

'I wanted Saba,' she said. 'And Danny knew who Saba was.'

'Ach, no, now, now,' said Uncle Solly. 'Suddenly this moves from being a treasure hunt with added spleen to a nasty political thing, *nu?*'

'Oh, yes,' she said.

'In that case,' said Saba, 'Yossi, where is your pool?'

'No, really,' I protested.

Every pair of eyes in the room looked at me in surprise. I felt myself in an alien universe. Surely they didn't mean to kill her?

'What are you going to do?' I asked.

'You want to know?' Uncle Solly smiled at me.

'Yes,' I said. 'On balance, I am involved in this, I want to know.'

'We put her on the plane to London tomorrow,' he said. 'She is now someone else's problem.'

'I won't go,' she said.

'You will,' I replied. 'Or Senior Constable Bray will hear all about the soul cakes. You wouldn't like an Australian jail. It would be full of Australians. Goodbye,' I said, suddenly so tired I couldn't keep my eyes open. 'We will never meet again.'

'And that will be too soon,' she said wearily.

Daniel put an arm round my shoulders. Georgiana Hope closed her eyes. Outside, a car was waiting, and the witches were singing songs to the descending moon. I wanted to go home. So I went home.

Chapter Twenty

I had made all my arrangements very carefully. Jason and I had scrubbed Earthly Delights throughout, using sugar soap, in case so much as a snake scale remained of our recent history. Meroe had visited with the news that Barnabas had died suddenly; a heart attack, she said.

'In the old days,' she told me, speaking slowly, 'one member of the coven used to go naked, that is, ungreased, in the snow at Samhain.'

'They'd die!' I protested.

'Yes,' she agreed. 'Of exposure. One volunteer to explain to the Goddess that we still loved her and worshipped her and needed her help.'

'That's sick,' commented Jason, who had been listening. I still hadn't sorted out when 'sick' was an approving comment and when it meant what I usually meant by it.

'Better a volunteer than a sacrifice,' Meroe told him. He took a pace backwards and fell over his mop.

'Yes, all right, agreed,' I said, helping my apprentice up. 'Are you saying that Barnabas was such a volunteer?'

'No, I think the Goddess took him,' said Meroe.

'I can't congratulate her on her choice of consorts.'

'He won't be a consort,' said Meroe wolfishly. 'He'll be lucky if he gets to—'

'Mop floors?' asked my irrepressible Jason, ducking out of cuffing range.

We did not comment further. Meroe had censed the entire place, and we now had a talisman in the bakery and an angel in the shop. I had risen at three to begin the baking, and the bread was rising like a revolution. The girls had put on their prettiest frocks, Jason had clean overalls, and the Mouse Police had been given treats, that apply-between-the-shoulderblades flea treatment, and new collars. They were presently engaged in attempting to remove their bows, which Kylie had tied very securely on said collars. Blue for Heckle and green for Jekyll. Went very nicely with their black and white colour scheme. Horatio had a new royal blue collar from which the intrusive bell had been removed.

Outside in the alley the cobbles had been soused and swept free of any biological debris. The gas-fired barbecue was all fired up. The paper plates, the ketchup, the onions and the French mustard were all available. Therese Webb, in a hand-embroidered calico apron, stood behind the grill with an array of sausages. The shutters were up, the lights on, the door open, the till supplied with its float. Bread steamed on the racks. Jason's muffins sat lightly on the glass shelves. Earthly Delights was reopening with a sausage sizzle. If only someone would come.

Daniel munched on the first beef and tomato sausage and said, 'It's very early yet. Have a sausage, they're good.'

'Not hungry,' I replied. 'Hello, Meroe!'

'Blessed be,' she said. 'Are those leek and cheese? Cook one for me, Therese?'

'Right you are,' said Therese.

Around us the city was waking up. It was past All Saints Day, clean washed of ghosts. Spirits had gone back to their haunts, veils had closed. And I was back where I belonged. I hoped.

Mrs. Dawson, returned from her daily walk, accepted a pork sausage with onions and bought a loaf and two muffins. The Professor liked weisswurst with mustard. Mistress Dread demanded chili. Kylie and Goss nibbled away at a lo-fat sausage which Daniel had found somewhere, and the sun came up, at last, at last, on a lot of people who wanted to buy my bread.

I was swamped. When Kepler was observed trying a sausage and not immediately spitting it out, for he was very polite, I barely had time to giggle. Therese was relieved by Daniel, who took over the barbecue and the apron, in which he looked quite chic. I barely had time for a word with Vin Wyatt.

'Going back to Shep,' he said. 'That's where I came from. Got a new job with a mate at Kentucky Fried for Eddie. Janelle's gone to Sydney. The franchise is closing Best Fresh, so your competition is gone, Corinna. Bloke I know grows pigs. Needs a partner who can cook for all his workers. Always liked pigs,' he said, biting into his sausage and walking away.

Muffins, cakes, slices grew legs and walked out. And the demand for sausages continued. Trudi liked the lamb and rosemary ones. So did Lucifer, once he was persuaded not to try immolation on a pyre. Cherie Holliday bought her father a ferocious chili sausage as a hangover cure. All my favourite people were supporting me and so were my customers. Mr. Benson sent his PA for his usual muffins. Everyone was pleased that Earthly Delights was open again and after a while we ran out of bread and it just became a street party. Jason was sent to the Pandamuses' for more food and came back with a message.

'Yai Yai says, did you find them? And are they punished?'

'Yes and yes,' I said. He ran back with the news and returned with a heavy load of Greek kebabs to grill.

In the middle of it, someone delivered me a large box of Heavenly Pleasures chocolates. With it came a note in the same hand as my other mysterious gifts: *I thought you needed a treat, and perhaps your young man needed a rival. I would be him, if I was twenty years younger. With love, Dion.* I sought out my Professor and kissed him.

When Uncle Solly strolled down the lane we were just running out of everything at last. It was past one o'clock. The shop was empty. Jason was sweeping away crumbs and wrappers and I was sitting on a chair in the bakery door, overwhelmed with joy and relief. He grinned at me.

'All right, dollink?'

'All right,' I said. 'Have a sausage, Saba?'

'Don't mind if I do,' he said, indicating a chicken one. 'You don't need to worry,' he told me. 'You did the right thing, you and that Daniel of yours. A good boy, no matter what his mother says.'

'What will happen to Georgiana?' I asked.

'I don't know,' he said. 'But she is gone now. And everything's back to normal, *nu?*'

I looked around. The bread was sold, tomorrow's mix was already started, the shop was clean, the business was booming, and all around were smiling faces. I had come very near to losing all the things I valued and I valued them more now that I knew how very much I would miss them. I grinned up at the man who did not come from Mossad.

'Yes,' I said. 'It's all right now.'

Afterword

Strange as it may seem, almost the whole story of Max Mertens and the Salonika treasure is true. You can Google it. It will be one of those stranger-than-fiction moments for you, as it was for me. I'm sorry that I cannot name the people who told me about Greece and the Shoah, but they were adamant about this.

Sources

For Greece and the Holocaust
Isser Harel, *The House on Garibaldi Street*, Corgi, London, 1985
Anne Michaels, *Fugitive Pieces*, Bloomsbury Press, London, 1997
Nicholas Stavroulakis, *The Jews of Greece,* Talos Press, Athens, 1990
Various documents and displays from the Jewish Museum, Athens, Greece.
Personal reminiscences told to the author by persons who wish not to be named but are greatly thanked.

For boats and boating
Many thanks to Greg Blunt of Blunt's Boatyard, a Williamstown institution.

For magic of any kind
Dion Fortune, *Psychic Self-Defence*, Samuel Weiser Inc, Maine, 1997 (first printed 1930)
Michale Streeter, *Witchcraft: A Secret History*, Quarto, London, 2002

For ergot poisoning and the most recent outbreak in Europe
John G Fuller, *The Day of St. Anthony's Fire*, Hutchison, London, 1969

Recipes

Mary Phillipou's Wonder Cake

This is a fantastic recipe. As long as you keep the proportions balanced you can make any kind of cake, using fruit, dried fruit, nuts, chocolate, lemon or orange peel, grated carrot, mashed banana, spices—whatever you like. As long as the additions include one cup of chocolate bits, it will rise very reliably. I like that in a cake.

2 eggs
1 cup caster sugar
300 ml cream
1 teaspoon vanilla essence
1 3/4 cups self raising flour, sifted
1 cup frozen berries
1 cup white chocolate bits

Grease a 20 cm baking tin and line it with baking paper.
Preheat the oven to 180 degrees.
Beat the eggs and sugar together until thick. Add the cream and vanilla essence and mix well. Add the sifted flour and fold in until the mixture is smooth. Fold in the berries and chocolate bits.
Pour the mixture into the prepared tin and cook for approximately 50 minutes. It's cooked when a skewer inserted in the

middle comes out clean. Allow the cake to cool in the tin, then turn it out and dust with icing sugar or top with your favourite icing.

Yum.

Boiled Chocolate Cake

From the same admirable source, for when you unexpectedly have a children's party arriving on your doorstep or a lot of relatives who didn't mention that they were on their way...

4 tablespoons butter
3/4 cup caster sugar
1/4 cup drinking chocolate powder (milk)
1/4 teaspoon bicarb of soda
1/4 cup of water
1/2 cup of milk
1 egg
1 1/2 cups self raising flour

Preheat oven to 180 degrees.

Grease a 20 cm cake tin and line it with baking paper. Combine the butter, sugar, chocolate, bicarb of soda, water and milk in a saucepan. Stir and bring to the boil. Take off the stove. Allow to cool to room temperature. Add the egg and flour and mix well. Pour into the prepared tin and bake for about 30 minutes. It's cooked when a skewer inserted in the middle comes out clean.

Allow the cake to cool before icing.

Icing

2 cups pure icing sugar
3 tablespoons milk chocolate powder
Melted butter
Milk

Mix together the chocolate powder and enough melted butter and milk to make it smooth—about a teaspoon of each to start, then add more little by little until the paste is sturdy but not stiff.

Ice cake when cold. A studding of smarties is always popular. Or hundreds and thousands. Or grated chocolate.

You can make a grown-up version of this for a very fast and impressive dessert cake by using baking cocoa or grated dark cooking chocolate instead of milk chocolate powder. When the cake is cool pour over it a tablespoon or two of Kahlua, rum or brandy and then either ready-made chocolate syrup or chocolate ganache, made by melting equal quantities of good dark chocolate and cream in a microwave. Add a handful of glacé cherries or candied peel or sugared violets or walnuts and serve with heavy cream and strawberries.

It's a flexible recipe. Play with variations on one of those cold dark Sunday afternoons when you feel like cooking and your undeserving household is watching the cricket/football. If the experiment fails, they still have to eat it. And like it.

Cheesy Muffins—a very reliable recipe.

3 cups plain (all-purpose) flour
Pinch of salt
4 teaspoons baking powder
1 cup grated Parmesan cheese
2 eggs
2 tablespoons of finely chopped basil
1 teaspoon thyme
1/2 cup virgin olive oil
2 cups (approx.) of warm water

Preheat oven to 190 degrees.

Mix the flour, salt, baking powder, cheese and herbs in a big bowl. Mix the egg, water and oil together in a small bowl. Stir the wet into the dry mixture quickly and thud them into a 12-cup muffin tray. Cook for about 25 minutes. Wonderful served with soup.

Chicory and Onions (Mark Deasey's recipes)

Chicory is that stuff that looks like dandelion leaves. You need a bunch of it, one onion and half a cup of good olive oil.

Chop the chicory stem ends off, rinse the leaves and wash out any grit. Cut the whole bunch in half and drop into a big pot of boiling salted water and cook until tender—about five minutes—allowing the stems to retain a bit of bite. Drain the chicory and refresh it under cold water.

Peel and slice the onion, fry in olive oil until dark brown and caramelised. Add the drained chicory and stir until the leaves are coated in oil and the onions are mixed through. Serve warm or at room temperature. Sweet and comforting.

To receive a free catalog of Poisoned Pen Press titles, please contact us in one of the following ways:

Phone: 1-800-421-3976
Facsimile: 1-480-949-1707
Email: info@poisonedpenpress.com
Website: www.poisonedpenpress.com

Poisoned Pen Press
6962 E. First Ave. Ste. 103
Scottsdale, AZ 85251